EVER
YOURS

Gabriella Anderson

S0-ARD-438

ZEBRA BOOKS
KENSINGTON PUBLISHING CORP.
http://www.kensingtonbooks.com

ZEBRA BOOKS are published by

Kensington Publishing Corp.
850 Third Avenue
New York, NY 10022

Copyright © 2003 by Gabriella Anderson

All rights reserved. No part of this book may be reproduced
in any form or by any means without the prior written consent of the Publisher, excepting brief quotes used in reviews.

If you purchased this book without a cover you should be
aware that this book is stolen property. It was reported as
"unsold and destroyed" to the Publisher and neither the
Author nor the Publisher has received any payment for this
"stripped book."

All Kensington titles, imprints, and distributed lines are
available at special quantity discounts for bulk purchases for
sales promotions, premiums, fund-raising, and educational
or institutional use.

Special book excerpts or customized printings can also be
created to fit specific needs. For details, write or phone the
office of the Kensington Special Sales Manager: Kensington
Publishing Corp., 850 Third Avenue, New York, NY 10022,
Attn: Special Sales Department. Phone: 1-800-221-2647.

Zebra and the Z logo Reg. U.S. Pat. & TM Off.

First Printing: August 2003
10 9 8 7 6 5 4 3 2 1

Printed in the United States of America

To the other members of the Fabu Five:
Judy Ballard, Nancy O'Connor, Brenda Schetnan,
and Barbara Simmons
Thank you for the laughter, the advice, the chocolate,
and the word "naked."
I couldn't have done this one without you.

Chapter 1

London, 1854

"Are you sure you haven't made a mistake?" Ivy sat up in the spoon-backed chair.

The solicitor peered through his spectacles at her. "You are Lady Ivy St. Clair, daughter of Gerald and Phoebe St. Clair, Earl and Countess of Dunleigh?

"Yes."

"Then I've made no mistake."

Ivy glanced at her brother, who shrugged. He folded his arms across his chest and leaned against the wall.

"But a bequest? I didn't even know Lord Stanhope." Ivy shook her head. "Why would Lord Stanhope leave *me* anything?"

"It is not my place to answer such questions." The solicitor removed his spectacles and wiped the lenses with his handkerchief.

Ivy thought Mr. Jenkins suited his office. The burgundy striped wallpaper with the walnut wainscoting was ever so formal. She could say the same of the solicitor.

"What has she inherited?" Christopher asked.

"A house in Devon and one thousand pounds." The lawyer replaced his glasses.

"Not bad, Ivy," said Christopher.

Not bad? It was amazing. The bequest wouldn't make her rich, but it was enough to take her breath away. It was downright perplexing.

"There is, however, a stipulation, a task you must perform before you inherit," said the solicitor. He removed an envelope from his desk and placed it on the table.

From her seat, Ivy could read the name on the front—her own.

The lawyer rose from his place and crossed the room to a small closet. From the recess, he pulled a slim, rectangular package covered in brown paper and returned to his visitors. "Lord Stanhope instructed me to show you this before you read his letter."

With meticulous care, he unfolded the brown paper from the package. As she had suspected, the lawyer revealed a portrait, but Ivy stopped thinking of the lawyer the moment she saw the painting. Clear blue eyes stared at her from the canvas. The man in the portrait was young, but past the awkward stages of youth. The sharp lines of his jaw denoted strength, whereas the seriousness of his expression bespoke intelligence. Yet the sparkle in those eyes hinted at mischief and something she didn't quite understand.

Nonsense, Ivy. It's a painting, nothing more. Anything you see in the expression, the artist put there.

"I haven't seen *him* during the season," said her

brother. "Good thing, too. Wouldn't want to have competition for the affection of the ladies."

"Who is he?" asked Ivy.

"Lord Stanhope did not make me privilege to that information. Perhaps he mentions something in his letter." The solicitor pushed the envelope toward Ivy.

Christopher grabbed it. Ivy tsked at him, then held out her hand. Her brother handed the letter to her, and she glanced at the bold writing on the front.

"Lord Stanhope further instructed me to give you one week to decide if you agree to his stipulation."

"I suppose the task is in his letter." Ivy tucked it into her reticule.

"I was assured it is so. You must understand I have not read the letter."

"And if I do not agree to Lord Stanhope's request?" asked Ivy.

"The house and money shall revert to his nephew, the new earl."

"That would be a pity," said Christopher.

"You are to take the portrait with you. One of my boys will carry it to your carriage. At the end of the week, sooner if you wish, you are to relate your answer to me." The lawyer smiled and stood, a sign that indicated the meeting was over.

Ivy rose from the chair. "Thank you for your time, Mr. Jenkins. I suppose we shall meet again in a week."

"Shall I reserve this same time again for you next week?"

"Yes, thank you."

The solicitor opened the door to his office and

bowed to her as she passed him. Christopher followed her out.

As their driver guided the carriage toward home, Ivy stared at the portrait. Those blue eyes couldn't be real. His gaze drew her in, called to her, stirred something within her that she couldn't name.

"Who do you suppose it is?" asked Christopher.

Christopher's question roused her from her musings. "I expect he's someone important. It's a very nice portrait."

"I don't think Mother and Father will approve of bringing a strange man into the house. Especially by you. I'm not sure I do, either."

"Don't be a goose. I'm not bringing a strange man into the house."

"His portrait, then. I don't want you mooning over him."

"You're sweet, Christopher, but it's just a painting."

"Sweet? If anyone overheard you, 'twould ruin my reputation." But he kissed the top of her head anyway. "Read the letter, wench. Let's find out who he is." Christopher leaned back against the cushions of the carriage.

Ivy removed the letter from her reticule. She broke open the seal and pulled three sheets of parchment from the envelope.

My Dear Ivy,

Forgive me the informal greeting, but I feel I know you well enough to forgo the nuisance of titles. In any case, it is too late to reprimand me for my manners. (A little jest. I always thought one should never spend a single day without laughter.)

What a strange man, thought Ivy. Certainly he had a strange sense of humor.

"What does it say?" asked Christopher.

"I haven't finished it yet."

"Hurry up. I want to know what this is all about."

"If you don't stop pestering me, I won't read it until we reach home and I can lock myself in my room."

"I'll be quiet." Christopher crossed his arms and struck a pose of disinterest, but watched her with an unwavering gaze.

Ivy laughed at his antics, and continued with her reading.

> *By now I'm sure you're wondering why I left you this strange bequest. Many, many years ago, I fell in love with a beautiful woman. Imagine my joy when I learned she returned my feelings. I've never forgotten the season we spent in each other's company—the dancing, the secret whispers, the stolen moments. But I was the second son of my father. With nothing to my name and few prospects, her parents didn't approve our match and wed her to someone else. That woman was your mother, Phoebe. I watched her with a broken heart as she wed your father. Vowing never to bring her as much pain as she brought me, I thought it best I never intrude upon her life again. But I never forgot her.*

That explained her mother's reaction. When Ivy had received word that Lord Stanhope had left her a bequest, her mother had sighed, said, "Harold," then left the room, dabbing tears from her eyes.

I heard of the birth of her son, then you, then your sister. By that time, my brother had died, and I stood to inherit the title. I had the title and wealth now, but I had lost my love. One of life's little ironies. I did tell you I like a jest, didn't I? Life is capable of jokes as well.

Do not think me bitter. On the contrary. I do not believe in railing against what I cannot change. Phoebe was happy in her life, and I was content in mine. But I followed the lives of her children from afar, never stepping forward, but always interested.

You, Ivy, I found the most fascinating by far. Your brother and sister are fine individuals, but you showed a sparkle, a zest for life your siblings lacked. You handle your admirers with kindness, yet give them no encouragement. None has stolen your heart yet. I imagine your parents have responded with dismay over your behavior.

Ivy let out a soft chuckle. Lord Stanhope did indeed know her and her parents.

So I'm leaving you a little house and a little money so you can continue to feel independent even if you marry. But I have a request first. Travel sometimes makes many things clear. And many times you will find your heart's desire at the end of your journey.

Her heart's desire. Ivy shook her head. Her heart's desire wasn't what waited for her at the end of her journey. Duty awaited her. Duty in the form of Neville Foxworthy, Earl of Wynbrooke. She frowned, then continued reading.

By now Jenkins has shown you the portrait. I want you to deliver it to a friend of mine in Wales. He won't be happy that I've kept it so long. I believe you are the only one who can carry out this task.

My former housekeeper, Mrs. Pennyfeather, has agreed to accompany you. She is a fine woman and would make an admirable chaperone. A driver and carriage stand ready for your use. Jenkins knows the details. Dear Ivy, I hope you accept this proposition from a well-meaning friend you never knew you had. I wish you all the best in the future. I only wish I were there to witness it.

Yours, Lord Stanhope

The last page of the letter gave the name and address of the man to whom she was to deliver the portrait. Auburn Seaton, Earl of Tamberlake, Gryphon's Lair, Betws-y-coed, Wales. If her sense of geography served her, Lord Tamberlake lived in Snowdonia.

Funny. She had never heard of Lord Tamberlake.

She folded the letter and placed it back into its envelope. Extraordinary. Any delivery service could have taken the portrait to Wales. Why her? Lord Stanhope never explained why he chose her for the task. And yet, Ivy no longer needed a reason.

Her mouth curved into a little smile. If she went, the party would have to be postponed.

Her smile grew broader. Ivy placed the letter in her lap.

"Well? Who is he?"

"Who?"

"The man in the portrait." Christopher gazed at her as though she were daft.

"Lord Stanhope doesn't say."

"Then what does he want?"

"He wants me to deliver the portrait to a friend of his in Wales."

"Impossible."

"Impossible," said Phoebe St. Clair, Countess of Dunleigh. "I won't hear of it, Ivy. You can't miss the beginning of the season."

"What do I care for a few silly balls?"

"Silly? Ivy St. Clair, I will not have you—"

"Now, Mother, remember your dyspepsia." Ivy patted her mother's arm. "It isn't as though I've decided to call off the betrothal."

"Don't say such a thing, Ivy."

"I was joking."

"Don't even joke about such things. You know you must marry first. Then we can find a suitable husband for Georgina."

Ivy wished she were the younger sister. "I said I would marry Lord Wynbrooke."

"We've delayed the announcement long enough." Lady Dunleigh fanned herself. "What will people say?"

"They won't say anything because no announcement has been made. I'll only be gone for a couple of weeks." Ivy rose from the settee and crossed to the window. She stared toward the west. She wanted to go, but her mother was proving difficult to convince. A moment later an idea struck her. "I should think you'd like me to do this favor for an old friend. But he probably doesn't mean as much to you as I thought."

Lady Dunleigh sighed. "Dear Harold." She pulled

out a handkerchief and dabbed the corners of her eyes.

Although her estimation of her mother had grown since the discovery of her lost love, Ivy had no qualms in using Lord Stanhope's memory to weaken her mother's resolve. She turned back to her mother and took her hands. "We can announce the betrothal as soon as I return, I promise. And I'll even let you pick out my dress."

Ivy's mother brightened at once. "I know just the color I'll pick to offset your eyes. It's a shame you aren't blond like your sister."

Ivy gazed out the window again to hide her smile. She didn't care that her hair was brown, and her eyes matched its color. Her sister, Georgina, received enough simpering poetry for the both of them.

"But it's impossible. I can't chaperone you myself, and I can't spare your maid. Georgina has several balls to attend. She can't miss the beginning of the season because you choose to traipse about in the wilds."

"I don't need my maid. Lord Stanhope has arranged for his housekeeper to accompany me. And Christopher said he would like to come as well." *And I think the wilds will be tamer than the season,* she added to herself.

"A housekeeper as a chaperone? That's hardly acceptable."

"We could tell everyone she's impoverished nobility or some such tale. And Christopher will be there, too. Please, Mother? You wouldn't want me to neglect Lord Stanhope's memory."

"No, I wouldn't. What a dear man to remember you in his will." An enigmatic smile lit upon her mother's face. She fingered the lace at her collar and gazed off into the air. "And he left you the cottage in Devon."

"Yes, but only if I carry out this task."

"It's hard to imagine he's gone."

"Then let me honor his last request." Ivy held her breath.

Lady Dunleigh nodded. "Yes, we must honor his memory. You will go to Wales. I'll settle it with your father and Lord Wynbrooke."

Ivy bit her lip to keep from shouting with joy. Three more weeks of freedom before she had to settle into the yoke her parents had fashioned for her. She would wed as her parents had arranged, but she didn't have to like it. And if her soon-to-be-betrothed didn't care for her absence, well, she had time enough to obey after they wed.

"Tell me again what you need to do."

"I need to deliver a portrait to the Earl of Tamberlake."

Lady Dunleigh gasped and grew pale. "You never told me his name."

Ivy rushed to her mother's side. "What's the matter, Mother?"

"My darling girl, I can't let you go."

"Nonsense. It's a simple task." Ivy crossed her arms. "Besides, you've already agreed that I may go."

"No, you don't understand. It isn't the task. It's the man."

"Who?"

"Tamberlake. The monster earl."

Chapter 2

Monster Earl.

The words echoed in Ivy's head as she stared through the wrought iron gates at the gray stone manor house. No hint of light came from any window. A turret on each end of the house gave an impression not of whimsy, but of a fortress. Lichen grew on the stones, and chimneys rose from the roof without any attempt to conceal them. No adornment graced the outside, save the image of a griffin on the gates.

"Doesn't look very friendly," said Ivy.

Christopher glanced out the window of the carriage. "What did you expect? We *are* in Wales."

Mrs. Pennyfeather patted her arm. "I'll wager it keeps one safe and warm in the winter." The housekeeper tried to find the positive aspect in everything. The woman had proven to be an amusing companion on the trip. She was bright, quickwitted, and a good conversationalist. Lord Stanhope had chosen his help well. Ivy would be sorry to see her go at the end of their journey.

Ivy glanced up at the sky. It showed no sign of welcome, either. The weather wasn't helping her mood. Sullen, gray skies had followed them for the past week, slowing the journey by dumping their rain and turning roads into bogs of mud and mire. Today looked even worse.

In this setting, Ivy could almost believe in a monster earl. If she were some kind of horror, she would choose this remote area with the looming gray mountains to make her home. In fact, she might just need to take refuge in these mountains. Her mother wouldn't be happy when she learned the trip was taking longer than planned. But the weather wasn't her fault.

She hoped the rain wouldn't stop for weeks.

With a sigh, Ivy pulled back from the carriage window and rested her head against the cushions. The journey had been uncomfortable at best—the many inns whose cleanliness was sometimes questionable, the bad food, the tedium of the drive. The roads had deteriorated once they left England, but she had to say this last hour had been the worst. With every bump, Ivy wondered if she'd ever be free of the bruises she'd incurred.

The driver climbed from his perch and unlatched the gates. A few minutes later they stopped again, this time in front of the house. Ivy waited for the driver to open the door. Christopher climbed from his seat with apparent reluctance, then helped her out. He stood by the coach. "If you don't mind, I'll wait here." He lit a cheroot and leaned against the side of the carriage.

"Suit yourself." She climbed the steps to the front door. Mrs. Pennyfeather followed her while the driver remained by the coach.

Ivy spied the ornate brass knocker. It was a griffin. A ring hung from its sharp beak, and its raised claw looked ready to strike. If she were at all timid, the knocker would have been enough to send her on her way. She lifted the ring. It creaked and groaned as if protesting its use.

That's your imagination talking again.

Ignoring her fanciful thoughts, she rapped twice.

For a minute, nothing happened. Ivy frowned. "Do you suppose no one is home?"

"I was told the earl never leaves," said Mrs. Pennyfeather.

"That's what I thought." Ivy lifted the knocker again.

The door opened and wrenched the ring from her fingers. She let out a little cry of surprise. A heavyset, gray-haired man stood in the doorway. "May I help you?"

"I'm here to see the Earl of Tamberlake. I have—"

"His lordship sees no one. Good day." The butler shut the door.

Ivy gaped at the griffin knocker, which seemed to be laughing at her. She turned to Mrs. Pennyfeather. "He shut the door on me."

Mrs. Pennyfeather looked as surprised as Ivy felt. "I can see that."

Letting out a puff of air in exasperation, Ivy faced the door. She knocked again.

The butler opened the door in less time. "His lordship does not wish to have visitors."

"But I'm not here to visit, I'm—"

The door shut with a bang.

"Of all the rude, ungracious—" began Ivy.

"Now, now, my lady. Calm yourself." Mrs. Pennyfeather patted her arm. "It won't help to lose your temper."

Christopher pushed himself off the side of the coach. "Let's head back to the village and find lodging for the night. We can come back tomorrow."

"I most certainly will not come back. I can be as stubborn as he. We'll wait right here until he has to let us in."

Mrs. Pennyfeather raised her eyebrows. "As you wish, Lady Ivy."

Ivy knocked again and shouted at the door, "I haven't left. I'm still here."

Christopher shrugged his shoulders and returned to his cheroot.

Ivy looked at the house. She thought she saw movement in an upstairs window, but she couldn't be sure. She crossed her arms and resisted the urge to stick out her tongue at the window.

For half an hour she stood in front of the door, standing on one foot, then the other, but she didn't budge. Mrs. Pennyfeather had abandoned her efforts to draw her back into the carriage. Christopher ignored her entirely. Ivy was determined to stand on these steps until the butler let them in. Nothing would stop her.

Not even the rain, which started to fall.

Ivy glanced at the gray sky with a frown. Were the heavens conspiring with the earl against her? Well, she could out-stubborn the rain, too.

"Ivy, come into the carriage," said Christopher. "You'll get wet."

"I don't care." Ivy resisted the urge to stomp her foot. "I'm not leaving this step."

"Don't be a fool. We can still find some nice rooms in the village," said Christopher.

"No." Ivy stared at the door.

"Don't expect me to stand in the rain with you."

Ivy gave him a withering look. "I don't."

Christopher climbed into the carriage. Mrs. Pennyfeather sighed, then wrapped her shawl over her head and around her neck.

"I can't ask you to stand in the rain with me. You go into the carriage with Christopher, Mrs. Pennyfeather." Ivy gave her companion a gentle push toward the conveyance.

"Oh, no, I couldn't." Mrs. Pennyfeather stopped on the top step.

"Please, there's no sense in both of us getting wet. I could order you." Ivy gave the woman a wink.

"But you'll get ill."

"From a little water?" Ivy lowered her voice. "Besides, he's bound to let us in now."

"Then I shall stay with you." Mrs. Pennyfeather frowned.

The driver offered Ivy his umbrella, but she refused. An umbrella might be viewed as a sign of weakness.

Fifteen minutes later, Ivy shivered on the top step. She had started doubting her plan long ago, but the hope that the butler would open the door in the next minute kept her from retreating. She thought she spied movement in the same window, but when she looked up, rain fell into her eyes and obscured her vision.

Foolish. That's what you are. Foolish. Just as Christopher says. Just as Father says. Any sane person would have given up long ago. Ivy sighed. She was cold, wet, and hungry. Her hair had long since fallen from its coiffure, and her skirt clung to her crinoline with a weight she thought would bend the hoops. Mrs. Pennyfeather looked miserable. Guilt assailed her as she saw the woman's suffering. Even knowing she had urged her companion to take shelter in the carriage didn't assuage her conscience.

She sighed again. They could come back tomorrow.

Just as she was about to turn from the door, the griffin swung away from her. The butler stood in the doorway. "The master says you are to come in."

Ivy bit back a cry of triumph.

The two women stepped into the entrance hall. No lights lit the corridors leading from the door. Ivy moved from the door to leave room for Mrs. Pennyfeather. Her foot slipped on the wet parquet, but she caught herself before she fell.

Christopher ran in behind the women. "I have to give you credit, Ivy. I didn't think you'd ever get inside." He shook the few drops of rain from his hair.

"I'll tell the driver where to take his carriage." The butler turned to the door.

"Have him bring our luggage in first," said Ivy.

The butler raised an eyebrow.

"We must have dry clothes, or do you prefer having a pool in your entry hall?" Ivy placed her hands on her hips.

In the first sign of propriety he demonstrated, the butler said, "Very well."

"And have him bring the package in as well."

"Very good, miss."

"My lady," said Mrs. Pennyfeather, correcting the butler.

The butler said nothing, opened an umbrella, and left to talk to the driver.

A *drip, drip, drip* filled her ears. She glanced down. Although she couldn't see in the dim light, she knew the dripping came from her skirt. She moved her foot to stop the noise, but the slosh that replaced the dripping sounded worse to her ears.

The butler returned. "I've instructed the driver to move the carriage to the back of the house. You may use a room to change your attire."

"What of me?" Christopher asked the man with a cheery smile.

The butler looked him over. "You may wait in the salon. Follow me, please." He led them down the hall.

Ivy shook herself, then grabbed her sodden skirt and trailed after the butler. The hallway grew no brighter as they went deeper into the house. Mrs. Pennyfeather came after her. After leaving Christopher in the salon, they climbed the stairs. The second story of the house was as dim as the first.

Pausing by a door, the butler turned to them. "You may change here. I'll bring your trunks up in a moment. We don't have any maids to help you, so you will have to manage on your own." He pushed the door open.

Ivy entered the room, followed by Mrs. Pennyfeather. She turned to the butler. "Where shall we go—"

The door closed.

"Humph. They have something to learn about manners in this house," said Ivy. She started to unbutton her bodice. "He didn't even tell us his name. Probably doesn't think we'll be here long enough to use it."

Mrs. Pennyfeather crossed behind her and untied the laces at her waist. "They are a little strange. But perhaps they are unused to such excitement."

"Excitement?"

"Visitors, my lady. We are the excitement."

"Wet excitement." Ivy shrugged out of her bodice and held the soaking garment from her. Then she stepped out of her skirt, leaving the wet mass on the floor. She peered around the room. A single table with one chair stood in the corner. No fire burned in the grate, and draperies covered the windows. At least the butler had left a single candle. She shivered and gooseflesh rose on her skin.

Ivy hung the bodice of her dress on the back of the chair and lifted the skirt from the floor. She spread it over the table like a tablecloth. Water dripped from the hem. "I suppose we should be glad there is no rug we can ruin in this room."

"A fire would have been nice," muttered Mrs. Pennyfeather.

The sparse furnishings made Ivy wonder about the earl. Perhaps he couldn't afford a house full of furniture. Or perhaps he had an aversion to comfort. She shivered. She had seen little in this house to offer comfort.

Her mother's words leaped unbidden to her mind. *Monster Earl.* What sort of man lived in a house he kept dark?

A knock at the door made Ivy jump.

"Yes?" said Mrs. Pennyfeather.

"It's the housekeeper. My husband has put your trunks in the adjacent room."

"Thank you."

"Ring the bell when you've finished changing, and I'll come for you."

Ivy heard the footsteps of the woman disappear. She turned toward the door to the adjacent room. "Dry clothes will bring us some relief, at any rate."

In half an hour, they had dried themselves and dressed. Ivy even managed to twist her wet hair into some semblance of a coiffure. Her appearance would appall her mother, but it would do for a visit in the remote mountains of Snowdonia after a rain. Ivy rang the bellpull.

The housekeeper appeared in a few minutes. She was short and stocky. "I see you've dried off. Come along then. The master will see you soon." She led them down the stairs.

The hall was just as dark as before. Ivy's skirt brushed against a stool in the hallway and sent her hoops flying. With a frown, she tamed them with a touch and wondered where the sense was in putting things in a hallway where one couldn't see them anyway. Someone could trip and hurt themselves.

The housekeeper paused in front of a door and opened it. "You may go in."

As Ivy started into the room, she stopped short. "Oh dear. The letter from Lord Stanhope to the earl. It's in the box in the carriage."

"Can't it wait?" asked the housekeeper.

"No," replied Ivy. "I'm to deliver it with the package."

"I'll fetch it," said Mrs. Pennyfeather.

"Suit yourself," said the woman with a shrug. "The rain has stopped, but you'll find the yard full of mud and puddles. I'll show you the way." The housekeeper turned to Ivy. "You may wait here."

Ivy entered the room. A fire in the hearth was the sole source of light. The drapes let no light from outside through the windows. *Goodness, if the earl has tried to make his house gloomy he has succeeded.*

Christopher sat in one of the two chairs that stood near the hearth. He held out a snifter. "The earl sure has nice brandy."

"I'm glad you're comfortable."

"A fire, good brandy, and a comfortable chair. What more does a man need?"

"I'm happy you're so easily satisfied." She turned her back to him and tried to make out the rest of the room. As her eyesight adjusted to the dim light, she realized shadows claimed most of the room. No sounds reached her save the crackle of the flames in the fireplace. If not for Christopher, she could imagine she was alone in the house, secluded from the world, a prisoner of the evil Lord Tamberlake.

Ivy almost snorted as she held back her laughter. She walked to the far wall, then back. The package she was to deliver leaned against the wall near the hearth. She noticed no paintings on any of the walls. What a shame to leave such a lovely portrait to a man with no appreciation for art.

For another few moments, she waited for someone, anyone, to come to her. Mrs. Pennyfeather was taking her time as well. Christopher looked content, sucking on his brandy. Letting out a puff of air in impatience, Ivy crossed to the door and looked out.

"What are you looking for?" asked Christopher.

She pulled her head in, feeling as guilty as if she were, well, guilty. "Nothing. Go back to your brandy."

Christopher lifted an eyebrow, then did as she said. She poked her head out again.

In the hall, light spilled onto the floor from beneath the door to the room opposite her. Curiosity beckoned her to action. She crept across the hall, inched the door open, and poked her head in.

Whatever she had expected, this room wasn't it. It was a library. Shadows claimed most of the room, but a cheery fire glowed and a lamp illuminated one part of the room. Shelves lined every wall, and books filled every shelf. Her mouth opened in surprise. Her father had a library, but he kept his guns and cigars there.

The comparative brightness of the room welcomed her. She walked inside. The sound of a book snapping closed startled her. She spun around. Although she didn't see anyone, her heart pounded as though she had done something terrible. Ivy shivered and hurried to the fire. She held out her hands to warm them.

"You wouldn't be so cold if you had sense enough to get out of the rain."

Ivy whirled around at the man's voice. She peered into the corner shadows and saw a pair of legs wearing fawn-colored trousers and black boots emerging from a deep winged chair. Darkness covered the rest of him. "Wh-who are you?"

"I believe I am the person you've come to see," said the voice in the dark. The man stood and retreated further into the shadows. "I am Auburn Seaton, Earl of Tamberlake."

Chapter 3

Tamberlake took in the startled look of the woman. From the shadows of the corner, he watched her digest the information of his identity, then pull herself upright. Her thoughts played out on her face. She wasn't sure whether to seek him out or follow convention. Convention won out.

She sank into a deep curtsey. "Lord Tamberlake. I am Lady Ivy St. Clair."

"Pleased to meet you."

"I doubt that." The woman rose from her curtsey. "You've gone out of your way to make us unwelcome and uncomfortable." She took a step toward him.

He countered with one of his own. "No, please stay by the fire and warm yourself," he said.

She stopped and turned back to the hearth. "You might have thought of my comfort before you let me stand in the rain."

Tamberlake chuckled. This woman was most unusual. "Since, as you said, I didn't make you welcome, why would you risk pneumonia to see me?"

"Lord Stanhope sent me."

For a moment, the memory of friendship recalled long-buried feelings. "How is old Stanhope?"

Lady Ivy paused. "I'm sorry. I thought you would have heard. He died."

He had not expected this news. The one man who had stood by him despite everything was no more. Tamberlake cleared his throat. "I shall miss him."

"Perhaps you can tell me about him. I never met the man."

"But you just said he sent you—"

"I know. It's most perplexing. He left me a bequest in his will with the stipulation that I deliver a package to you." She shrugged.

"A package?"

"The reason for my visit."

"Indeed?" He didn't know what Stanhope might have sent him. "And where is this package?"

"In the salon."

"The room where you were supposed to wait?"

Her cheeks reddened, and he had the most unexplained urge to touch them and feel their heat.

"Why don't you return there? I shall be along in a moment and we can discuss this further."

Ivy fled back through the door. Tamberlake sighed. Reaching for his cane, he followed slowly. He entered the salon without greeting his . . . he supposed he could call them guests. Lady Ivy stood by the fire, and the young man stood beside her. Who was he? His proximity to Ivy showed some level of intimacy, which troubled him.

"Lord Tamberlake," said the young man. "I am Ivy's brother, Christopher St. Clair, Viscount Styles."

Her brother. A sense of relief shot through him. "I trust you are enjoying my brandy, Styles."

Swirling the amber liquid in his glass, the young man grinned. "You do serve an excellent vintage."

The brashness of the young man amused him. Tamberlake moved to the sideboard. Mrs. Beaker had left a pot of tea there, as was her custom. He ignored it, as was his. Sloshing brandy into a snifter, he glanced back at Lady Ivy. She had moved away from the fire and was approaching him.

"Do take a seat, Lady Ivy. That chair by the fire should be warm enough to dispel any chill that lingers."

She peered toward him. "But I—"

"Shall I pour you some tea? I'm afraid I haven't had visitors in some time, and I'm not used to entertaining."

"Tea would be lovely."

Placing his brandy on the sideboard, he lifted the cozy from the pot and poured the still-warm liquid into a cup. "Milk and sugar?"

Lady Ivy settled herself into the chair. "Milk only, please."

He walked to the chair, careful to stay out of the brightest parts of the room, and stood behind the chair. Reaching over the top, he offered her the cup with his left hand. "Your tea."

She looked up. She couldn't twist her neck enough to see him, but he did glimpse the puzzled expression on her face. She reached for the cup from his outstretched hand. "Thank you."

Her fingers brushed his as she took the cup. Their softness surprised him. He snatched his hand away and returned to the sideboard. Lifting the snifter, he took a long swallow. The brandy warmed his stomach as no fire could. He looked back at Lady Ivy. Her brown hair gleamed in the firelight like finely polished wood. For a moment, he wondered if her hair was softer than her hands.

"Lord Tamberlake," she said.

"Yes?"

"I feel quite silly speaking into the shadows. Won't you join us by the fire?"

A chilled resignation crept down his spine. He had known he couldn't avoid this moment, but he had hoped to delay it.

Before he could step into the light, the door to the salon opened. Lady Ivy's companion came in. "I have it." She waved an envelope toward Ivy.

"Thank you, Mrs. Pennyfeather. You were gone quite a while. I almost despaired of seeing you again," said Lady Ivy, taking the letter.

"It was muddier than I thought." Mrs. Pennyfeather sat in the empty chair.

Ivy looked back toward him, then frowned. "Mrs. Pennyfeather, may I present our host, Lord Tamberlake?"

Mrs. Pennyfeather shot to her feet. "Good heavens, I thought we were alone." She squinted into the darkness, then dropped into a deep curtsey. "Forgive my impertinence, Lord Tamberlake."

"Don't trouble yourself, Mrs. Pennyfeather. Please sit." Tamberlake stood back in the shadows, hating the relief at the brief delay of his exposure.

"Come join us by the fire, Tamberlake," said Christopher. "I'd like to lift my glass to my host."

"I fear I prefer the shadows."

A moment of silence descended upon the room. Then Lady Ivy stood and faced toward him. "Lord Stanhope wrote this letter for you. I was to deliver it along with the parcel."

She held out the letter toward him. He could

delay no longer. Tamberlake placed the now-empty snifter on the sideboard. Grasping his cane, he walked toward the three.

His cane came into the light first. He leaned on it as he placed his weight on his weak leg and stepped out of the darkness. As the light of the fire hit him, Mrs. Pennyfeather gasped. Christopher forgot to drink from the snifter. It sat at his lips, until he took a huge gulp and swallowed in a hurry.

When Ivy looked up at him, her eyes widened. He waited for the look of horror to cross her features, followed by the fruitless attempt to control her revulsion.

The look never came.

Ivy looked into his right eye, then to where his left should have been, but now a half-mask of porcelain covered the spot. "Your letter, Lord Tamberlake."

He reached out to take it, expecting her to shrink back from his touch. Instead, his fingers brushed the back of her hand. His fingers lingered for a moment, but she still didn't pull away. He took the envelope from her and tucked it into his vest pocket.

"Aren't you going to read it?" she asked.

"Perhaps later." He couldn't take his gaze from her. She hadn't reacted at all as he'd expected.

She shrugged. "The portrait I am to deliver is here as well." She pointed to the parcel.

"Portrait? I thought you were to deliver a package." He glanced at the paper-wrapped parcel and froze. A sense of foreboding rose in him.

"Yes. The package is a portrait."

He strode to the slim, flat package and ripped

the paper from it. His own face—his face as it used to be—stared back at him. He pivoted to her. "I had hoped you weren't capable of mockery, Lady Ivy."

"I don't understand."

"Take a good look at the painting, Lady Ivy. Then amuse yourself some more at my face."

Ivy gasped. "The portrait. It's of you."

"Yes. I trust you're enjoying this."

"I didn't know." She looked up at him, her eyes welling up with tears.

"Do you expect me to believe that?"

Before she could deny her duplicity, Beaker entered the room. "Forgive me, my lord. There is a problem."

"In addition to the one I'm looking at?" As he turned from Ivy, he heard her utter a small cry in protest. He ignored it. "What is it, Beaker?"

"Their carriage, sir. It's broken."

"That isn't my problem."

"No, sir, but it's too late to send to the village for parts. Shall I ready yours for their use?"

He faced Styles. He never wanted to see Ivy again. "My carriage shall take you to your accommodations."

"We have none." The man's expression was disapproving.

"We thought to carry out my errand and return in time to find an inn," said Ivy. "We hadn't counted on your games delaying us for so long."

She sounded angry. Before he could stop himself, he looked at her. The tears had dried, and indignation pinched her lips. What right had she to anger?

"Prepare rooms, Beaker. They may stay one night." He gave her a curt bow. "Forgive me if I don't play the host for you."

Without a backward glance, he strode from the room.

Ivy tossed in her bed. She didn't know whether to be furious or miserable. Dinner had been a sullen affair. The housekeeper, whom she now knew was Mrs. Beaker, served them a cold supper. Only Mrs. Pennyfeather and Christopher had eaten. Of her host, she had seen nothing. They retired early, but Ivy couldn't sleep. Although she knew she wasn't guilty, she couldn't help but feel disturbed over the portrait. How could she not have recognized Lord Tamberlake? A deep chagrin filled her. She had been dreaming of the portrait for two weeks. A mask covered half his face now, but the similarities were there.

She thought back to their meeting. The timbre of his voice had warmed her more than the fire, and his touch had been so gentle, she shivered at the memory. Of course, his manners needed much improvement. How could he think she'd be so cruel as to make sport of him?

With a groan, Ivy tossed the covers from her and left the bed. Pulling a wrap around her, she lit a taper from the small fire in her room. She welcomed the light after the day she'd had.

Ivy remembered the one room that shone with comfort. The library. If she couldn't sleep she might as well read.

With a silent tread, she made her way down the stairs to the library. Cracking open the door, she saw the room was lit as bright as before. Strange that he should want it so light even at night. She slid inside and turned to the shelves.

"Do you always sneak about in the homes you visit?"

She let out a sharp cry and clasped her hand to her throat. "You startled me."

Lord Tamberlake stepped from the corner of the room. "I? I've been here all along. You are the one creeping through my house in the middle of the night. Haven't you done enough harm for one day?"

The guilt she knew she needn't be feeling flooded her. "I couldn't sleep and . . ." She paused. "I suppose it doesn't interest you anyway. With your permission, may I find a book and return to my room?"

"By all means." He bowed to her.

His false politeness irritated her. She turned her back to him and tried to read the titles on the shelves.

"Why couldn't you sleep? Were you afraid of the monsters in this house?"

She didn't turn around. "Don't be ridiculous." She concentrated on the books.

"Or perhaps just this particular monster?" His voice sounded nearer.

"I don't believe in monsters," she said in a huff.

"Don't you?" His breath breezed against her neck.

She whirled around and found him less than a foot from her. She leaned against the books.

"I am well aware of what they call me in the *ton*. Isn't this why you came? To see the monster?" His breath smelled of brandy.

"The only thing monstrous about you is your behavior." Ivy straightened and shook her finger in his face. "You may choose to withdraw from society, but that doesn't excuse your lack of manners."

He raised his eyebrow. She couldn't tell if he raised both, for the porcelain mask concealed his left one. A pink shine shimmered from the surface. It looked cold and uncomfortable. Before she could stop herself, she asked, "Do you wear that mask all the time?"

His fingers touched the hard shell that covered a quadrant of his face. "The mask is for visitors and my mother. I usually wear an eye patch when I'm alone."

"But why are you wearing it now? We've all gone to bed."

He just looked at her.

Ivy felt a blush creep into her cheeks. "You couldn't have expected to run into me."

"No, but I wouldn't have wanted to shock you if you were a sleepwalker."

"You wouldn't shock me."

"Perhaps not, but you have me. It isn't often I find half-clad women wandering about my house." He lifted the filmy wrap that covered her nightgown.

Good heavens, she had forgotten her state of undress. Although her nightgown buttoned high on her neck, long sleeves covered her arms to her wrists, and not even her toes poked out from the hem, a man shouldn't view her in her nightclothes. Her cheeks burned now.

Tamberlake chuckled. "Find your book. This monster won't eat you . . . tonight." He leaned forward and drew a line with his finger along her jaw.

Ivy grabbed the first book she saw and fled the room, running until she shut her door behind her. She leaned against the wood to catch her breath.

Her lack of modesty troubled her less than the strange sensations that his touch stirred in her. Her heart pounded in her chest, yet she felt sure the dash up the stairs didn't cause it. Something about Lord Tamberlake spoke to her soul, although she wasn't sure what it was saying.

She clutched the book to her chest and climbed into the bed. Settling herself against the pillows, she looked at the title. Mary Shelley's *Frankenstein*.

With a groan, she dropped the book and blew out the taper.

Chapter 4

Tamberlake watched Ivy run from the library. *Damn it.* He reached up to rub his forehead and touched the mask. He ripped it from his face and threw it onto a chair. The cold, painted eye looked back at him as if in mockery. *Damn it.*

Limping back to his chair, he flopped onto the seat and grabbed the snifter at his side. He took a swallow of the brandy, then grimaced. He had had enough to drink today. Of course, today had been no ordinary day, and if any man had a reason to drink, he did.

He placed the snifter to his side anyway.

The glow of the lamp and fire bathed the room in light. He reveled in it. The library was his sanctuary, the one room where he allowed light to touch his face. And now she had invaded it.

He rubbed his face. His fingers bumped over the puckered scars and ridges that lined his cheeks and forehead.

Closing his eyelids, he leaned his head back. Unbidden, the memories sprang into his mind.

The sudden jolt; the carriage toppling onto its side; the pain as his leg twisted beneath him; the sound of shattering glass; the fear as the fire spread from the small lamp onto the upholstery toward his face; the smoke choking him, blocking everything from his vision except the orange flames—

He bolted upright, and his eye shot open. He hadn't relived those images as vividly in years, except in nightmares. And he knew whom to blame. Lady Ivy.

With a grunt of discontent, Tamberlake admitted he was being unfair. He should hold Stanhope accountable. But his friend was dead, and Lady Ivy was here.

What had Stanhope been thinking, sending her to Gryphon's Lair? She neither shied away from an argument nor from his face. She was the first woman to look at him without flinching or revulsion. Even his erstwhile fiancée, who had claimed to love him, wouldn't look at him after the accident. Why wasn't Ivy afraid? He didn't know what to make of her.

She wasn't a beauty, with her plain brown hair and brown eyes, but something in her glowed with life. He felt himself drawn to her, basking in her company just as he basked in the light of the library. She brought life into a room with her, where he thought no hope of life existed.

He wanted her to leave. He wanted no reminders of life outside Gryphon's Lair, a life denied him by the very society that had embraced him when he was beautiful. And whole.

With a growl, he fetched the painting from the salon and set it up opposite him. Returning to his chair, he stared at the portrait. He was younger then—six years younger than his current thirty. No mirror hung on any wall, but he knew how he looked. Half his face showed little of the six years, the other half showed how much could happen in the same amount of time.

What sort of joke was Stanhope playing on him? Tamberlake tapped his vest pocket. The letter crinkled when he touched it. Pulling it from his pocket, he glanced at the writing on the front.

It was Stanhope's hand. He ripped the envelope open.

> *Dear Tamberlake,*
> *I wager you're ready to kill me, my friend. Of course, if you are reading this, it is too late.*

Tamberlake shook his head. Stanhope had always made inappropriate jests.

> *In all seriousness, I hope you will forgive my intrusion into your life. I know how you value your privacy.*
> *How I have missed you, my friend. London is dull without your scintillating conversation and quick wit.*

Tamberlake nearly snorted. Stanhope had spent most of their time together ribbing Tamberlake about the way women flocked around him, hoping to gain his attention. Stanhope claimed they were attracted by his brilliance.

> *It is in the hope that you remember our friendship that I send you the portrait. You wanted to destroy it after the accident. I wouldn't let you. Look*

*at it, Tamberlake. Look into the face of the man you
once were and ask yourself what you see.*

Tamberlake set the sheets onto his lap and
gazed at the portrait. What did he see? A man with
a near-perfect face, a man with his life ahead of
him, a man who had never tested his strength of
will or been tested. His single-eyed view caught the
glint in the blue gaze on the canvas. What had he
been thinking when he sat for the painting? He
couldn't remember. Tamberlake shook his head.
The portrait meant nothing to him. It was the em-
bodiment of a memory, little else, and the image
of a man long gone. He picked up the letter again.

*If you are half the man I believe you are, you
will see what I do. A fine portrait, nothing more,
nothing less. The man on the canvas doesn't exist,
and I don't believe he ever did, much to the dismay
of all those unmarried girls pining away for him.*
*Lady Ivy isn't like those girls. She neither pines
nor follows. Treat her well. She doesn't deserve your
scorn. I chose to send her on this errand, so save
your scorn for me.*

Tamberlake chuckled. Stanhope knew him too
well.

*I shan't lecture you, my boy, but embrace living.
You don't need to hide.*

Hide? He wasn't hiding. He was avoiding the id-
iots of the *ton*. The ones who couldn't see past the
scarred face and limp. As Lady Ivy had done.
That thought stopped him. He didn't want to

think of her. He didn't want to think of anyone. Stanhope didn't know what he was talking about.

Live well, my friend. I treasured our friendship, and I hope when you think of me, if you think of me, it is with fondness.
Stanhope

Tamberlake crumpled the letter and made to toss it into the fire, but stopped himself. He smoothed out the sheets and folded them with care, then stood. He placed the letter between the pages of a book. *Don Quixote.* Stanhope would have approved.

Ivy woke early the next morning. She corrected herself as she stretched in bed. She couldn't say she woke. To wake one must sleep, and Ivy most definitely had not slept last night. When the sky turned from black to gray, she climbed from the bed and dressed. She didn't bother to hope for a blue sky.

After her adventure of the previous night, an easy familiarity with the house greeted her steps. Tamberlake wouldn't welcome her ease with his house. With little difficulty, she made her way to the dining room. The sideboards were bare, and no aromas tickled her nose. Gryphon's Lair must have no early risers.

Ivy shivered. Welsh mornings were chilly, and she had yet to find a welcoming hearth. Ivy wandered toward the library. It was the brightest room in the house. Maybe its fire could provide a little warmth. In any case, she could read while she waited for breakfast.

She hesitated at the door. If Lord Tamberlake was inside, she wasn't sure she should disturb him. Then again, he had been awake as late as she last night. He had to be still asleep now. What reason had *he* to lie awake all night? She pushed the door open.

The library's hearth had no fire, but the embers still glowed from the previous night. She crossed to the fireplace and held out her hands. Enough heat rose from the banked ashes to warm her.

Turning, her gaze fell on the portrait. She thought he might have destroyed it, but instead it leaned against the wall as though it had a place of honor. *As well it should. What a beautiful man. And quite a good likeness as well.*

She turned from the hearth to search for a book, remembering too late that she had failed to return the one from the floor in her room. No lamps burned, but light filtered around the edges of the draperies. She crossed to the window and pulled the curtains back, letting the windows showcase the sharp hills of Snowdonia.

Ivy caught her breath. The landscape seemed all the more wild in the gray weather. From the top of a mountain, a stream cascaded over boulders and rocks as it crashed its way to the bottom. A few scraggly bushes grew in defiance of the winds, but she could see no trees. Low stone fences marked the land into grids, and sheep dotted the hillsides. In the distance, she could see a stone cottage, but the view was spectacular in its loneliness. Little wonder Lord Tamberlake made his home here.

As she took in the view, she noticed a lone figure climbing a path alongside the stream. His black cloak flapped in the wind, and his dark hair whipped around his neck. A thick staff aided his walk, and his steps were slow, but sure.

Tamberlake.

Her gaze riveted on him. He seemed such a part of this wild beauty, tears came to her eyes. A deep longing filled her. She wanted to be a part of it as well.

She hurried from the library and dashed up to her room. In her trunk, she found a pair of leather boots. *These should suffice.*

Exchanging her slippers for the boots took but a few minutes; then she rummaged through her trunk again for a thick cloak. Wrapping it around herself, she ran to the entryway and opened the door.

The brisk morning air stole her breath for a moment. She stepped outside and huddled into the wool of her cloak. At least it wasn't raining.

She ran around the side of the house to the rear, where a low iron gate opened onto the mountainside. Squinting up the path, she could just make out Tamberlake as he climbed. She hastened onto the path and started to ascend.

The rocks and damp ground caused her to slip once or twice, but they didn't deter her. Her legs ached, and the stitch in her side stabbed her with every breath, but she didn't let that slow her down. She had never climbed a mountain before, and she was enjoying herself, even if the experience left her gasping for air. The gap between herself and Lord Tamberlake diminished.

"Lord Tamberlake," she called out.

The figure in front of her didn't turn.

She quickened her pace and shortened the distance between them. "Lord Tamberlake."

He straightened, then turned. Ivy could see he wore only his eye patch today. She waved, then bunched her skirt in her fists and closed the space between them. When she reached him, she grinned with the exhilaration she felt. "Good morning. You look just like a pirate in that eye patch. I imagine the children of the village love to play with you."

"What the devil are you doing here?" Tamberlake scowled at her.

"I saw the mountains from the library window and then you." She clasped her hands in front of her. "I've never climbed a mountain before, and I took the opportunity presented to me."

"And you thought that gave you the right to bother me?" He turned his head so that she could view only the undamaged side of his face.

"Must you always be so rude?" Her cheeks, already pink from the climb, grew redder. Her brows drew together in a look of stern disapproval.

He stared at her. Surprise flooded him. She hadn't cowered from him. He had used his angriest tone, one that sent most men scurrying from his path, and she hadn't moved. "You're chastising me?"

"Someone must. Did you never learn manners as a child?" She planted her fists on her hips.

He leaned forward. His soft voice didn't disguise his irritation. "Manners are wasted on those who ignore the wishes of others."

Her eyes widened. "I haven't ignored your wishes. You never said I couldn't climb a mountain."

"Have I not made it clear I don't wish for your company?"

"That, sir, you have made clear." She grabbed her skirt again. "If you will excuse me, I wish to reach the summit."

He watched as she started higher up the mountain. "You'll get lost or slip and break your skinny little neck."

"Why should that bother you?" she called back over her shoulder. "Either way, you'll be well rid of me. And my neck is not skinny."

He chuckled. The girl had no sense, but she amused him. He braced himself on his staff and followed her. If something did happen to her, he would only have more visitors asking questions and disrupting his peace.

Her skirts didn't hamper her movement. She clutched them in her fists and lifted them above her feet. He wondered how she would respond if she knew she exposed more than her ankles. They were enclosed in boots, to be sure, but a proper lady never showed her ankles. Of course, he would be the last to call her a proper lady.

She clambered ahead of him, never giving him a backward glance. Because she didn't depend on a staff to aid her steps, she outdistanced him. "Lady Ivy," he called.

Her skirts fell around her feet as she stopped. For a moment, she didn't turn, then she faced him. "Did you call me?"

"Would you slow your pace?"

"Why?"

"I cannot climb as fast as you."

"I thought you had no wish for my company."

She turned back to the mountain and climbed a few more steps.

He sighed. "Lady Ivy, I would love to accompany you on your climb. Will you wait for me?"

She stopped. "Please."

"What?"

"Say *please.*"

"I won't ask permission to climb my own mountain."

She climbed a few more feet.

He bit back a roar. Through clenched teeth he said, "Please?"

When she faced him, a brilliant smile lit her face. "Why, yes, Lord Tamberlake. I should be happy to wait for you."

He grumbled with every step he took. When he reached her, he looked at her for a moment. "Has anyone ever told you how exasperating you are?"

"Oh, yes. My father says so often. My mother says the same. She claims I am the cause of her gray hair because she simply cannot understand me."

"I can believe it," mumbled Tamberlake.

"Pardon me?"

"Surely not." He leaned on his staff and strode forward. She matched her pace to his.

They climbed in silence for a few minutes. He noticed the lace on the hem of her dress grew muddier with each step. A wide band of moisture ringed the bottom of her gown. "Your dress will be ruined if we continue much farther."

Ivy glanced down, then waved her hand in dismissal. "What care I for a dress when I can climb a mountain? Papa can buy me a new one, but I shan't have another mountain for ages."

"As long as you don't expect me to replace it."

"Never. Mother is always trying to get me to wear prettier clothes anyway. She'll be happy to see one of my gowns ruined."

"That dress is pretty enough."

"I suppose, but Mother would have me dress in something more suitable than burgundy or green. I think she likes to pretend I am still in my first season."

"Aren't you?"

"Heavens, no. I've had three."

"And you haven't married yet."

"No, not yet. Papa had begun to despair, not to mention he'd tired of the tantrums thrown by my younger sister. Papa insists I marry first, and Georgina finds that tremendously unfair."

"I see." He couldn't explain it, but the news she had no prospects pleased him.

"What of you?" she asked.

"Me?"

"Yes. Why haven't you married?"

"I?" The question startled him.

"It's surprising. You are an earl. Many girls would love to be a countess."

He paused. "I had a fiancée once. She cried off."

"Why?"

As they had climbed, he had stayed on her left side. Now he faced her. "You need to ask?"

"You're right. Forgive me. Sometimes my curiosity gets the better of me. And to think I lectured you on your manners."

He stared at her in amazement. She really couldn't understand why Daphne had cried off.

She gazed back. "Do I have something on my face?"

"What?"

"You're staring at me. Do I have something on my face?"

He shook his head. "No."

Ivy looked up. "Then come on. We're almost at the top."

With a burst of speed, she clambered up the last hundred feet. He had to laugh at her exuberance. Lady Ivy was unlike anyone he had ever met. No one had accepted him this easily except Stanhope.

He froze. Oh, no. Stanhope had sent her. Stanhope probably had some other purpose in mind besides the delivery of the portrait.

Stanhope, you are a devil. But he wasn't interested in marriage.

He climbed up beside her and looked at her. Her face held an expression of awe as she took in the view.

"I can see why you climb here. I would want to scale the mountain every day to see this."

He tried to see the sight as she must. Other mountains rolled farther into the mists of the morning, climbing higher until one couldn't see their peaks. In the other direction lay the green trees of Betws-y-coed. In a few months, carriages carrying London folk who had discovered the joys of wandering would fill the village. Until then, these hills were his to wander. He had chased more than one trespasser from his lands in the past few summers.

"I come for the exercise."

"Liar." She grinned at him. "I can see it in your face. You love this spot."

For a moment, he couldn't speak. Her smile warmed him as the sun never had. He couldn't take his gaze from her. Then he shook himself and gave her an answering smile. "You're right. I do love this spot."

"I knew it." She spread her arms wide and spun around. "Now I can tell my children I have climbed a mountain. Thank you for letting me."

"I don't think I could have stopped you."

"No, you probably couldn't have." She laughed. "I'm hungry. Do you think they'll have breakfast ready by the time we return?"

He couldn't prevent the laugh that rose from his throat. "Yes, but I had better warn you. Mrs. Beaker isn't the best cook."

"Right now, gruel would sound wonderful. I'm famished."

"Watch what you wish for. Gruel is Mrs. Beaker's specialty."

Chapter 5

Tamberlake had been correct. Mrs. Beaker had made gruel. It was soggy and tasteless, and Ivy couldn't even find sugar on the table with which to sweeten it. She stirred and stirred, but the porridge only clumped together more. Mrs. Pennyfeather wasn't eating, either. She was staring at the lumpy mess in her bowl. Christopher lifted spoonful after spoonful above his bowl and watched it plop back into the congealing mass.

Lord Tamberlake, porcelain mask back in place, sat at the head of the table, eating one bite after another.

Ivy leaned toward Lord Tamberlake. "Do you eat this every morning?" she asked in a loud whisper.

"No," he whispered back. "Sometimes I have burnt toast to go with it."

"Why don't you hire a real cook?"

"She came with Beaker."

"You might consider replacing Beaker as well. A more surly butler I have never met."

Tamberlake narrowed his gaze. "Beaker is loyal."

"I meant no offense." She stirred the gruel again. Was it her imagination, or was the slop changing color?

Beaker entered the room and stood beside Lord Tamberlake's chair. "A message from the village, my lord."

"Thank you, Beaker." Tamberlake took the folded paper and opened it. He scanned the contents, then frowned.

"Bad news?" asked Christopher.

"Yes. Your carriage won't be ready for at least a week. The wheelwright says he's surprised you made it here at all with all the parts that have broken off. He needs to order several pieces from the blacksmith to make the repairs." He looked at Ivy.

"Don't scowl at me. It isn't as if I planned it." Ivy lifted a spoonful of the gruel to her nose and sniffed it. It smelled worse than it looked.

Christopher pushed his bowl from him. "A week of this?" he whispered.

Tamberlake glanced at him and lifted his spoon again. "You're welcome to stay in the village."

"Are you throwing us out?" asked Christopher.

"By no means. I am merely pointing out your alternatives," said Tamberlake in an even tone.

"At least I'd get a decent meal."

"Christopher." Ivy frowned at her brother, then caught sight of Mrs. Pennyfeather. The woman was pale, except for two spots of color in her cheeks. "Mrs. Pennyfeather, are you ill?"

"Pardon?" Mrs. Pennyfeather glanced at her, then averted her gaze to the table. "No, I'm fine. The news just startled me."

"There now, Mrs. Pennyfeather. No need to be

afraid. We came to no harm, and we shall return home in safety as well once the carriage is fixed." Ivy sighed and turned to Tamberlake. "I suppose we've imposed on your hospitality long enough. Would you be kind enough to lend us the use of your carriage to carry us into the village?"

"No," said Tamberlake.

Ivy's gaze shot to him in surprise.

"What I mean is that you don't need to stay in the village. My house is yours as long as you need it. I was making a poor attempt at jesting with your brother."

Ivy didn't believe him, but smiled at his attempt at gallantry.

"Then if I might make a suggestion . . ." Mrs. Pennyfeather folded her hands on the table.

Tamberlake raised an eyebrow. "Mrs. Penny-feather?"

"I have some experience in housekeeping. Perhaps I might be allowed to offer my abilities in the kitchen for the length of our stay."

"Yes, please," said Christopher, desperation in his voice.

Tamberlake coughed into his napkin, but to Ivy he looked more like he was hiding a laugh. A moment later Tamberlake said, "An excellent suggestion, Mrs. Pennyfeather. I'm sure Mrs. Beaker will appreciate the help."

By late morning, Mrs. Pennyfeather was ensconced in the bowels of the house, and Christopher and Ivy waited in the salon. Curtains blocked the window, but a fire glowed in the hearth. Ivy noticed a few lamps in the room that hadn't been there the previous evening. Christopher shuffled a deck of cards he found, while Ivy tried to read a book.

"What do you suppose he's up to?"

Ivy looked up from the page. "What do you mean?"

"Tamberlake. What do you think he's doing? He sure isn't providing entertainment for his guests."

"We're hardly his guests. We intruded into his home."

Christopher riffled the cards. "Nevertheless, one would expect a modicum of decency from an earl. 'Course, his behavior is hardly a surprise, given who he is."

Ivy frowned. "What does that mean?"

"Well, look at him. I can see why he hides out here in Wales, but you'd think he could get a haircut."

"I think his hair looks fine."

"Really, Ivy. The last time I saw hair that long was on some self-proclaimed colonel from Georgia, who was trying to drum up custom for his cotton crop. Tamberlake is an earl, not some drawling colonial." Christopher dealt out the cards for a game of patience. "I suppose the hair does help hide his face."

"There's nothing wrong with his face," said Ivy.

Christopher chuckled. "Only you, Ivy. Only you would consider the man's face not a problem."

"He has a beautiful face." She felt the heat rush into her cheeks.

"Half of it." Christopher looked up at his sister and paused. "You're blushing."

"I am not." Her countenance grew hotter.

"You find him some kind of tragic, romantic character."

"I do not. He's rude and arrogant, and his manners are nonexistent." She tossed her head. "Much like a viscount I could name."

"I wouldn't leave my guests without anything to do."

"Really, Christopher. Lord Tamberlake probably has more important things to do than see to our entertainment. I'm sure he has correspondence, or accounts from his holdings to look over, or papers to read, or—"

"Correct, Lady Ivy," said Lord Tamberlake from the doorway.

Ivy whirled around. The blush that had just started to abate returned full force to her cheeks.

Tamberlake walked into the room, leaning on his cane. "But I have finished my morning business. It wasn't my intention to ignore you this morning."

"We quite understand, Lord Tamberlake."

"Speak for yourself," said Christopher under his breath.

Ivy glanced at him. "Our father spends much time taking care of his affairs. We often go days without seeing him."

"And Lord Styles, here, must have his own responsibilities." Tamberlake watched Christopher place a card on top of a pile.

"Hardly. Father isn't likely to let me run any of his estates until he's dead," muttered Christopher.

"That's unwise of him. What better way to teach a son than to give him responsibilities of his own."

His eyes wide, Christopher stared at Tamberlake. He placed a card on the table without looking at it.

"I believe you've misplayed, Styles." Tamberlake tapped the card.

"What?" Christopher looked down and snatched up the card. "Right. Don't know what I was thinking."

"Do you play chess?"

Christopher shrugged. "Not very well."

"Would you be interested in a game?" Tamberlake moved to two chairs by the window. A chess table stood between them. "I would enjoy playing again. Beaker didn't come with knowledge of the game."

Christopher abandoned the cards and took the chair opposite Tamberlake.

"And what should I do while you play?" Ivy asked with her arms crossed over her chest.

"You may watch, or start your own game of patience," said Christopher.

"Which leaves me as little to do as before," said Ivy. She picked up her book and flopped into a chair. The book failed to hold her attention. The two men drew her gaze time and again. From this angle, she couldn't see the mask that hid Tamberlake's face. His mouth curved downward in concentration as he considered his next move. His hair was decidedly long, but it gave him the air of some medieval hero. He was a beautiful man.

Soon she gave up all pretense of reading. Instead, she watched the two men. Her brother was younger than Tamberlake. His expression revealed his emotions as he played—consternation at a misplay, elation at the execution of a tricky maneuver. Tamberlake's face never changed. His concentration didn't waver. She wondered how it would feel to be on the receiving end of such attention. She sighed.

Tamberlake looked up. "Lady Ivy, are you bored?"

"No, I—I . . ." Her cheeks flamed. "I think I shall change for luncheon." She snapped her book closed. The clap startled her. Without waiting for any sort of response, she fled the room.

Tamberlake looked at Christopher. "Is she often so unpredictable?"

"Definitely." Styles moved his knight forward.

Tamberlake lifted his queen and took the knight. "Checkmate. Shall we play again?" Tamberlake replaced his pieces on the board.

"Yes. Give me a chance to get even," said Styles.

"We didn't wager."

"I know. Pride and all that." Styles finished setting up the white men.

Now, how to approach the information he wanted. "Of course, I've heard of your family. Your father stands in high repute in London. I'm surprised he allowed you to come so close to the season."

"Father had little to say about it. Mother convinced him." Styles lifted a pawn from the board and moved it forward two spaces.

"Your mother? I didn't realize she wields such power over your father." Tamberlake countered Styles's move, but didn't take his gaze from his opponent's face.

"No, I didn't mean that at all. Mother wheedled, but Father wouldn't have let us come if it wasn't convenient. I don't mind missing a few balls. After all, I'm not planning to settle down anytime soon. And Father doesn't think much about Ivy. I mean, he doesn't think about her often."

Somehow Tamberlake believed the first choice of words.

"She's only his daughter, after all," continued

Styles, "and as such is only important for the match she will make in her husband. Connections, you know."

"But she will miss the beginning of the season. She can't make a match if she doesn't meet any bachelors."

"Her betrothal is already decided. Father wouldn't have let her come if it wasn't."

That news sent a queer tightening to his stomach. "Lady Ivy is betrothed?"

"Not officially. We shall hold a ball to announce it after we return." Styles chuckled. "No doubt Wynbrooke is anxious. Our trip has already lasted longer than planned."

"Wynbrooke?" Tamberlake moved his rook, exposing his knight.

"Neville Foxworthy, Earl Wynbrooke. He's the man Father has chosen for Ivy." Styles captured the black knight.

"Good move," said Tamberlake. He racked his brain for any memory of this Wynbrooke, but failed.

"Of course, Georgina must be biting her nails at our delay."

"Who is Georgina?"

"My youngest sister. Father won't let her accept suitors until Ivy is married."

Tamberlake was forming a good picture of Ivy's family. "And Georgina is . . ."

"Quite the beauty," said Styles. "She's only eighteen, but she was afraid Ivy would never marry. At twenty-one, Ivy seemed in danger of being put on the shelf, and Georgina feared Father wouldn't ever let her get married, either. And judging from the amount of poetry she receives already, many of the bachelors would have also suffered."

"Lady Ivy has never had suitors?"

"A few who were interested in her dowry, but they disappeared soon after speaking with her. Ivy isn't one to refrain from voicing her opinion."

"I've noticed." Tamberlake took Styles's castle, leaving himself open for checkmate.

"Wynbrooke outlasted the others. Finally Father talked to her and announced his approval of the match." Styles pounced. "Checkmate."

"Well played. We shall have to battle again." Tamberlake placed the pieces in the drawer and rose from the table. He walked to the fire. "Did you know Stanhope?"

"Stanhope? Oh, you mean the chap who left Ivy the bequest. Didn't know him at all." Styles joined his host by the fire.

More and more, Tamberlake understood Stanhope's purpose in sending Ivy. But what could the man do now? Unless he was a ghost, he couldn't meddle in their lives, and Tamberlake didn't believe in ghosts. He had enough trouble with monsters. "But he left her a bequest?"

"Yes. Rum story, that one. Seems he was in love with my mother, but couldn't marry her. He left Ivy a house in Devon and some money if she delivered a package to you. Strange stipulation, especially from a man we never met, but now she's done it." Styles leaned against the hearth. "Can't imagine why the fellow would do such a thing. It isn't as though she hadn't any prospects."

"Perhaps she hadn't at the time Stanhope wrote the will. Has this Winthorpe been around for long?"

"Wynbrooke, and, no, come to think of it. Wynbrooke and my father first talked about a month ago. Never saw much of him before. Not even at the clubs. He wasn't an ardent suitor. He was just there at times."

Tamberlake was more convinced than ever of Stanhope's plan of bringing Ivy and himself together. Tamberlake shook his head. As if a monster was the worthy companion to a lady.

"Wonder where Ivy has gotten herself to." Styles glanced toward the door. "She doesn't usually take this long to dress."

"Perhaps she has hidden herself in fear of Mrs. Beaker's cooking." Tamberlake placed his weight on his cane and took a step toward the door. "I shall see if she is in the library. She seems to find herself there often."

He crossed the hall to the library and opened the door. For a moment, he didn't recognize the room. The draperies were pulled back. Although he kept the library brighter than the rest of the house, the light that did pour in was more than the room had seen for some time.

She stood by the window, forgotten book in hand, staring at the mountains.

"What are you doing?"

Ivy whirled around. "I? I'm not doing anything."

He crossed to the drapes and released them from their ties, first one side, then the other. The heavy cloth swished back into place.

"Why did you do that?" she asked. "If I had such a view from my window I would never cover it."

"I don't like the light." Tamberlake scowled at her.

"Well, of course you don't. Not with that atti-
tude." Ivy didn't flinch under his glare.

He looked away first. "My apologies."

"Accepted." Ivy smiled at him.

A rush of warmth filled him at her smile. With
some irritation, he noticed his heart beat faster as
well. "I thought you were changing your dress."

"I decided against it." She crossed to the bookshelf and tucked the novel into its place. "Why?
Have you decided we're dining formally?"

"No, you look fine. Shall we rejoin your brother?"

"By all means."

He leaned on his cane and took two steps toward the door. Ivy didn't move. He looked at her
for a moment, wondering what she waited for. She
stood with her hands folded in front of her.

"Shall we go?"

"Yes."

She didn't move, but only looked at him with
that smile.

"Luncheon." He took another step.

"Indeed. And I am famished." Ivy didn't stir.

He came back to her, and her smile grew
broader. She took his free arm. "Thank you, Lord
Tamberlake. I knew you wouldn't allow a lady to
go in to lunch without the proper escort."

Chapter 6

He cried out in pain as his leg snapped.

Move, you foolish boy.

But he lay still as the carriage settled on its side.

Get up.

The smoke came first, choking him, blinding him, until he saw the flames. Then he screamed.

Tamberlake's eye shot open. He bolted upright in his bed, clawing at his throat and face. His breath was ragged, and his heart raced. Sweat plastered his hair to his forehead and neck. The panic gripped him for another moment before he realized he was safe.

A gap in the curtains let a ray of bright sun into the room. It hit him in the eye. He winced.

Damn sun.

He climbed from the bed and crossed to the washbasin. His leg always hurt more following the nightmare. He poured water into the basin. Cupping his hands, he splashed the cool liquid on his face, then dried it with a towel.

He sat in a chair and let his head fall back. He

hated waking this way. It was always a portent of
the day to come.

Ivy stretched her hands over her head and
blinked in surprise. The sun shone through her
windows. She hadn't seen such light in days.
Perhaps the change in the weather would chase
away the chill or improve the mood of their host.
Either way, Ivy was glad of the brightness.

As Ivy dressed, she realized she didn't miss the
scurrying of servants carrying the morning trays
or wood for the various fires. Although she couldn't
tighten her corset as well by herself, she had Mrs.
Pennyfeather's help if she wanted it. She didn't
miss her family, either. No one telling her where to
go, or what to do, or how to dress. Or expecting
her to be like someone else. Or chiding her for
her lack of beauty.

Ivy sighed as she adjusted her skirt. There was
something to be said for a life in isolation. Georgina
was beautiful, but Ivy couldn't remember the last
time her sister read a book. And the comfort of a
looser corset was worth mentioning again.

Ivy made her way to the breakfast room and
stopped in surprise. Bread and jam waited on the
sideboard. Two carafes held steaming liquids. She
sniffed each one. Tea and coffee. She poured herself a cup of tea and took one of the rolls. With a
little butter and jam, this would hold her until a
proper breakfast with the rest of the household.

The roll was still warm as she broke it open. She
inhaled its yeasty aroma. She didn't know what
miracle Mrs. Pennyfeather had wrought in the
kitchen, but she was grateful for it.

"Good morning."

"Oh." Ivy jumped. Lord Tamberlake stood in the doorway.

"I didn't mean to startle you."

"No, I wasn't . . . I hadn't expected anyone else to be up so early. Christopher usually sleeps until noon at home, and . . ." She eyed his sturdy boots and the thick cloak draped over his arm. "You're going out again."

He nodded. "I always take a morning constitutional. I find my leg is less stiff throughout the day if I exercise it." He looked at the sideboard and raised his eyebrow. "Edible?"

"Delicious." She took a bite of the roll.

"Amazing." Tamberlake helped himself to coffee and a roll. As he bit into the bread, his expression changed from wariness to enjoyment.

"Will you climb the mountain again today?"

"No." He offered no further explanation.

"Then where shall you go?"

He paused for a moment as if reluctant to tell her. "If one follows the brook, it leads to the edge of the woods."

"I'd love to see them. May I join you?"

He examined her with a look of annoyance. "If I turn you down, you'd probably follow anyway."

"Most likely." She smiled at him.

"Very well, but don't be surprised if we are gone for a while. The hike up the mountain is more strenuous, but this walk takes longer. Take your wrap. The sun might be shining, but it's still cold outside."

"I'll return in a minute." Ivy dashed from the room.

When she returned, Tamberlake was waiting by the door.

"I had to change my shoes before we left," said Ivy. She poked out the toe of her boot from under her skirts. "These should prove better for a long walk."

"Mmmm." He drew on his cloak.

Ivy unfolded hers, but was surprised to feel it rise from her hands.

"Allow me." He held out the garment.

"Thank you." Ivy turned her back to him as he draped the cloak over her shoulders. His manners were improving.

Tamberlake opened the door for her, then followed her out into the sunshine. He blinked into the brightness.

"It's a beautiful day, isn't it?" Ivy turned her face toward the sun and closed her eyes.

"Too bright," said Tamberlake. "Come along."

She opened her eyes to see him walking away from her. So much for thinking his manners had improved.

They strolled beside the brook without talking. The only sound she heard was the gurgling of the water and the occasional cry of a bird. Tamberlake moved with a sure, steady pace, relying on his walking staff when he stepped on his weak leg. Although the cold in the air stung the back of her throat as she breathed in, the sun on her back warmed her.

Ivy enjoyed the wild look of the land. An occasional stand of trees sprouted from the side of the mountain they walked beside, but mostly scrubby little plants covered the hillsides. Half an hour later, she wasn't admiring the view any longer. She struggled to keep up with Tamberlake. Her shopping forays into London with her mother and Georgina hadn't prepared her for this excursion. She glanced up at him. His steps hadn't slowed.

She gave out a loud puff of air, picked up her skirts, and hurried after him. Her rapid breath gave evidence to her efforts, but Tamberlake didn't glance at her. She kept her pace even with his through sheer determination. He was the one with the weak leg. Why was she so slow? On the mountain yesterday she had been faster. Of course, she hadn't walked for half an hour at a brisk pace to reach him.

Her boot slipped on a loose rock. Ivy cried out and stumbled forward.

Tamberlake whirled with a grace she didn't think him capable of, and caught her in his arms before she could fall. "Lady Ivy, are you hurt?"

She didn't move. His leg might be weak, but nothing but strength dwelt in his arms. He held her so that her feet barely touched the ground. Her hands were trapped against his chest. Nothing weak there, either. In fact, she rather enjoyed the sensation of being held up to such a strong man.

"Lady Ivy?" He placed her on the ground and held her away from him to gaze into her face.

She blushed. Heat flooded into her cheeks and flamed onto her skin. Oh Lord, what must he think now?

"Are you hurt?"

"N-no." Ivy remembered to speak. She shrugged off his hands and righted herself. She turned her face from his so he couldn't see her. "I stumbled over a stone. I'm fine."

He said nothing for a moment. "Perhaps we should turn back."

"No. I wish to see the woods." She faced him again, hoping the color had abated enough to be taken for the pink of exertion and not mortification. He looked disturbed. "Truly, I'm not hurt. Are they very much farther?"

"What?"

"The woods?"

"No."

"Then shall we continue?"

"Yes."

"Unless you wish to return."

"No."

She wondered what she'd done to earn his single-word responses again.

The brook veered to the left as they followed its bank. Rounding the bend, Ivy stopped. Ahead stood an expanse of trees, bushes, and greenery. Although far from full leaf, the trees held the new green of early spring. She imagined it was beautiful in summer.

Something brown darted in front of them and disappeared into the underbrush.

Ivy let out a startled cry. "What was that? It looked like a weasel."

"A polecat, most likely, or a small fox." Tamberlake continued toward the woods.

Birds called around them. Ivy glanced from one bush to another, hoping to catch a glimpse of whatever creatures might lurk therein, but she saw nothing. Tamberlake pushed forward through the trees. Ivy followed behind him, gazing from side to side. When he stopped, she almost bumped into him.

"Why have you . . . Oh." She took in the view of a small lake. The water was as still as glass and reflected the sky on its surface. She didn't speak for a minute or two, then smiled. "I can see why you come here."

Tamberlake looked out over the water. "It's peaceful." He glanced at her. "Usually."

Ivy placed her fists on her hips. "I haven't done anything to disturb the quiet."

"You just did." He laughed.

"You provoked me. It's hardly right, accusing me of—"

He held up his hand. "I was thinking back on last summer. I found a group of picnickers along the shore. They were throwing their trash into my lake."

"What did you do?"

Shrugging, he said, "I frightened them away."

"How?"

Tamberlake stared at her, then shook his head. "Lady Ivy, you are a wonder."

"Stop looking at me as if I were a freak."

He let out a sigh of exasperation. "Do you know why I allowed you to accompany me this morning? You do remember you are a single woman in the company of a bachelor without any sort of chaperone?"

Her stomach cramped at the thought. "Oh, dear. You're right. Mrs. Pennyfeather should be here. Mother would have an apoplectic fit if she knew."

"Do you know why your reputation won't be harmed by our stroll?"

"Because you are honorable and won't tell anyone of my indiscretion."

"No, because your reputation is safe with me.

No one would believe I am capable of leading you astray with this face."

"Why not?"

"Open your eyes, Lady Ivy. Who would willingly kiss this face?" He stepped closer, leaning over her. She stepped back. "I could ravish you right here, and no one would believe you."

"Rubbish."

He stepped even closer. "Shall I prove it to you?" He encircled her with his arm, pulled her to him and kissed her.

Ivy's senses whirled. The warmth of his lips stole her breath. She closed her eyes as the wonderful vertigo grew. When his tongue entered her mouth she let out a little moan of pleasure. She had never been thoroughly kissed before, but she certainly was now.

He released her. The sudden cold air where once his warmth had been shocked her.

"Tell your brother, and wait for his reaction." He turned from her and started back through the woods.

She gaped after him. He hadn't meant to kiss her except as an experiment. He had just wanted to prove his point. Well, she would tell her brother and prove him wrong.

Dashing a tear from her cheek, she didn't know whether she was angry or devastated. He didn't like her. Damn female sensibilities. She wouldn't cry. She wouldn't.

With a sniff, she lifted her chin higher and followed him, wiping an errant drop now and again.

They didn't speak the entire way back. Ivy made no attempt to catch Tamberlake. She was content to march behind him as her fury grew.

They didn't speak at the house, either. She was in high dudgeon when they reached the steps. Tamberlake opened the door, and Ivy flounced through the portal. She threw her cloak off her shoulders and tossed it to a startled Beaker.

They also didn't speak through breakfast. Ivy chewed in silence, ignoring the questioning glances from her brother and Mrs. Pennyfeather. She didn't taste the eggs, or the ham, or the kippers, or the fruit tarts. With wry humor, she supposed she should have saved eating in this manner for Mrs. Beaker's gruel.

Tamberlake disappeared from the table first. In a few minutes, Mrs. Pennyfeather muttered something about seeing to the kitchen and left as well. Ivy laid her napkin on the table.

"Ivy, what is wrong?" asked Christopher.

She glared at him. "Tamberlake kissed me."

"Really, Ivy. If you don't want to tell me, just say so."

Ivy's anger ebbed from her. Tamberlake had been right.

"Did he say something to you? Something about the ideas women get when they read too much?"

"Ugh, men." Ivy gave a withering look to her brother, then left the room.

She wanted solitude. The library should be empty. Tamberlake was probably in his study. She wasn't disappointed. Glancing around to ascertain the room was empty, she spotted the window. Mischief beckoned her, and she flung the curtains wide. No one could tell her not to let the light in today.

Settling into a comfortable chair, she refused to think about Tamberlake, his kiss, or how her brother reacted.

Her book lay unread on her lap.

Tamberlake's kiss played over and over again in her mind. With a growl, she lifted the book in front of her eyes. She didn't see the words. Her heart hammered in her chest as she ran her tongue over her lips. If she closed her eyes, she could recall every riotous, wonderful sensation that had cascaded through her. Until his words ruined everything.

Ivy, you're a goose.

Luncheon was as silent as breakfast had been. Styles had tried to make conversation, but he hadn't bothered after a few minutes of unspoken rebuffs. Ivy never dared lift her gaze. Tamberlake enjoyed the silence. He cherished it. It was almost as though his guests had never arrived, as if he had never kissed her.

Tamberlake dropped his spoon. It clattered against the china with a sharp ping. He snatched it up again and fought the annoyance that flooded him.

Why was he thinking about the kiss? He shouldn't have done it. He knew he shouldn't have touched her, but she looked so trusting, so innocent, so delicious, he had let his sensibilities rule. Even now he couldn't keep his gaze from her face. Thank heavens she wasn't looking at him.

Three more courses followed the soup. Tamberlake couldn't remember when he had eaten so well, and he hated every minute of it. He wanted his solitude. He wanted the darkness. He wanted . . .

He wanted Ivy to look at him.

Gad, what was he thinking? His fingers touched

the hard, cold mask. The last woman to look at him had been Daphne, a woman who was supposed to love him, and she had fled in terror of his face. Why didn't Ivy run away?

The interminable meal was nearly over when Beaker entered the room.

"Excuse me, my lord?"

"Yes?"

"Another carriage has arrived."

"What?"

"Two gentlemen. They wish to speak with you, sir."

"Did you tell them I won't see them?"

"Of course, my lord, but they claim they know Lady Ivy."

Ivy glanced up at this news. She looked as surprised as he felt.

"What are their names?"

Beaker handed him two cards. Tamberlake read the printing on the front, then looked at Ivy. "It appears they speak the truth."

"Who are they?" asked Ivy.

"I believe your betrothed has come looking for you." Tamberlake tossed the cards on the table.

The names, Neville Foxworthy, Earl Wynbrooke, and Roger Thorndike, Esquire, appeared on the cards for all to read.

Chapter 7

Tamberlake watched from a small gap in the drapes in an upstairs room. Ivy and Styles stood beside the carriage as two men climbed down. One man was taller than the other. He bowed to Ivy, then stepped to the side. The shorter man grasped Ivy's hands in his and greeted her with a wide smile.

Wynbrooke. Tamberlake didn't need an introduction to know which man was which. The familiarity of the greeting belonged to a betrothed. The man should have been an actor; his voice boomed across the drive. Tamberlake had no trouble hearing him.

"Lady Ivy, I have found you at last." Wynbrooke bent and kissed her hand.

Tamberlake scowled. He didn't like the man. His blond hair didn't look as though he had spent the last few hours in a coach. Neither did his clothes. They looked as if he just stepped from his tailor. The man was slender, too good-looking, and clearly had a happy disposition.

And he was whole.

Tamberlake let the curtain drop into place, blocking his view. Beaker would take the new arrivals to the salon. He would wait there. He hurried down the stairs to beat the newcomers to the room.

As he entered the salon, he noticed the extra lamps burning. He'd ordered them for Lady Ivy. Now he didn't want them. As he extinguished the flames, the room fell into its customary darkness. The heavy damask drapes let in none of the sunshine. He moved to the corner of the room where a high-backed chair stood bathed in the shadows. He sat and waited, feeling much like a spider waiting for a fly.

As expected, Beaker showed the small group into the darkened room. From his hidden recess, he watched surprise flit across Wynbrooke's face.

"Rather dark, isn't it? I would think a man as rich as Tamberlake could afford a few lamps."

"Rich?" said Ivy.

"I made some inquiries about the man. His fortune makes your father's look paltry."

Tamberlake glanced at Ivy. Her gaze never rose from the floor.

"We did hear the man was eccentric, Wyn. Looks like the rumors were true," the taller man said, leaning against the mantel as though he were lord. Tamberlake knew this must be Thorndike. Arrogant. He didn't like him, either.

"What are you doing here, Wynbrooke?" Styles took a seat by the hearth.

Tamberlake wanted to know the answer to that as well.

"Your mother sent for me. She didn't like the tone of your last letter, Lady Ivy."

"My letter?" Ivy glanced up at Wynbrooke. "I suppose you mean the one I sent from the inn when the weather delayed us."

"Your mother felt that as your betrothed I should be aware of your difficulties. And rightly so. She seemed terribly distraught over your journey, so I thought it my duty to ease her mind and travel with you."

"Besides, Wynbrooke wouldn't want the earl to steal you from him. Would you, Wyn?" Thorndike chuckled.

"Most definitely not." Wynbrooke pulled on his cravat. "Are there no servants here? I could use a brandy."

"Not many," said Styles with a grin.

Thorndike snorted. "I expect the man's stingy despite his wealth."

"He is not," said Ivy. "He gave us lodging when our carriage broke."

"Your carriage broke? Then it's quite right that I followed you here. We can ride back in my coach," said Wynbrooke.

Tamberlake's stomach cramped at the thought.

"We wouldn't all fit," said Ivy. "And I won't ask Mrs. Pennyfeather to stay behind without me. No, I suppose we'll just have to wait until our carriage is repaired."

"How long will that be?" asked Thorndike. "I don't want to be stuck in this godforsaken spot for longer than necessary."

"They told us a week," said Christopher.

"A week?" Wynbrooke grimaced.

"It can't be helped, I suppose," said Thorndike. "Ah, well. Just think how we'll dine out on tales of our week with the monster earl."

Two spots of color appeared in Ivy's cheeks. "He is not a monster, and I won't have you speak of him that way."

Tamberlake rose from his seat. "Don't trouble yourself, Lady Ivy. I've heard worse." He limped toward the small group. Styles's face held a hint of amusement at the chagrin in Wynbrooke's expression, but Ivy looked ready to cry. "Welcome, gentlemen, to Gryphon's Lair. I'm sorry I wasn't able to greet you outside."

He stepped into the full light of the fire and waited for the reaction of the men. It came, and with it his wry satisfaction. Their mesmerized gazes fell upon the porcelain mask. "May I offer you gentlemen some brandy?"

Wynbrooke's Adam's apple bobbed up and down as he swallowed hard. "Yes, thank you. Brandy would be welcome."

"I'll get it." Styles jumped up from his seat and crossed to the sideboard. He winked as he passed Tamberlake.

Tamberlake took a position by the fire. Thorndike scurried out of his way. Tamberlake smiled as he leaned against the mantel in an exact imitation of Thorndike's former pose. "Lord Wynbrooke, a pleasure to meet you. I must admit your name is unfamiliar to me."

"I came into the title only recently when my father died after a long illness. He wasn't in society much."

"And, of course, I haven't been in society much myself recently." Tamberlake chuckled at his own joke.

Wynbrooke laughed with him. At least Tamberlake believed it was a laugh. It sounded more like a squeak.

"Mr. Thorndike," said Tamberlake, "I hope the journey wasn't too tiresome."

"Not in the least, my lord. The changing landscape was fascinating."

With a nod, Tamberlake said, "I believe it takes a special individual who can appreciate the unique beauties of Wales. Wouldn't you agree, Lady Ivy?"

Ivy hid a smile behind her hand. "Most definitely."

Styles returned with four brandies. He gave one to each of the gentlemen, and returned to his seat. He lifted his glass. "To your health, gentlemen."

Tamberlake waited until the two men had lifted their glasses to their lips. "And to the health of Lady Ivy."

As he expected, the two men snatched their snifters from their mouths. The brandy sloshed along the sides of the glasses.

"To the Lady Ivy," said Wynbrooke in hasty agreement. Thorndike nodded.

Ivy coughed into her hand. Tamberlake saw the crinkle at the corner of her eyes that indicated her laughter.

"I'm sorry you traveled all this way to retrieve us, Lord Wynbrooke," said Ivy. "I will not think ill of you if you wish to return without us. Christopher will see me home."

"I wouldn't dream of abandoning you, Lady Ivy. I have nothing pressing in London. The season can start without me." Wynbrooke looked at Tamberlake, then glanced away. "Perhaps you could recommend a suitable inn for us?"

"Since it seems your departure has been delayed for a few days, may I offer you accommodation in my home?" Tamberlake watched Wynbrooke as a look of relief crossed his face.

"Thank you, my lord. We are in your debt."

"I'll have Beaker make up two more rooms," said Tamberlake. "I can't remember the last time he's had so many guests to care for. He'll be thrilled."

"Beaker?" said Styles. "I would pay to see that."

Within an hour, Beaker had shown the new guests their rooms, and Tamberlake retreated to the sanctuary of his study—the wood paneled walls, the paintings he never tired of examining, the heavy desk, his notebooks filled with ideas for his estates—his place, where no one intruded except Beaker on occasion to bring him his brandy. Although he was resolved to prove Ivy's words about his generosity correct, he nevertheless couldn't shake the discomfort that seized him knowing so many people were in his house. He looked over the papers on his desk. A few hours of going over account books should sufficiently numb him to the presence of others.

He had every intention of setting to work, but his gaze landed on his copy of *Burke's Peerage*. He flipped through the pages until he found Wynbrooke. The family's history was illustrious. The line went back several centuries. Reading the various exploits of the Wynbrooke family, Tamberlake felt his mood growing more foul. When he finally reached the present Earl Wynbrooke, he read with interest. Only the book didn't cover this Wynbrooke, just his father.

He snapped the book shut and shoved it onto the shelves.

Muttering to himself, he sat behind his desk

and stared at his account books. Forcing himself to concentrate, he started on the figures, but then a knock on his door pulled him away from his work. "Come."

To his surprise, Mrs. Pennyfeather entered the room. "Forgive my intrusion, Lord Tamberlake."

He shook his head. "No bother. How may I help you?"

Mrs. Pennyfeather pursed her lips for a moment, then faced him with a slight frown. "It isn't my place to tell you how to run your house, but . . ."

Tamberlake raised an eyebrow. "But . . . ? Do go on, Mrs. Pennyfeather."

"With the new arrivals, Mr. and Mrs. Beaker need help. You can't expect them to see after the rooms, the food, the laundry, the heating of water, and everything else alone."

Tamberlake leaned back in his chair. "What do you suggest?"

"You must hire a few girls from the village as chambermaids and sculleries. Perhaps a few men as well for the care of the horses and as valets for the gentlemen."

"And what if no one will come work for the monster earl?"

"Pshaw. If you offer them a decent wage they will soon forget their fears. It's amazing how money overcomes superstition."

"You seem to have thought the situation out."

"You forget I used to be a housekeeper. It was my duty to think things out."

He nodded. "Very well. Send Beaker to the village and hire whomever you think we need."

A hesitant look flitted across her features.

"A problem?"

Mrs. Pennyfeather shook her head, but paused for a moment. "Mrs. Beaker would make an admirable housekeeper with a little more training. Perhaps you should send her instead. I'd be happy to accompany her and give her the benefit of my years in service."

"Isn't it customary for the butler to do the hiring?"

"Yes, but I think the villagers might find Mrs. Beaker less formidable than Mr. Beaker."

"As you wish." Tamberlake returned to his books, only to look up in a minute. Mrs. Pennyfeather had not left. "Is there something else?"

She nodded. "Mr. Beaker is an admirable servant."

"And loyal. I believe we had this conversation at breakfast yesterday."

"Yes, my lord, but when I went to the kitchen, I noticed Mr. Beaker had quite a talent for cooking."

"What?" He stared at her.

"Mrs. Beaker has been cooking for you all this time, because Mr. Beaker was your butler and had other duties. When I went to the kitchen to speak to them about the food, Mr. Beaker seemed to understand what was needed at once. He has prepared the last few meals."

"Beaker?"

"Yes, sir. I believe he enjoys it. I found him singing in the kitchen this morning."

"Beaker?"

"Yes, my lord. I think he would make a fine cook."

"*My* Beaker?"

"All the finest chefs are men, my lord."

He blinked several times, hoping to clear his thoughts.

"If you were to ask him . . ."

He shook his head. "Then I would be without a butler. In your experience, wouldn't you agree every household needs a butler?"

Mrs. Pennyfeather smiled. "Of course. But Mr. Beaker needn't be that butler. If you'll permit me, I know a man who is in want of a position."

"Aha. He has been let go. He can't be reliable."

"His employer died, and the new earl had his own butler. He worked for Lord Stanhope."

Tamberlake sat back, dumbfounded.

"I should perhaps warn you of the man's unconventional appearance."

He raised an eyebrow. "His appearance?"

"Yes, sir. Mr. Fletcher is highly capable, but many prospective employers are put off by his looks."

Mrs. Pennyfeather was warning *him* of the man's appearance? This day grew more strange by the minute. "If I choose to hire a new butler, his appearance shall have no bearing on the post."

"Thank you, sir. Shall I send Mr. Beaker?"

His shoulders slumped. "Yes."

"As you wish." Mrs. Pennyfeather gave a quick curtsey and left the room, but the image of her all-knowing smile lingered.

Any thought of returning to the books vanished. What manner of chaos had invaded Gryphon's Lair with the arrival of Ivy? And how could he fight against it? Oh, he could ignore Mrs. Pennyfeather, but what if she was right and Beaker would prefer to cook? He clenched his fists and waited for Beaker.

Chapter 8

When Tamberlake came down the stairs the following morning, Ivy was waiting for him.

"Where are we going today?"

He rubbed his forehead to ward off a nonexistent headache. His world was in enough turmoil without having to worry about Ivy. Beaker had indeed preferred to remain on as cook, and Mrs. Pennyfeather had sent off a letter to her former butler acquaintance. Plus, he knew he'd think of nothing but the kiss if Ivy was alone with him. "I didn't think you'd want to accompany me this morning with the others in the house."

She frowned. "My brother? No, thank you. I'll spend plenty of time with him in the future."

"What of your betrothed?"

"I'm sure he's still sleeping. Besides, he won't miss me even if he does wake. Mr. Thorndike will keep him entertained." Ivy wrapped a scarf around her neck and pulled her cloak around her. "Shall we go?"

Tamberlake didn't speak. He grabbed his own cloak, pulled it on, and opened the door for her. Another glorious day. He frowned. Perhaps rain would have put her off.

They headed in the opposite direction of their previous walk. He led the way, following the brook upstream. Scrub covered the terrain, and the occasional sheep looked up at them as they passed. High above, a hawk searched for its breakfast. No welcoming wood waited at the end of this ramble. Tamberlake hoped Ivy would become discouraged and avoid his company in the future. He was having trouble enough untangling his life from the complications she had brought.

He didn't look at her, he didn't speak to her. He quickened his pace. She followed without a complaint. When he glanced back at her, the sight of her nearly stole his breath. Her cheeks were pink from exertion, her lips were parted just a tad to help her breathe, and she tilted her face to the sun. The expression of enjoyment on her face reminded him of a child at Christmas, only Ivy was no child.

He groaned.

Ivy hurried to him. "Are you hurt?"

He turned his gaze from her. "A rock, a small one. I stumbled."

"I didn't see you stumble."

"I mean a sharp one. I stepped on it."

"Oh. Shall we return then?"

"No." He glanced at her. Her face was a mask of concern. When was the last time anyone had cared if he was injured? After his accident, his mother worried more about the reaction of her friends to his new face. His fiancée wouldn't even look at him. But Ivy never averted her gaze. "I'm fine. Do you wish to continue?"

"Oh, yes. I don't imagine you have such beautiful weather often."

He started forward, but he waited for her and slowed to a leisurely pace.

"Has Mrs. Pennyfeather worked for your family long?"

"She doesn't work for us at all. She was Lord Stanhope's housekeeper. His will specified she was available to help me as I needed. I needed a companion." Ivy glanced at him. "I suppose I shouldn't have told you that. Mother was adamant that no one learn she is hired help. 'A housekeeper isn't a proper chaperone.' So Mrs. Pennyfeather has been elevated to the position of poor relation for the duration of this outing."

Tamberlake laughed. "Are you always this forthright with your answers?"

Ivy shrugged. "I know I shouldn't be, but I find it too troublesome to lie or disguise the truth, as my mother would say. Although it was my idea in the first place."

"What was?"

"Telling people Mrs. Pennyfeather was a poor relation. I knew Mother wouldn't let me come if I didn't. She worries overmuch about what people think."

And she probably doesn't want to think about her daughter with the monster earl. No wonder the woman sent Ivy's betrothed after her.

Without warning, he turned and started back.

Ivy stopped in surprise, then scrambled after him. "Must we go so soon?"

"Yes." He didn't alter his pace.

"Why?"

He frowned at her. "I have guests. Or had you forgotten?"

"No, I hadn't forgotten, but I'm surprised you remembered." She frowned back at him.

His abrupt mood changes baffled her. Not that it mattered. She wasn't staying long enough to master his moods.

Due to the narrowness of the path, she walked behind him. He never turned to see how she fared or if she followed at all. With a loud puff of air, she trudged after him. Why she bothered to try to befriend him escaped her.

Even if she secretly hoped he would kiss her again.

She stared at the broad back in front of her and wondered how a man so contrary could kiss with such passion.

A shot rang out.

She let out a little yell, but Tamberlake glanced at the sky in the direction of the shot. With a growled curse, he strode off in the direction of the sound. Despite his limp, Ivy struggled to keep pace with his long strides. When he stopped, Ivy almost collided with his back.

"Damn. Poachers."

A kestrel lay on the ground. Blood oozed from a spot near the bird's breast, and its wing dangled useless from its side. It screeched at the humans and flapped its good wing in a vain attempt to escape.

"The poor thing," said Ivy. She took a step toward it.

"Not yet." Tamberlake grabbed her and moved

behind a boulder. He crouched down, pulling her with him. "Be quiet and don't move."

Ivy opened her mouth, but he placed his hand over her mouth. "Be quiet."

Within a few minutes, she heard the tromp of boots.

"Here it is." The rough voice didn't belong to anyone from the house.

"It'll make a fine dinner," came a second voice.

"Stay down," whispered Tamberlake. In the next moment, he jumped up from his hiding place. With no hint of weakness in his twisted leg, he bounded to the top of the boulder. He spread out his cloak as if he were a bat.

"Merciful heaven, the monster," screamed one.

Ignoring Tamberlake's directive, Ivy stood to watch the unfolding scene.

"Begone," said Tamberlake in a voice that boomed across the valley.

"Don't hurt us," yelled the second man. He fell to his knees, raising his arms to ward off an attack.

"Get off my land, poachers." Tamberlake jumped from the boulder, his cloak unfurling behind him like great wings.

The man on the ground screamed.

"Look, the monster has captured a woman." The first man pointed at Ivy.

"Better her than me," said the second as he scrambled to his feet. "What about the bird?"

"Leave it for the monster," yelled the first over his shoulder.

The second wasted no time in following his retreating companion.

Ivy came out from behind the boulder.

"I told you to stay down."

"And miss the excitement? I should say not. Can you believe the unmitigated gall of those fellows? They thought you had captured me."

The falcon screeched on the ground and flopped farther from them.

"They didn't get the bird," said Ivy.

"Sometimes it helps to be a monster," said Tamberlake.

"You are not a monster."

But she didn't think he heard her. He was bending over the panicking fowl. He removed his cloak and spread it over the wriggling bird. Then with gentle hands, he scooped the falcon up and wrapped it into the folds of cloth until the bird stilled. Cradling the small bundle in his arm, he retrieved his staff in the other and started walking again.

Ivy hurried to follow him. "What will you do with him?"

He didn't turn to her. "Eat him."

She gasped. "You wouldn't. How could you? You've just saved him."

"Maybe I just let the poachers do the work for me."

Ivy frowned until she realized he carried the fowl with inordinate care. And wasn't the bird bleeding? Tamberlake wouldn't ruin his cloak if he meant to eat the bird. Hastening to his side, she gave him a triumphant smile. "I don't believe you."

"Why not?"

"You didn't wring his neck back there. If you meant to eat him, you wouldn't go to all this effort to keep him safe."

"Perhaps I'm saving that pleasure for Beaker."

"You're not."

He stopped. "How can you be so confident?"

She ignored his question and continued to walk. "Hurry up. You don't want the falcon to suffer more than it must."

When they reached the house, Tamberlake didn't go to the entrance. Instead he circled to the back and strode across the yard toward a small barn. She didn't even consider returning to the house. She picked up her skirts and followed him. The door was ajar, and Ivy could hear the rustle of hay and low squeaks as they entered. What sort of animals did he house here?

A row of metal cages lined a shelf against the far wall. Not one held an animal, but a layer of straw covered the bottom of each. He lay his bundle on the ground. A duck waddled to him and quacked.

"Not now, Humphrey." He pushed the duck away and unfolded his cloak. The kestrel began to call out as soon as it saw the light. A cow in the corner stall lowed, and the duck flapped its wings and quacked again, but Tamberlake ignored the cries of the animals. He lifted the falcon to a waiting cage. The bird struggled in his grasp, lashing out with its beak, but Tamberlake didn't let go. He lay the bird onto the straw, then released it. The kestrel struggled to right itself as Tamberlake closed the wire door. He grabbed a dish from beside the cage. "Fill this for me."

Ivy glanced around and saw a water trough. She filled the dish with water and returned it to him.

Holding the water in one hand, he opened the cage and placed the dish inside. The bird screeched again, but Tamberlake never spilled a drop. Then he picked up a large cloth and covered the cage.

"Darkness will calm him." Tamberlake lifted his cloak from the ground and shook the hay from it.

"Will it live?"

"I don't know. I can only give it food, water, and warmth and hope that it doesn't die." He examined the cloak. A small spot of blood stained the lining. "Mrs. Beaker should be able to clean this."

"You're hurt," said Ivy. She took hold of his hand. A long welt rose along his thumb and extended farther over the skin. Blood seeped from the scratch.

He snatched his hand back. "It's nothing."

"Yes, it is. You need to bandage that." She looked around for something to wrap the wound with, but saw only filthy rags and old horse blankets.

With a sigh of resignation, Tamberlake pointed to a box under the shelf. "There."

Opening the box, Ivy found all sorts of medical supplies—scissors, string, bandages, various tins of powder.

"It's for the animals," he said without looking at her.

She pulled out a roll of gauze, unrolled a length, then ripped it. Taking his hand again, she wrapped the gauze around his thumb and wrist until the bandage covered the wound. "That should work until you get inside and wash it."

"Thank you."

For a moment neither spoke. She was so close, if she tiptoed she could touch his lips with hers . . .

Quack.

The duck waddled to Tamberlake's legs and quacked again. Tamberlake scooped up the bird and smoothed its feathers.

"A pet?" she asked with some laughter.

"In a way. Humphrey was injured last year, and the fool doesn't seem to realize that he's free to go."

She didn't believe his annoyance with the duck. He was holding the bird far too fondly. From the corner of her eye she saw a movement. Ivy looked toward a beam that ran beneath the roof and gasped. "Is that a polecat?"

Tamberlake cast a lazy glance toward the roof. "Yes. That's Shylock."

Ivy raised her brows. "Another pet?"

He shrugged, but said nothing.

Ivy eyed the animal that poked its nose toward Tamberlake. "He only has three legs."

"I know."

She gave him a look of exasperation. "What I should have said was, 'What happened to his leg.'"

"Caught in a trap. He had almost chewed himself free before I came upon him."

"Chewed?" Her stomach lurched.

"His leg off."

"Oh, dear." Ivy slumped down onto a crate with a thud.

Tamberlake reached into his pocket and pulled out a small pasty. Shylock jumped from the rafter with surprising agility, leaping from spot to spot until he landed upon Tamberlake's shoulder. Tamberlake offered the treat to the animal, who stayed only long enough to seize it in his jaws then leap away to enjoy it in privacy.

"Oh, my," said Ivy. "I've never seen such a thing. Doesn't he bother the other animals?"

"Not really. Shylock keeps to himself, mostly. Mrs. Beaker blames him whenever a hen is missing or they haven't laid their usual number of eggs, but he rids the barn of mice and pests better than a cat."

Ivy shook her head in wonder. "You have hidden depths, my lord."

He raised an eyebrow.

"Most people would have little regard for these creatures."

"I suppose." He set the duck on the ground and adjusted the cover on the falcon's cage once more. "I need to tell Mrs. Beaker to save some meat for the bird." He started for the door, then stopped. "I mean, I need to tell Beaker."

"Mr. Beaker?"

"Haven't you heard? Beaker is my new cook."

"Pardon?"

"Your Mrs. Pennyfeather has wrought great changes in my house. Apparently Beaker grew up the son of innkeepers. He learned to cook at an early age. So now I'm waiting for a new butler, whom Mrs. Pennyfeather highly recommends."

Ivy examined his expression for a moment, then smiled. "I was, at first, about to apologize for Mrs. Pennyfeather's intrusion, but now I believe you've decided you like the changes, despite your desire to be contrary."

Tamberlake stared at her. "Lady Ivy, what does your betrothed say to your forthrightness?"

"I doubt he's even realized it. We aren't very well acquainted. Besides, it will hardly matter. I expect we shall have separate lives as do most marriages in the *ton*."

"And this doesn't upset you?"

"On the contrary. I dreamed of love like any woman, but what can I do? My father wants this marriage, and I would like children. It isn't as if anyone else ever caught my attention." *Except you,* came the thought without warning. Ivy drew in a sudden gulp of air as if in pain and let it out slowly. She could only hope he hadn't noticed her discomfort.

For a few long seconds, he gazed at her without blinking. Then he turned away. "I believe breakfast should be ready."

"Excellent. I'm famished." Ivy hopped up and walked toward the house.

Tamberlake didn't follow right away. How did one cope with a woman such as her? He knew what he wanted to do. He wanted to kiss her until he forced her to admit that life with a monster would be better than a life in society.

He cursed under his breath. Humphrey quacked back. He looked at the duck.

"You're not the only fool in this barn, it seems."

Chapter 9

After she had washed up, Ivy joined the others at the table. They all rose as she walked into the room. Lord Tamberlake wore his mask again. She didn't like it. She much preferred the eye patch.

"Allow me to fill your plate," said Wynbrooke. He stepped to the sideboard.

"Thank you," said Ivy. She tamped down a pang of annoyance. Wynbrooke was just being kind, as a proper betrothed should, but she would have preferred Lord Tamberlake make the gesture. She shook the thought from her.

As she sat, Wynbrooke placed a plate heaped with food in front of her. Picking up her fork, she wondered how she could possibly eat this much.

"Where have you been?" asked Christopher.

"On a walk. We foiled a pair of poachers. They shot a falcon," said Ivy.

"Poachers?" said Christopher. "You weren't hurt, were you?"

"Of course not. Lord Tamberlake handled them

with great aplomb." Ivy glanced at the earl. "Only the poor little falcon was hurt."

"I hope you brought it back for the cook. I'll wager it'll make a tasty pie," said Wynbrooke.

"Certainly not," said Ivy with a severe frown. "Lord Tamberlake brought it back so that it might recover."

"How very unusual of you, sir," said Wynbrooke. "Do you gather strays often?"

"Only the odd one that crosses my door," answered Tamberlake without a change in expression. A slight red tint crept into Wynbrooke's face.

"What shall we do today?" asked Thorndike, bringing their attention to him. "What sort of entertainment can you offer us, Lord Tamberlake?"

"None whatsoever," answered Tamberlake. "I'm afraid I have no activities scheduled for guests. However, this area is known for its spectacular nature walks. If you go into the village, I'm sure someone there can help you."

Neither Wynbrooke nor Thorndike looked enthusiastic.

Tamberlake pushed himself back from the table. "If you will excuse me, I have business to attend to." He left the room.

"The fellow has no sense of propriety," said Wynbrooke. "I can see why he keeps himself hidden out here."

"His face, of course," said Thorndike.

They both laughed. Then Wynbrooke said, "No, it's more than that. Although I must admit it's decent of him to leave the table so we don't have to look at him while we eat. Can you imagine staring at that every morning? It's enough to put me off food entirely." He stuffed a large piece of ham into his mouth.

Thorndike laughed. "Thank goodness we only have to bear this boredom for a few more days. When did you say the carriage would be ready?"

Christopher didn't answer, but a surge of pride ran through Ivy as he looked with disapproval upon the two men's mirth.

Wynbrooke waved his hand. "Never mind, Thorndike. Let's go into the village and see what sort of diversion we can find. We'll ask the wheelwright while we are there. Would you care to join us, Lady Ivy? Styles?"

"No, thank you, Lord Wynbrooke. I find I am fatigued after my walk." Ivy lifted a bite to her lips.

"I believe I promised the earl another game of chess," said Christopher.

"As you wish. I can't imagine the village will offer better entertainment in any case." Wynbrooke rose and brushed crumbs from the front of his shirt.

As the two men left the room, a sense of relief washed over Ivy. How would she stomach Lord Wynbrooke as her husband if she didn't like the man now?

Christopher wiped his mouth on his napkin. "I'm sorry, Ivy. I know you're to marry the man, but sometimes Wynbrooke irritates me."

"Me, too." Ivy sighed. "Perhaps I should have accepted one of those earlier suitors."

"No, they were worse." Christopher pushed back from the table and crossed to his sister. He pulled out her chair for her.

"I wish Father weren't so insistent that I wed. I

would be happy reading my books and being a good aunt to your children."

Christopher raised his hands as if to ward off a blow. "Hold off on wishing me children. I have a few good years left before I find myself shackled to some woman."

"Shackled? I like that. As if we women have any freedom before or after marriage."

He chuckled. "I suppose I should be thankful at that. And that Father thinks I'm too young to worry about making a good marriage."

"Would that I were."

"Don't fret, Ivy. You'll be a magnificent countess. I can picture you surrounded by all sorts of silly young things asking for your wisdom."

Ivy jabbed him with her elbow. "Don't make me out to be a *grande dame* just yet."

Christopher let out a small chuckle, then became serious. "You don't really mind getting married, do you, Ivy?"

She shrugged. "Even if I did, there's little I could do."

At the struck look on her brother's face, she patted his arm. "I shall have a house, a family, and be a countess. Besides, can you imagine how Georgina would act if I didn't marry soon?"

Christopher laughed. "I don't know how you've retained your humor. But if you ever need me, I'll rescue you."

"I know, Christopher. And I love you as well." She kissed his cheek.

Christopher took her arm. "What do you say I show you Lord Tamberlake's gallery? He has an amazing collection of arms and armor."

"I thought you had promised to play chess."

"No. That was just an excuse to get out of going anywhere with Wynbrooke and Thorndike."

Ivy laughed. "Then lead on, brother dear. You know how I like to view arms and armor."

Two days later, Tamberlake sat behind his desk again. Two new girls helped Mrs. Beaker with the housekeeping, as well as a man for the garden. Mrs. Pennyfeather had been correct. A good salary overcame most fears of the monster, although the girls flinched whenever he came near.

The weather had returned to its customary rain, but Ivy had walked with him the past two mornings despite the gray skies. Wynbrooke and Thorndike had reported that the wheelwright was nearly finished with the carriage repairs. His house would once again be empty of intruders and he could relish the silence of his home.

Strange that the thought brought him little pleasure.

Tamberlake looked at the papers on his desk. He had retreated to his study so many times in the past week that he no longer had any work to take care of. He had read these papers—twice. Leaning back in his chair, he gazed at the ceiling. What was Ivy doing now? Was she touring his house again? He had seen her with her brother in the gallery the other day, but didn't disturb them. Was she reading another of his books? He had discovered more than one volume out of its place in the library.

A knock jarred him from his reverie. "Come in."

Mr. Beaker entered. He looked apprehensive. "Sir, I've bad news."

"The carriage isn't ready."

"No, my lord. The carriage is finished, but . . ."

He arched an eyebrow. "But?"

"The driver seems to have disappeared."

"Pardon?"

Beaker shrugged. "The man never came to his bed last night. He went into the village to visit the pub. I went to ask after him this morning, and the innkeeper said the man was celebrating a sudden abundance of wealth and caught the post coach this morning."

"What?"

"I don't know what to say, my lord. Lady Ivy's driver is gone."

"This is impossible." Tamberlake paced the room. Thoughts tumbled through his mind, but foremost came the repeating words: *Ivy isn't leaving*. He ignored the relief that accompanied that thought and concentrated on the annoyance he felt.

"What shall I do, sir?" Beaker watched his employer with a wary expression.

Tamberlake threw his hands into the air. "Make lunch. You are my cook now."

"Yes, sir, but I thought I could be of service until the new man arrives."

He stopped and drew a deep breath. "Forgive me, Beaker. I was taking my anger out on you."

"Think nothing of it, sir."

Tamberlake pondered the situation for a moment. "I suppose we'll have to find them a new driver."

"Yes, sir. Shall I make inquiries in the village?"

"By all means. But it can wait until tomorrow. I still need you to make lunch."

Beaker grinned. "As you wish, my lord." He gave a quick bow and left the room.

What madness had come over him? Tomorrow? A week ago, he would have done everything in his power to make sure his guests left that day. But today?

He started to pace again.

A second knock interrupted him. "What now?"

Mrs. Pennyfeather came into the room. "Pardon me, my lord. Mr. Fletcher is here."

At last a little good news. "Send him in."

Mrs. Pennyfeather ushered in a man not much taller than herself, then pulled the door closed as she left. The man's hair was gray, but it looked as though it had been cut with gardener's shears. Tufts stuck out at various angles in uneven lengths. Thick spectacles perched on his nose, and a definite hump protruded from his back.

Mrs. Pennyfeather had warned him.

Tamberlake took a place behind his desk. "Mr. Fletcher?"

"My lord."

His voice was crisp, pleasant, with the intonation of one accustomed to the upper classes.

"I understand Lord Stanhope was your employer."

"Yes, my lord. I served him for many years."

"And he was satisfied with your work?"

"Never a complaint, sir. You may ask Mrs. Pennyfeather."

"I have." He sat back and crossed his hands in front of him. "I'll give you a trial, Fletcher."

"Thank you, my lord. May I be so bold as to say you won't be disappointed."

Tamberlake smiled. "Somehow I don't think I will be. I have a few rules which you may find unusual."

"Unusual, sir?"

"Yes. I don't like the sun coming into the house. You will keep the drapes closed."

"Of course, my lord."

"And few lamps."

Fletcher nodded.

"Beaker can show you everything else."

"As you wish, my lord." Fletcher bowed his head and turned toward the door. As he left, Tamberlake noticed the man's shoes were of different thicknesses. He wondered how the man would walk without the corrective shoes.

Before Fletcher reached the door, Tamberlake stopped him. "Oh, Fletcher."

The butler turned. "Yes, sir?"

"I do need you to do something. As soon as you've settled in, I need you to find a driver for our guests."

"Yes, sir. It will be an honor to serve you." With a deferential nod, the butler left.

Only after the door closed behind the man did Tamberlake realize the man had not reacted to his face. *Curious.*

He didn't spend more time wondering about it, for a third knock came at the door. "Who is it this time?"

Ivy poked her head into the room. As she walked in, he fought the urge to rise, but she would only scold him if he didn't, so he rose.

"Forgive the intrusion, Lord Tamberlake, but may I speak with you for a moment?"

"If you must." He tamped down the jolt of excitement her presence brought.

"Has Mr. Beaker spoken to you yet? About the driver?"

"Yes."

"He isn't a member of our household, you know. Lord Stanhope had arranged for me to use his coach and driver. A lucky thing, since Father couldn't spare ours."

She waited for some response, but he sat in silence.

Ivy sighed. "I know you can't be happy with our prolonged presence here. I thought perhaps someone could drive us to the inn, and we shall take up residence there until a new driver can be found."

Here was the opportunity to reclaim his life. He could send the entire group on their way and be rid of them. All it would take was a few simple words.

"I won't hear of it, Lady Ivy. You must stay. Besides, who would accompany me on my walks should you leave?"

Where had those words come from? He grimaced, or at least he would have if the smile of pure delight on Ivy's face hadn't stolen his ability to reason.

"Thank you, Lord Tamberlake. You've been too kind to us."

"Not at all," he muttered.

"Won't you join us when you've finished your business? We're having a rousing game of forfeits."

"I'm not much for parlor games."

"That's all right. I can teach them to you."

He nodded. "Very well. I shall come presently."

"Excellent." Ivy left the room with a decided bounce in her step.

Tamberlake sunk into his chair. Parlor games? Had he just agreed to play parlor games? There could be no doubt.

He must be going mad.

Chapter 10

Tamberlake sat in a large armchair, savoring the darkness. The guests had long since scattered for the night, but he wasn't ready to sleep. He had retreated to the salon for a brandy and a few minutes of contemplation in silence. The uproar in his house left him with a disquiet he couldn't shake.

He had played forfeits with the others, then joined them at dinner. Fletcher served them with impeccable style, even if his shuffling gait and crooked back were peculiar. Ivy had led them in conversation, speaking on topics from philosophy to the latest play in London. Just as though she belonged at the head of his table.

Banish that notion, Tamberlake.

He took a large swallow from his snifter. More and more, Ivy invaded his thoughts, and he wasn't enjoying the sense of rushing toward a crashing disappointment.

The door to the salon opened. For an instant his heart beat faster in anticipation of seeing Ivy again, but it was only her brother. "Good evening, Styles."

Styles peered through the darkness. "Is that you, Tamberlake?"

"Pour yourself a brandy and join me." He surprised himself with his words. Being the genial host was becoming easier. Of course, he couldn't say how he might have behaved if his nighttime visitor had been Wynbrooke. "How are you enduring your forced exile in the wilds?"

The younger man sloshed a bit of drink into a glass and crossed to his host. "I have to say it is a change, but I find myself enjoying the peace."

He cocked an eyebrow. "Really?"

Styles laughed. "I know. It's hard to believe. But Father can't yell at me while I'm in Wales."

"Does your father yell at you often?"

"Only when I've lost at the gaming hells. He just paid off one of my debts before we came. He wasn't happy."

"Then perhaps you shouldn't gamble."

"What else is there to do?" Styles took a swallow. "I've finished my schooling, I'm too young to search the marriage mart, and I have little else to do. This trip was a godsend."

"For whom?"

"Both of us, really. I can't accrue any debts while I'm here, and Father can't watch over my every step. And Ivy doesn't have to worry about the upcoming hullabaloo. Father didn't want to let Ivy leave. He's eager to see the ties between Wynbrooke's family and ours. He thinks it will yield more power in parliament for him. Father likes to think he's influential, but really he's just loud and arrogant."

"Yet he let her come."

"Yes, well, he couldn't fight both Mother and his sense of outrage at his son." Styles laughed again. "Wynbrooke's as eager to wed Ivy as Father is to see them wed. I don't blame him for coming after her."

"Does he love her?"

"I don't believe so. They hardly know each other. Wynbrooke wasn't an ardent suitor, but he did approach my father first. I think Father was so happy to see Ivy wed to a good family, he didn't care if Ivy wanted to marry."

Why was Wynbrooke so eager to wed? Tamberlake frowned and drank his brandy. Why did it matter? He didn't want to embroil himself in their affairs. Ivy wasn't his concern.

Styles yawned. "Must be more tired than I thought. Thank you for the brandy." He rose. "Good night."

"Good night."

Even after his glass was empty, Tamberlake didn't leave his chair. He wasn't sleepy. Visions of Ivy played in his head like a never-ending panorama— her concern over the falcon, her animation at the games, her lively conversation . . .

Enough. She isn't yours to think about.

Despite the warning to himself, he found himself pulled deeper and deeper into his thoughts of Ivy throughout the night.

Ivy carried the small storm lamp from one painting to the next. The gallery had fascinated her since she had come here with her brother to view the arms and armor. She gazed at the heavy drapes that shrouded the windows. If Tamberlake would just open them, she wouldn't need this light. Lifting the lantern to give the painting better light, she saw the face of an Elizabethan gentleman looking back at her. He wore a broad smile. Probably some ancestor of Lord Tamberlake, but she had never seen him look so happy. On the other hand, the portrait beside the gentleman was of a sour-looking woman from the same period. Ivy could believe this woman was an ancestor. She didn't appear to worry about manners, either.

Ivy giggled and moved along the wall. Each painting depicted a face from a different era. Some were formal sittings of individuals, some were family groups. Her own family had such a rogues' gallery at their house. As a child, she remembered inventing stories about the people she saw on the canvases.

The glow from the flame fell upon a painting that hadn't been there the last time she had visited. It was the portrait of Lord Tamberlake she had delivered. Lifting the lamp higher, she examined the face staring back at her. The clear blue eyes of the painting twinkled with mischief. The earl she had met didn't have a spark that she could notice.

"Mourning the difference?"

Ivy let out a small cry. The lamp wobbled in her grip. Tamberlake's hand shot out to steady it, then took it from her and placed it on a pedestal.

"Great heavens, you startled me." Ivy let out a deep breath. "You should give a person notice before you sneak up on them."

"Ah, but that doesn't garner the same results."

She shot him a wary glance. The lamp reflected on the shiny surface of the porcelain mask. "What results would those be?"

He didn't answer. Instead he turned to the painting. "Not a good likeness after all."

Ivy looked at the portrait. "It looks just like you. A bit younger perhaps."

His head whipped around to her. "Are you mad, Lady Ivy? Or just enjoying a bit of cruelty perhaps?"

Ivy's mouth gaped open. After a moment, she closed it. Anger roiled within her as heat rushed into her cheeks. "If you wish me to leave, you have but to ask. There's no need to insult me."

"Insult *you?*" He let out a low, mirthless chuckle. "I couldn't begin to top your efforts."

"I? I haven't insulted you."

"No?" His hand grabbed her chin and twisted her head to the portrait. "Gaze at the painting, and tell me again how you think it a good likeness."

She wrenched her face free. "It is."

He let out a snort of disgust. "Then you must be blind."

"I am not the blind one in this room."

"Ahh, finally the truth. My missing eye troubles you."

"No. 'Tis the other I speak of." She glared at him.

His expression slipped from anger to disbelief. "Explain yourself, my lady."

"Your eye fails to see your face as it is."

"You mean the scars. I assure you, I see my scars every time I look in the mirror."

"No, I mean you fail to see anything *except* your scars."

Tamberlake whipped the mask from his face.

Tiny shadows marked the valleys formed by the puckered ridges, and spots of shiny skin glowed in the lamplight. A deep scar slashed through where his eye might have been. "Take a good look, Ivy. These are the scars you claim you can't see."

Ivy took a step back, but not from revulsion. The rage in Tamberlake's face frightened her.

"Finally. Even *you* are repulsed." Tamberlake lifted the mask to replace it.

Ivy couldn't tell what drove her, but she dashed forward and snatched the mask from his hand. "I am not repulsed."

"Give me the mask, Lady Ivy." He stepped forward.

"I shan't." As she moved back, she hid it behind her back. "Not until you've let me see you as you've asked."

"You wish to gawk at my face?" He took another step forward.

As if in some sort of bizarre dance, Ivy countered by moving back again. "You claim to be a monster. Let me see if you are correct."

"My mask," he said in a low growl. He pressed ever closer.

"I think you fear being seen, so you hide behind a bit of china to keep the world away."

"What would you know of it? Give it to me." He came ever closer.

Ivy's back hit the wall. She could retreat no farther. "I don't fear the monster."

"Perhaps you should." Tamberlake's hand shot out and encircled her throat.

Ivy let out a little cry but never averted her gaze. "I don't fear you." She brought the mask out from behind her back and dashed it to the floor.

A loud, bell-like tone rang out; then the sound of shattering echoed through the gallery.

Tamberlake leaned into her face. "What have you done?"

Without thinking, Ivy lifted her hand and ran her fingers over the scars on his cheek. He pulled away, but Ivy reached for him. With both hands, she cupped his face. "You are a beautiful man."

A guttural moan tore from his throat. He leaned in and kissed her.

For an instant, she thought he was killing her, but then her mouth welcomed his. She clung to him, reveling in the racing of her heart. A heady vertigo enveloped her. She tilted her head to fit her lips better to his. When his tongue slipped past, she opened her mouth to let him taste of her. And she of him. He pressed himself against her, hip to hip, so that his warmth seeped through her skirts.

His hand slid up, across her waist, to cup her breast. His touch burned through the material of her dress. Heat pooled between her legs, an unfamiliar but breathtaking feeling. A longing she didn't recognize grew within her, pulsing through her in a sweet ache she didn't know how to subdue. She didn't *want* to subdue it. She wanted it to swell, to engulf her, to overcome her.

What seemed a moment later, he pulled away from her. He stepped back suddenly, dropping his hand from her throat. His breath was ragged and his eye shone as brightly as the sun off a mirror. "Forgive me." His voice was gruff. He gave a stiff bow and hastened from the gallery.

As his warmth left her, her body filled with what she could only describe as discontent. She sagged against the wall. "No, I shan't forgive you," she whispered to the empty space. "I shall never forgive you if you're sorry you kissed me."

Ivy moved away from the wall and straightened her dress. Her shoes crunched beneath her. Her gaze fell to the floor. Shards of porcelain lay around her slippers. "Oh dear. I shouldn't have done that." She pushed some of the larger pieces with the toe of her shoe.

"But I can't say I'm sorry I did."

Tamberlake retreated to his study. He poured a generous amount of brandy into a snifter and sat behind his desk. He stared at the brandy, but didn't drink it. For a moment, he sat unmoving, then he dropped his head into his hands. What had he done?

He reached into a drawer and pulled out an eye patch. He preferred the comfort of the patch to the cold, heavy mask, but he had become accustomed to wearing it in the presence of others, however seldom people came to see him.

He slipped the patch over his head. Ivy had said he used the mask to hide. Did he? Was he hiding or was he turning his back on a world that had only tolerated him when he was beautiful?

Bah. He wasn't hiding. His life in Wales was free of the hypocrisy of the *ton*. Of the men preaching morality, then slipping away to be with their mistresses. Of the women who cried for love, but married the first decrepit old man who offered for them. Of polite pretense in front of one's face, quickly changing to gossip when one turned one's back.

He didn't fear the world as much as hated it.

With a wide sweep of his arm, he sent the brandy crashing to the floor. Ivy was wrong. He was no coward. But she had done him a favor. He would never wear a mask again.

What would his mother say?

That thought brought a laugh to his lips. She visited him twice a year, but he didn't fool himself by thinking she came out of some misguided sense of motherly love. She came to make sure he wouldn't cut off her generous allowance. He was the earl, after all, and she lived on his estates at his largesse. His appearance would scandalize her. He would enjoy that.

Against his will, Stanhope's memory taunted him. Stanhope had been neither a hypocrite nor a shallow member of the *ton*. In fact, the man had amused himself at the games being played around him. And from what Tamberlake could see, Ivy didn't fall into those two categories either.

Tamberlake grimaced. He didn't want to be fair. He wanted to remain angry at the world. But he felt his anger sliping away despite his efforts.

He rose from the desk and surveyed the damage. The brandy left wet splotches on the rug, and the snifter had broken into four large pieces. He shook his head. Such a waste of fine cognac.

His hand reached for the bellpull, but before he could ring it, a knock came at the door.

"Come."

Beaker entered the room. He carried an armload of a mud-covered mess.

Tamberlake raised an eyebrow. "You've come to add to the mess I've made?"

"No, indeed, sir. I was looking for eggs and

found these in the mud of the chicken yard. Nearly tripped over one."

"What are they?" he asked, peering closer.

"Near as I can tell, they're carriage parts. Like the ones from *their* carriage."

Tamberlake had no need to ask who "they" were. "What are you saying?"

"I'm thinking it were deliberate, their carriage breaking down like that. And now with the driver gone . . ." Beaker looked at him over the end of his nose and nodded.

"You think they wanted to be stranded here? Why?"

"Wouldn't know. Can't say how the nobility thinks."

Tamberlake looked at the muck-encrusted metal. Who would have, or could have, removed these parts? He hated a mystery.

"Excuse me, my lord." Fletcher's precise tones came from the doorway.

"Yes?"

"There is a trail of mud through the house, which I followed to your study, sir." Fletcher eyed Beaker with a frown.

"Come in here and tell me what you make of this, Fletcher." Tamberlake waved him in and pointed to Beaker's hoard.

Fletcher crossed to Beaker, eyeing the mass of mud with disdain.

"Well?"

"I wouldn't know, sir. Metal parts to something."

A glob of mud plopped to the floor.

"Perhaps Mr. Beaker would be kind enough to remove these things before I have more of the floor to mop up . . ." Fletcher turned his huge gaze to Tamberlake.

"I'm going. I've got dinner to prepare anyhow. Just wanted to show his lordship what I found." Beaker took his armful of metal and left the room, leaving a new trail behind him.

Tamberlake crossed to his bookshelf. Why would someone deliberately strand himself here?

"Sir?" Fletcher moved into his range of sight. He had forgotten the man was still there. "Yes?"

"May I send a girl to clean your floor?"

"By all means." Tamberlake eyed his new butler. "Fletcher, you haven't heard any of our guests say something peculiar?"

"Several times, my lord. What sort of peculiarity do you mean?"

"I'm not sure exactly. Something about the source of a broken carriage, or wanting to stay far from society."

"No, sir. Nothing like that."

He hadn't expected to find the answer so easily. "Thank you, Fletcher. If you do hear something, tell me."

"Of course, sir." Fletcher bowed and left the room.

Tamberlake returned to his seat, then stood again. He wouldn't stay. Neither maid had stopped flinching at his appearance, and he felt in no mood to deal with their silliness. He would check on the kestrel.

Avoiding the noise emanating from the parlor, he passed through the house toward the kitchen. With a wry smile, he entered the room. He doubted many aristocrats even knew where their kitchens existed, but he wanted to grab a treat for Shylock and something for the bird. The room was empty. Beaker had to be washing up after his muddy encounter. On a cutting board lay a mound of kidneys. Perfect. After placing two on a small plate, he grabbed a crust of bread and left by the back door.

Humphrey waddled to him almost as soon as he stepped out. Shaking his head, Tamberlake tossed the bread to the bird. With a quack, Humphrey picked up the crust in his bill. The duck would never be safe in the wild now. Humphrey would probably walk up to any hunter, expecting the man with a gun to feed him.

Tamberlake crossed the yard toward the barn, Humphrey waddling behind him the entire way. The door to the barn was ajar. As he approached, the kestrel screeched. In the next instant, he heard a woman cry out, followed by a man's laugh.

"What the devil?" He ran the last few steps and threw open the door.

Chapter 11

"What in the blazes is going on here?"

Ivy whirled toward the door, sucking on her finger. She pulled the digit from her mouth. "Lord Tamberlake."

Christopher grinned as he moved away from the cage. "Ivy was showing me your kestrel."

"He's not my kestrel." Tamberlake stepped forward. "Are you hurt, Lady Ivy?"

As she remembered their last encounter, her heart sped up and heat filled her cheeks. "I'm not hurt. He only snapped at me. He's getting quite strong."

"Why did you open the cage?"

She pointed to the plate Tamberlake carried. "For the same reason as you were about to, it seems. Do you think Mr. Beaker will forgive me for taking some kidneys?"

Tamberlake crossed to the kestrel's cage. "He will."

"If he doesn't, I shall. I'm not fond of kidney pie," said Christopher.

Tamberlake peered into the cage. The kestrel hopped about in agitation. He stretched his wings in an effort to escape the scrutiny.

"He won't need care for very much longer," said Ivy.

"No, his wound is almost healed—healed enough, at any rate, to release him soon. Two days, maybe three."

"May I watch when you do?" asked Ivy.

He nodded. He dropped a kidney through the openings in the wire. The bird screeched again, but eyed the meat with interest.

"I brought something for Shylock as well."

"Yes, that's what I wanted to see. The tame polecat," said Christopher.

"I'm not sure I'd use the word 'tame' for Shylock. 'Tolerant' might be better," said Tamberlake. He tapped a spot on a low beam and tipped the second kidney onto the spot. "Put the food here. But he might wait until we're gone to get it."

Ivy left the small pasty on the wood and backed away. Her gaze searched the high beams and corners for a glimpse of the polecat, but she saw nothing. "I suppose he's too shy to come out for strangers."

"We'll come again before we leave," said Christopher.

"Leave?" The earl's head snapped up.

"Yes. Mother wrote to say she's found us a new driver. She's sending him on the mail coach." Christopher headed for the barn door.

"You'll soon be rid of us. This has to be welcome news," said Ivy in a low voice.

Tamberlake averted his gaze, then turned back to the bird. "Aye. Welcome news indeed."

"Shall we see you at dinner?" asked Ivy.

"Yes."

She waited for a moment, but he said nothing else. Crushing disappointment weighed down her thoughts. He was happy to see them leave. She had been foolish to think he might feel otherwise.

Following Christopher, she slipped through the barn door and crossed the yard to the house. A tidy little garden surrounded by low hedges lay off to the left. She hadn't noticed it the day they'd brought the falcon home. A narrow opening in the hedge led to a stone path. The path wove in and around low shrubs. The first hint of flowers appeared on some of the plants.

It's a maze. From where she stood she followed the path with her gaze. The path meandered by the face of a woodland god, past a small cherub fountain, to reach the center circle where a mosaic displayed the image of a griffin. The touch of whimsy in the earl's garden delighted Ivy. She never would have expected it of Tamberlake. Then again, the earl never ceased to surprise her.

A wave of sadness engulfed her. Her stay here was coming to an end. All too soon she would have to face society on the arm of Earl Wynbrooke and then take her vows with him. All too soon this last foray into freedom would come to a close.

"Lady Ivy, what a happy chance." Wynbrooke called out to her. He and Thorndike walked toward her from the side of the house.

Ivy dipped into a quick curtsey. "Lord Wynbrooke, Mr. Thorndike. What brings you this way?"

"We have just returned from an excursion to see the Waterloo Bridge. Designed by Telford, you know," said Wynbrooke. "Not very interesting, I'm afraid, but there's little else to do."

"One wonders how Nelson would feel to know such a memorial for his great battle exists," said Thorndike.

Lord Nelson would probably appreciate the efforts of a small town like Betws-y-coed, thought Ivy.

Wynbrooke approached the low hedge. "Ah, a maze."

"How rustic," said Thorndike. He cast his gaze over the stone path. "We could tarry here for . . . minutes before we solved it."

Ivy fought the urge to give a sharp answer. "I find it rather lovely."

"Yes, well, the god is impressive enough. Rather grim-looking. I shouldn't like to meet him in a dark corner," said Wynbrooke.

"Much like our host," said Thorndike. The two men chuckled.

"I don't find our host frightening," said Ivy. "I think he has been generous, considering we all descended upon him without invitation."

"I think your mother was correct in sending me after you." Wynbrooke pulled a box of snuff from his pocket. "You've obviously been far too long out of polite society. You need someone to remind you of decent behavior. Your brother can hardly offer a decent example. Your father despairs of his peccadilloes."

"What peccadilloes?"

Wynbrooke pinched a bit of snuff between his fingers and raised it to his nose. With a polite sniff, he inhaled the stuff and reached for his handkerchief. His sneeze was oh-so-proper and delicate.

He replaced the accoutrements of his habit in his pocket. "I'm not sure such news is fit for your ears, my dear Lady Ivy."

"If this is about his gambling debts, I know all about them. Christopher told me himself."

"Proof of his unacceptable behavior. No lady should hear of such things."

"He's my brother."

"There, there, my dear, you needn't worry about Styles," said Wynbrooke and patted her arm. "As my wife you won't have to deal with such distasteful thoughts. Rest assured that your father and I shall look after your welfare and protect you from unpleasantness."

"Yes, Lady Ivy. You have no inkling of the depths of depravity in society," said Thorndike.

She didn't like the way Wynbrooke patronized her. Or the way Thorndike looked at her and then laughed behind his hand with Wynbrooke. Perhaps when she was mistress of her house she could influence her husband to find new friends.

Nothing could prevent the sheer bleakness the image of their marriage called forth in her.

"Shall we go in?" Wynbrooke looked to the sky. "The weather seems to be turning worse."

Indeed, black clouds rolled through the grayness above, mirroring her own feelings.

"Does the rain never stop here?" asked Thorndike. "I shall be glad of our departure."

"As shall I, my friend." Wynbrooke held out his arm for Ivy.

She took it, but glanced back at the maze with the fervent desire to linger at that picturesque spot despite the threatening weather.

* * *

The thunder rolling through the house gave the only evidence of the storm outside. The drapes that kept out the sun also kept out the lightning, except for the occasional hint of light around the edges of the heavy fabric. Tamberlake took the opportunity dinner provided him to examine each of his guests in turn. Beaker's pile of parts left no clue who might have tampered with the carriage, but only one explanation made sense—someone had not wanted to return to London. But which one?

His gaze landed on Wynbrooke. No, he had not arrived until after the damage had already been carried out. That eliminated Thorndike as well.

Mrs. Pennyfeather ate her meal with refined manners worthy of a duchess. What reason would Mrs. Pennyfeather have to delay their journey? Admittedly she needed employment, but Tamberlake had no doubt Ivy would find her a position. The delay had allowed Pennyfeather to find a position for Fletcher, but he couldn't imagine her staging such an elaborate ruse just to find a position for a butler.

Styles? Perhaps. Perhaps his father was angrier than Styles had intimated. Perhaps his debts were more than money, and he needed a safe place to hide for a while.

Great heavens, his thoughts were beginning to sound like one of those emotional novels written by the Brontë sisters.

And what of Ivy herself? She seemed resolved to marry Wynbrooke. And yet . . .

And yet his hopes wouldn't relinquish their grip

on his imagination. The image of her on the mountaintop, the look of admiration when he rescued the kestrel, and her honest reaction to his kisses were never far from his thoughts. She embraced her time in Wales with a joy he hadn't seen in anyone. But was that enough reason to suspect her?

Beaker wouldn't have tampered with the carriage. He was as eager to see the guests leave as he himself had been. Mrs. Beaker was as unlikely as her husband to want guests. She had no reason to make herself more work.

And himself? He knew he hadn't damaged the carriage, but given the chance, he wondered if he might be tempted now.

Gad, what was he thinking?

He clenched his jaw in anger. She should leave before he became accustomed to her company, before he forgot she wasn't part of his world. Their driver should arrive in the next day or two, and he would be rid of her family, her friends, and most especially her.

"Lord Tamberlake, are you ill?" asked Mrs. Pennyfeather.

"Bit my cheek," he said. He gazed at his plate to avoid the stares of the others.

Fletcher circled the table, clearing the dessert plates. His demeanor and manners were impeccable. Nevertheless, Tamberlake couldn't help but fear he would drop the plates as he walked away on his shuffling gait. No crash came from the pantry. The interminable meal was at last at an end.

Fletcher reappeared. "If the ladies wish to retire

to the salon, I shall serve tea and coffee. Gentlemen, the port is coming."

Port? When had he acquired any port?

Ivy and Mrs. Pennyfeather left the room, and Fletcher placed a salver with a decanter and glasses on the table. "If you will excuse me, my lord, I shall see to the needs of the ladies."

He nodded, and Fletcher disappeared. Wynbrooke poured himself a glass of the dark wine, took a deep sip, and leaned back in his chair. "Ahhh, the niceties of a good meal."

Thorndike followed Wynbrooke's actions, but Tamberlake noticed Styles didn't drink this evening. He helped himself to half a glass. He tasted the port. Excellent. And once again he wondered when he had acquired the wine.

"Tell me, Tamberlake. How do you keep yourself occupied so far from civilization?" asked Wynbrooke.

He took another swallow before answering. "Correspondence with my stewards on my other estates, and such. And I receive a box of books from London monthly."

"Reading. Never could see the point of doing much of it myself." Wynbrooke filled his glass again. "Either they write of people long dead or some new strange science, neither of which is any use to me."

"And you, Lord Wynbrooke? How do you occupy yourself?" Tamberlake placed his glass on the table and focused his attention on his guest.

"I have Rosmartin Park, of course. The land, the tenants, the upkeep, you understand. I also enjoy entertaining my friends, dinner parties and the like . . ." His voice trailed off as if he was trying to think of something more substantial.

"No gambling or other vices?"

Wynbrooke coughed on his wine. "Good heavens, no. You sound like the father of a prospective bride."

"Do I? How unfortunate. But you would know, having been through just such a conversation."

"Yes, and I must say Lord Dunleigh subjected me to many more questions." Wynbrooke let out a nervous laugh. "I must have answered to his satisfaction."

"Indeed. You did win the girl's hand, after all." Tamberlake lifted his glass again. "And you, Mr. Thorndike?"

"I?"

"What do you do when not traveling with your friends?" He finished off his port.

"I don't do much of anything," said Thorndike with a smile that held little charm. "I don't have a title or lands or responsibilities."

"But you must do something." Tamberlake eyed the man.

"Apparently I am amusing company. My friends have helped support me these past several years."

"Indeed. Thorndike has his own rooms at Rosmartin," said Wynbrooke. "I must say he more than earns his upkeep with me. The places I force him to accompany me."

"Like Wales perhaps?" said Tamberlake in an even tone. Styles snorted as he tried to prevent a laugh.

"Much worse places, I assure you," said Thorndike. "Such as visiting his mother."

Wynbrooke let out a guffaw at that. When he caught his breath, he said, "You see? He told you he can be amusing."

"Yes, he did warn me." Tamberlake couldn't identify what troubled him about this conversation, but he was sure he would with time. He rose from the table. "Shall we join the ladies? I'm sure we could persuade them into playing whist or another rousing round of parlor games."

Chapter 12

Two days later, the thunder and lightning had disappeared, but the rain remained. Tamberlake placed his forehead against the windowpane. After two days of forced confinement, the entire household was tetchy. Tempers at the breakfast table simmered beneath polite facades. If the weather continued to curtail their activities, he would have his food sent on a tray to his room to avoid his guests.

Turning from the wet view, he walked to the opposite end of his study. His steps were slow, and he leaned upon his cane. His leg ached. He had had to forgo his usual morning constitution because of the rain. He didn't mind damp weather, or even snow, but such downpours made his morning excursions all but impossible. And when he didn't walk, his leg pained him for hours.

He propped his back against the hearth and rubbed his thigh, hoping the heat of the fire would loosen his tight muscles.

"Sir?" Fletcher entered the room.

Lately his study had become less a place of refuge than a place to insure interruptions. "Yes?"

"I wanted to let you know that your guests' coachman has arrived."

Ivy was leaving.

He took a deep breath and chided himself. No, Lady Ivy wasn't leaving yet. The man had just arrived. And they couldn't leave when the roads were little more than mire. "Thank you, Fletcher. Make sure he has a room and food."

"Yes, my lord."

"And tell me when the rain lets up."

"Yes, my lord." Fletcher bowed and left the room.

After three weeks of unexpected visitors, he would have his home back. The news should please him. He should be happy.

So why did this sense of panic have him in its grip?

He decided to search for Ivy to tell her the news of their driver himself. With a grunt of disgust, he pushed himself away from the hearth.

Without thinking, he made his way to the gallery. He knew she would be there, although he didn't know why he believed so. He saw her the moment he entered the long room. She stood in front of his portrait.

A rush of anger sped through him. Why couldn't she leave the image alone? "Lady Ivy?"

She whirled around. "Lord Tamberlake. You always seem to startle me."

"I don't see how. I'm not exactly nimble with my gait."

She looked as if she was about to speak, but he raised his hand. "I came by to tell you that your coachman has arrived."

She nodded. "I know. You must be happy to be rid of us soon."

He hesitated. "I haven't known much peace since you arrived."

She gazed at him, her brown eyes shining in the lamplight. Then she smiled. "I expect not. Well, we shall be gone soon, and you can return to your peaceful life." She turned to leave.

His hand shot out and caught her by the arm. "Wait."

Ivy looked back at him. His eagerness to see them leave hadn't surprised her, but his expression now did. An uncertainty wrinkled his brow, and he looked almost confused. He hadn't released her arm.

"Lord Tamberlake?"

He dropped his hand. "It's nothing."

She waited for a moment. "Very well." She took another step toward the door.

"I just . . ."

Ivy stopped. She didn't speak, she didn't move.

The moment stretched until he faced away from her. "I enjoyed our walks together. I believe I shall miss your company."

She wanted to cry out in joy. "As did I. I've seen so much that I've never seen before. I only wish the weather had allowed us a few more outings before I had to leave."

He nodded.

"I doubt I shall have the words to describe the beauty of your home."

"You find it beautiful?"

"Something in the mountains speaks of a wonderful freedom to me. It isn't a common beauty. I suppose many would find it stark and cold, but it's wild and strong and somewhat frightening, too. I don't suppose I would ever tire of looking at those mountains." She paused, then pressed her hands to her cheeks as a warmth crept into them. "I must sound like a goose."

"Not at all. Your words are honest. There is no shame in honesty."

"I say too much."

"You speak from the heart." He shifted his weight. As he stepped on his weak leg, he grimaced and clutched his cane until his knuckles were white.

"You are in pain." She hurried to his side.

He shook off her attention. "My leg is a little stiff, nothing else. The weather has prevented my morning exercise to loosen the muscle."

Ivy glanced up and down the gallery. "Why can't we walk now?"

"Pardon?"

"This is a gallery. They used these rooms to take exercise in centuries past. Why can't we use it now?"

His gaze took in the length of the room, and Tamberlake smiled. "I believe that's a splendid idea."

"But I must do one thing first." Ivy ran to the first set of windows and threw back the drapes. The sky showed nothing more than gray, and rivulets ran down the panes.

"What are you doing?"

"We must try to bring the outdoors inside, only we shall stay dry in the process." She waited for his reaction.

He shook his head, but shrugged. "As you wish, Lady Ivy."

She ran from one set of curtains to the next until all four windows loomed gray against the wall. Ivy looked around. The gallery was nevertheless brighter than she had ever seen it. She hurried back to his side. "I expect this walk shall disappoint me a little."

He raised an eyebrow.

She shrugged her shoulders. "No boulders to climb or rivers to cross."

Tamberlake laughed and held out his arm. "But perhaps it is the most civilized stroll you can expect from me."

She took his arm, and they started down the parquet. "You needn't worry. I shan't tell anyone."

He looked at her in confusion. "Tell anyone what?"

"That the monster is civilized. How would you frighten the villagers then?"

His eye widened for an instant, then he threw his head back and laughed just as she had hoped. "Lady Ivy, I don't believe anyone has dared as much as you."

"I know. My family complains to me all the time."

They circled the room, speaking of nothing and everything. He made her laugh with the stories of the ancestors whose portraits they passed with each round. She surprised him with her knowledge of books. His step grew stronger with each circuit until his cane barely tapped the floor.

Ivy had never spent such a morning. The easy conversation, the companionship, the laughter was something she had only shared with Christopher before. Yet here was a man, a virtual stranger, with whom she didn't feel the need to hide her love of books or her outlandish thoughts. And he had kissed her twice. That thought sent heat into her cheeks.

"Ivy, what are you doing?"

Christopher's voice halted her steps. She pulled her arm free of Tamberlake's and spun around. Christopher stood in the entrance. So did Lord Wynbrooke and Mr. Thorndike.

"Your cheeks are flushed," said Christopher.

"I'm afraid I am at fault," said Tamberlake. "Lady Ivy saw that my leg was troubling me this morning, so she suggested we use the gallery to take exercise. I usually take a morning constitution to loosen the muscles, but with this weather . . ." He gestured toward the windows.

"Right. I was going to show Wynbrooke the armor." Christopher gave his sister a look of doubt.

"You're welcome to examine all my collection." Tamberlake turned to Ivy and lifted her hand. "Thank you for your kindness, Lady Ivy. Forgive me if I overtaxed you."

He kissed her hand, then pivoted and left the room. Ivy stared at the spot on the back of her hand. A tingle had spread through her at his touch, and she didn't trust herself to move.

"He doesn't walk as though his leg troubled him," muttered Wynbrooke.

"Didn't you see him at breakfast?" asked Christopher. "He hobbled in on his cane."

"That's right. The man could scarcely walk this morning," said Thorndike. "Wyn, you are a lucky dog. Your betrothed is not only pretty, but compassionate as well."

Ivy said nothing. She glanced after Tamberlake and frowned.

"Will you join us in admiring the armor, Lady Ivy?" asked Wynbrooke.

"No, I believe I would like to rest," she said.

"Perhaps that would be best. Your cheeks are still flushed. I wouldn't want you to overexert yourself," said Wynbrooke.

"I'll come see you later," said Christopher. His eyes held questions that she didn't want to answer.

Forcing a smile to her lips, she nodded. "Enjoy yourselves, gentlemen."

She walked with deliberate steps from the gallery, fighting the urge to flee.

Ivy stood by the library window and watched the sun come out from behind a cloud. She couldn't remember a more unwelcome sight. The roads would dry soon if the sun stayed out.

Fletcher entered the room and crossed to her. "Lady Ivy, this arrived for you." He handed her a thin package wrapped in brown paper.

"Thank you, Fletcher."

The man bowed and left the room on his uneven gait. Ivy glanced at the package. She recognized the writing. It was her mother's. She tore open the paper. A newspaper appeared, and a letter flitted to the ground from between its folds. She picked up the letter.

My dear Ivy,

I thought you should see this. I regret I ever sent you on this ridiculous errand. You must come home.

Your loving mother

"Yes, Mother. I know I must come home," she whispered. She unfolded the newspaper and scanned the page. She found the item at once. "Oh, no." She balled up the paper in her fist.

"Is there a problem, Lady Ivy?" Fletcher crossed to her.

She had not realized the man had returned. "No, I just received some unpleasant news."

"I came back to see if you might like some tea or coffee."

Ivy tried to smile but her lips trembled, and she gave up the effort. "No, thank you, Fletcher. Do you know where my brother is?"

"I believe I last saw him in the gallery, my lady."

"Thank you." Ivy turned toward the door. As she passed the fireplace, she tossed the balled-up paper toward the flames and walked out. She didn't see the butler pick up the wrinkled sheet from the hearth and straighten it out.

Tamberlake came in from the yard. The kestrel was ready to fly, and yet he felt a strange reluctance to release it, as if somehow giving the bird its freedom meant he would lose so much more.

Ridiculous, he snarled to himself. He would find Lady Ivy and release the falcon this afternoon. He went into his study and rang for Fletcher.

The man came within minutes. "Did you need something, my lord?"

"Yes. Where is Lady Ivy?"

"I believe she is with her brother in the salon, my lord." Fletcher stepped closer to the desk.

"Thank you, Fletcher. I will go there now. If

you see her elsewhere, tell her to meet me there."

"Yes, sir." Fletcher stepped closer to the desk. "Is there something else?"

"Yes, sir. I found this paper, sir. I believe you should see it." Fletcher laid a sheet of newspaper on his desk. The paper showed signs of being crumpled up, but it lay flat now.

"What is it?"

"From London, sir." Fletcher bowed his head and shuffled from the room.

Odd man. Why did Fletcher think he'd be interested in the society pages? Tamberlake scanned the page. His eye fell upon a notice in the center.

> *The Earl and Countess of Dunleigh announce the betrothal of their daughter, Lady Ivy St. Clair, to the Earl Wynbrooke. They shall host a ball April 29 to celebrate the union of these two noble families. These two ancient lines . . .*

The rest of the words blurred in front of his eyes as Tamberlake fell into his chair. Ivy's betrothal had been announced. Until this moment he hadn't quite believed she would marry Wynbrooke, but now he could have no doubt. All the *ton* knew of the union now. He could no longer deny it.

Ivy was leaving—had to leave—his home, his life, and his dreams.

He snatched up the newspaper from his desk and tossed it into the fire.

Chapter 13

Tamberlake had every intention of heading straight to the barn and releasing the kestrel, but he paused at the door. Ivy wanted to see the bird released. He let out a blast of air in impatience. Since when had he catered to the wishes of others?

Nevertheless, he turned around and clomped to the salon. Ivy sat with her brother, heads bent together as if sharing secrets. For an instant, he envied their relationship. He had no brother or sister to commiserate with. "Lady Ivy?"

Their gazes shot to him. Her eyes looked red, but Ivy turned away almost at once. She fussed with a handkerchief.

"Afternoon, Tamberlake," said Styles. "Did you want to challenge me to a chess game again?"

"Actually I came to ask Lady Ivy if she wished to watch me release the kestrel. The rain has ceased; I fear if I keep the falcon caged for much longer, it might harm itself."

"Oh, yes," said Ivy. Avoiding his gaze, she stuffed her handkerchief into her pocket and rose.

"May I come, also?" asked Styles. "This kestrel rescue has intrigued me since I first saw the falcon in its cage."

"If you wish." Without waiting for them, Tamberlake turned to the door and left the room.

As he stepped into the yard, he paused. The air held a definite hint of spring. High on the mountain a fresh coating of snow glazed the peaks, but in the valley the land smelled freshly washed. He inhaled deeply, and the crisp air stung his nostrils. *He* could use a thorough cleansing to expunge his unwanted thoughts.

"Everything sparkles," said Ivy.

Most people would just notice the soggy ground and the damp hills. Ivy saw the magic. He scowled. He didn't need another reason to like her.

As he walked, the ground oozed from beneath his boots, but his cane steadied his gait. He turned back to see how Ivy fared. She wore slippers unsuitable for traipsing through mud. She slipped once, but Styles caught her. He said, "Watch your step. The yard is muddy."

"Yes, I believe we can see that," she answered. The determined look on her face nearly brought a smile to his lips, but he was just as determined not to let her encroach on his thoughts again. He slogged through the mire, leaving Styles to help Ivy.

Humphrey met them halfway to the barn and fell into line behind Tamberlake. Styles laughed. "This duck behaves better than a dog."

Humphrey quacked as if scolding Styles for the comment. Tamberlake ignored the words. At the barn door, he threw a crust of bread to the duck, then entered the structure. After the brightness of the yard, the barn seemed dark. Tamberlake crossed to the covered cage that housed the kestrel.

"Well, I'll be damned. You really do keep a polecat here," Styles said in a whisper. His gaze focused on the highest beam, where the three-legged polecat walked.

Tamberlake glanced at Shylock, then reached into his pocket. "I haven't forgotten you." He reached into his pocket and pulled out the chicken liver he had wrapped in paper.

Placing the meat on a shelf, he admired the grace that the sleek masked animal displayed as he climbed down to retrieve the treat. Shylock took the meat in his mouth, then darted back up the beams out of sight.

"Amazing," said Styles. "No one will believe me when I tell them."

"Then don't," said Ivy. "I know it sounds silly, but don't tell anyone, please, Christopher."

Styles gave her a smile. "I won't, if you wish."

Tamberlake didn't dwell on the reason behind Ivy's request. Propping his cane against the wall, he reached for the cage and lifted it, cover and all. The kestrel screeched, and Tamberlake struggled to hold the cage steady.

"May I help?" asked Styles.

"No, I'm fine." He limped to the door and out into the yard. Placing the cage on the ground, he waited until the siblings joined him before uncovering the cage. The kestrel jumped about in an agitated dance, screeching and stretching his wings.

Tamberlake pulled on a single leather glove and bent down to open the cage door. The kestrel snapped at him, but the glove protected him from injury.

"Angry little thing, isn't it?" said Styles, his eyebrows arched.

"I didn't expect gratitude," said Tamberlake. "It doesn't know I won't hurt him."

He opened the door of the cage and stepped back. The small falcon didn't realize for a few moments that his freedom lay in front of him; then he hopped through the open door and landed on the ground. The bird's head turned from one side to another. Then he spread his wings and flew. He rose into the sky and grew smaller and smaller until he appeared no more than a dot in the blue. In less than a minute, the kestrel disappeared from view.

Tamberlake turned to Ivy. Tears rolled down her cheeks as she stared into the sky after the bird. He pulled off the heavy glove, reached into his pocket, and removed a handkerchief. He offered it to her.

"What? Oh, good heavens," said Ivy, dashing the tears away with her hand. "Thank you, but I have my own." She pulled out the handkerchief he'd seen earlier. She blew her nose and gave him a tremulous smile. "That was beautiful."

Styles cleared his throat. "I've never seen anything like it. Thank you for letting me watch."

Tamberlake nodded. He cast a final glance into the sky, then bent to retrieve the cage.

Styles stepped to him. "I'll take that." Without waiting for an answer, Styles picked the cage up from the ground and returned to the barn.

Ivy handed him his walking stick. "I brought this out for you."

"Thank you." He took it from her.

"We leave tomorrow."

"I thought as much. The roads won't be dry yet."

"Lord Wynbrooke didn't want to wait any longer." Ivy glanced at the house. "We've been gone longer than planned, and my parents are displeased."

"I see." He didn't look at her. He couldn't look at her. The sooner she left, the sooner he could forget about her.

Styles came out of the barn. "Polecats and kestrels. I believe I shall remember this afternoon for the rest of my life."

"Your sister tells me you are leaving tomorrow."

"Indeed. I suppose it's time to face society again." Styles gave a wave of his hand. "But this adventure has been well worth the time. I enjoyed making your acquaintance, Tamberlake, and I hope if you ever travel our way, you'll allow me to play host to you."

"I never played host," said Tamberlake.

"You put us up. That's enough." Styles held out his arm to Ivy. "Come along, Ivy. I'm not sure I quite trust those girls to pack our things properly. We'll see you at dinner, Tamberlake, and say our good-byes then."

The brother and sister returned to the house. Silence descended over the yard. The wind was no more than a whisper, and the house swallowed any sound from inside. Humphrey waddled out to him, but even the duck remained silent. He cast his gaze around his house and land. The solitude and quiet he had sought these past weeks was at last his.

And it left him with a deep dissatisfaction.

* * *

Ivy lay on her stomach in her bed and stared at the space at the foot of the bed where her trunk had stood. The driver had already loaded it onto the carriage. Her travel clothes were draped over the back of a chair, but the rest of her belongings, save the nightgown she wore and a few items in a small valise, lay inside the trunk.

They planned to leave at first light, and travel as long and fast as they could. Even Christopher had acknowledged that the sooner they returned home, the easier they could soothe their parents' aggravation at the length of the journey. They had eaten dinner early to ensure that everyone would get to bed at a decent hour. Tamberlake joined them at the end of the meal. He didn't eat, but said his good-byes and accepted their thanks. Then he had disappeared, and Ivy hadn't seen him again.

She turned onto her back and closed her eyes. Sleep remained elusive. She couldn't prevent the thoughts whirling through her head.

Tomorrow she would return to the proper world of her parents, the world of rules and obligations, the world she would face as a betrothed woman.

And then? And then she would face the world as a married woman, no longer the property of her father, but the property of her husband. Earl Wynbrooke.

A shudder slithered over her.

The earl was a good man. He would treat her well. They would live at Rosmartin Park, and she would have her own house to run. Someday she would look back upon this little adventure with romantic nostalgia and sigh with fondness over her memories, just as her mother had sighed over Lord Stanhope.

What a horrible notion. Expelling a loud puff of air, she rolled from the bed and paced the floor. She wasn't ready to retire into domestic tranquility. She wasn't ready to return to her father's impatience with her or her mother's lack of confidence in her.

Face it, Ivy. You just don't want to leave Lord Tamberlake.

Ivy stopped pacing and flopped onto her bed. Why had she agreed to come on this errand? If she had never met Tamberlake, she would have no qualms about marrying Wynbrooke. That wasn't true. She hadn't looked forward to her marriage long before she met Tamberlake, but at least she could have performed her duty without the sense of loss she now felt. Her heart would not have awakened to joy, and her senses would not know the headiness of flight.

Ivy gave a little derisive snort. Since when was she prone to lyrical words of self-pity?

But even as she mocked herself, a sadness settled on her. Tamberlake was the first man who showed an interest in her without wanting to change her or control her. Well, other than Christopher, but he was her brother.

Tamberlake didn't treat her as some sort of ornament. He asked her questions and listened to her answers. He read books, had an innate kindness, and . . . and . . .

Ivy buried her face in her hands. *I've fallen in love with him. In less than three weeks, I've fallen in love*

*with an ill-mannered, contrary man who makes me for-
get propriety when I'm with him.*

How could she marry Wynbrooke when her
heart wanted to stay in Wales?

How can I not?

Father would never agree to call off the betrothal
now that it had been announced. A betrothal was
almost as binding as the wedding ceremony itself.
Her wishes in the matter counted for nothing now.

Besides, Tamberlake had made no promises to
her, had never once said a word of endearment.
He had kissed her—twice—and, although she wasn't
experienced in such things, she believed he had
enjoyed himself as much as she. But he had said
nothing more to her or even given her a hint that
he wanted her in his life.

In low, muted tones, the clock on the mantel
struck eleven. Ivy cast an impatient glance at the
timepiece. She didn't need a reminder that she
should be sleeping. The morning would arrive too
soon as it was.

Ivy rose from the bed. If she was to spend the
rest of her life living according to convention, she
wanted something to remember that belonged
only to her. She wanted a moment where she took
her freedom. She wanted to know she didn't lack
the courage to listen to her heart.

Pulling her wrapper around her, Ivy stepped into
the hallway. She tiptoed past Mrs. Pennyfeather's
room. Soft snores came from behind the door. No
light burned under Christopher's door. As she
passed the room allocated to Wynbrooke, she
stopped. Inarticulate voices drifted out to her. The
earl was awake and had company. Holding her

breath, she looked down the hall. Mr. Thorndike's door was ajar, and light spilled into the corridor. She crept past the open door, hoping Thorndike was with Wynbrooke.

She walked past the top of the stairs toward a section of the house she had never been in. Tugging on her lower lip, she turned down a dim corridor. A sconce on the wall gave out weak light, but enough for her to see her way. She could guess which room was her destination. The wide double doors could mean only one thing. This was the master's chambers.

Chapter 14

He wasn't asleep. How could he sleep when his thoughts continued to plague him? His safe, ordered world no longer existed, and the chaos that caused the destruction was leaving in the morning. And he found himself craving the chaos. The idea of a quiet existence didn't hold the same appeal any longer.

The latch clicked. His gaze shot to the door. By the light of a single taper, he could see the handle turn. What could require his attention at this hour? "Fletcher?"

"No," said the voice that had been tormenting him. "It's Ivy."

She slipped into the room appearing much like a spirit to his gaze. Her white nightgown floated behind her as she walked.

"Lady Ivy?" As Tamberlake sat up in the bed, he pulled on his eye patch. The blankets fell to his waist, exposing his chest.

"You've no clothes."

"I don't wear any when I sleep." He drew the

sheet up to cover himself. "You shouldn't be here." Even as he said the words, they sounded stupid to his ears.

Ivy sat on the edge of the bed. "I want to be here."

"Can I help you with something?"

"No . . . I mean, yes. It's difficult to explain." Ivy drew in a deep breath. "My betrothal has been announced. My mother sent me the notice that appeared in the newspaper."

"I saw it. Fletcher found it."

"He did? I thought I'd burned it." She frowned. "It doesn't matter."

"I don't see how I can help you with your betrothal."

"No, that isn't what I meant. I shall soon be the Countess of Wynbrooke. With the announcement, I'm as good as she already. Almost. But before I take my actual vows, I wish to do one thing."

Her gaze dropped to her hands. "Wynbrooke is my father's choice, but just once I want to choose for myself. And I choose you."

His heart pounded. Her words were the stuff of his dreams. He shook his head. "Lady Ivy, you don't know what you are asking."

"Oh, but I do." She leaned forward. With an ever-so-gentle touch, she placed her lips on his.

He groaned and pulled her closer, tasting her, trying to draw her essence into him. A moment later he broke it off. "No."

She smiled. "I knew you weren't indifferent to me."

"Indifferent? Hell. I can't seem to keep you out of my life." Tamberlake withdrew from her and eased out of the bed. He draped the sheet to cover his nakedness. He felt safer, somehow, with the bed between them. "Go before someone finds you here."

"I understand." She stood. "You fear the scandal if someone discovers us."

He stared at her. "No scandal can harm me."

"Then you won't risk your reputation."

He nearly laughed at that. "What reputation? No one would believe me if I shouted it from the top of St. Paul's."

"Do you protect my reputation then?"

"I am not that much a gentleman."

She walked around the bed, her gown fluttering out behind her like a wraith. "Then you don't wish to besmirch your honor. You won't touch another man's betrothed."

She stopped in front of him, just a few inches away from touching. Her eyes stared into his face. Her tongue licked the edge of her lip, the only sign of nervousness he had noticed from her.

" 'Honor' is an empty word to a man who disdains society. You should have care for your own honor."

"What honor is there in my father bartering me for his own benefit? What honor do I have in marrying a man I don't love?" She laid her hand upon his chest. "The greatest honor I can imagine is the giving of my heart. I choose to give it to you."

He couldn't speak. His throat grew tight, and his breath stalled in his lungs.

"Love me, Auburn. Love me tonight so I can take it with me for the rest of my days." She let her wrapper fall to the floor.

He drew her into his arms again, knowing he would

curse himself if he thought about his actions. With a fiery hunger, he kissed her. She was soft in his embrace. No corset or crinoline enforced a chaste distance. His hands slipped around her small waist and rested on the curves of her hips. Her breasts molded against his chest, searing him with their warmth. Her mouth scalded him, her fingers torched a path on the side of his face, her tongue smoldered against his as they tasted each other.

He lifted her from the floor and placed her on the bed. "Are you sure?"

Her answer was to take his hand and pull him toward her. Ignoring the final protest in his mind, he lay beside her. His hands unfastened the tiny buttons at her throat, and pushed the gown from her shoulders. His hands sought the skin beneath the gown, gliding over her collarbone, lower, until he brushed the top of her breast, lower still until he felt her nipple pucker into his palm.

Her sharp intake of breath stopped him for a moment. Then her hands traveled up his ribcage, over his back, and around again. "So strong," she whispered.

Still covered by the sheet, his lower body responded to her touch. His erection pressed against her thigh. Tamberlake wanted to see her—all of her. He pushed the nightgown to her waist, then over her hips down her legs until she was free of the garment. Ivy's cheeks filled with color, but she made no move to cover herself.

He lowered his mouth to her breasts. He sucked in one nipple while he played with the other, rolling it between the pads of his fingers. Her body bucked at the attention.

His kiss moved to the other nipple, and with his free hand, he delved between her legs. He ran his fingers through her feminine valley, searching out the bud and stroking it until her breath came in ragged gasps and her body trembled.

Ivy couldn't breathe. His fingers sent shots of sensation through her. She felt every pull of his mouth not only on her skin, but also at the very core of her. And every new touch astonished her and filled her with a jubilation she couldn't name. Her skin tingled so that even the touch of the bedding felt like a caress. Her blood bubbled through her as if it were made of champagne, and she didn't know how or even if she was breathing at all. When Auburn slipped a single finger within her, she thought she might scream.

He rolled away from her. Bereft of his warmth, Ivy felt a sense of loss, but the cold night air danced upon the heightened sensitivity of her skin with an odd sort of pleasure. Auburn stood beside the bed and discarded the sheet.

She leaned on an elbow and drank in the sight of him. He was a beautiful man.

The mattress dipped as he returned to her side. He raised himself above her and braced himself on his hands. "Tell me now, Ivy. Tell me now if you want me to stop. I won't have the strength later. I barely have it now." He stared down at her with an intensity she could feel.

She cupped his face in her hands. "I want you to love me."

A low sigh slipped through his lips. He pressed his hips forward until his erection brushed against the juncture at her hips. She opened her legs for him.

He reached between them, guiding himself to

the brink of her core. Then he pressed himself into her, hesitating only for an instant when he felt her maidenhead. When he broke through, she stiffened and cried out.

"Shhh, Ivy. It won't hurt anymore," he whispered. He offered small sounds of comfort and stroked her cheek until she relaxed.

He moved slowly, giving her body time to grow accustomed to his size, but her sweetness soon seduced him into forgetting his care. He thrust in faster, deeper, feeling as if he couldn't get enough of her. Through his haze, he noticed she met his every thrust, dancing in rhythm with him.

Ivy couldn't reason. Her senses whirled in a heady vertigo that was building toward some unknown finish. She clung to Auburn, reveling in his strength. She met him, hip to hip, wanting more of him. The sensation grew until she couldn't catch her breath. And then she shattered.

Above her, Tamberlake pressed into her, feeling her squeeze him. His control vanished and his body reveled in the release. A deep satisfaction rolled through his chest.

Her breath returned to her as the vertigo slipped away. Tamberlake gathered her in his arms, his own breath still heavy and warm. He kissed the tip of her nose.

"No wonder the poets write so much about love." Ivy snuggled deeper into his embrace.

He chuckled. "I knew you were dangerous."

She pressed herself up on her hands to look at him. "Dangerous?"

"Aye, dangerous. You are remarkably composed for a woman who just lost her innocence, and I am in grave danger of losing my heart."

"Oh no, you mustn't." Ivy moved away from him.

"I'm afraid it's too late." He reached for her, but she twisted out of his grasp.

"Ivy?"

She retrieved her nightgown from the foot of the bed and pulled it over her head.

"Where are you going?"

"Back to my room. I mustn't be found here."

"If you're found, I'll just have to marry you."

"I'm already to be married." She got up from the bed and picked up her wrapper from the floor.

"You can't marry Wynbrooke now."

"Don't you see? I have to. I don't want to, but I have to."

"Why?" Tamberlake grew angry. "Why would you marry him?"

Ivy turned to him, tears glistening in her eyes. "I gave my word."

"To hell with your word." He rose from the bed and wrapped the sheet around his waist.

"Do you think my father would release me from the betrothal after he had so much trouble finding someone for me? Do you think Wynbrooke would be the type to accept such humiliation?"

"I don't give a damn about them. I care about you. I care about me."

"And I care for you." Ivy started for the door.

"What if there's a child?"

She stopped. "A child?"

"Yes." He strode to her. "What if your desire for adventure produces a child? Will Wynbrooke marry you if you're carrying another man's child?"

"I don't know. I would have to tell him, I suppose."

"Oh, yes, undoubtedly. Perhaps you'll be good enough to tell me, too, since I would be the father."

"You needn't be hateful." The tears spilled over her lids.

He didn't want to see her cry. He couldn't bear to see her cry. "Ivy, I—"

"I must go."

"No." He reached his hand out.

"If I don't, I'd never find the strength later. I will let you know about any child." Ivy reached the door and hesitated. "If you care for me at all, you won't come after me. I gave my word."

She shut the door behind her. The latch clicked into place with a report as loud as a gunshot.

Tamberlake stared at the door. Damn her. Damn her father and Wynbrooke. And damn Stanhope for sending her here.

He pulled on a dressing gown. He needed a drink.

Wynbrooke entered the salon first. He drew his dressing gown tighter around him. "Keep your voice down. We don't want to wake anyone."

"No one will hear us. They're all sleeping. Like good little children." Thorndike laughed.

"You're terrible. Amusing, but terrible."

"That's why you keep me around."

Wynbrooke shook his head and crossed to the brandy. He poured the liquor into two snifters and handed one to Thorndike. "Thank God we leave tomorrow. Of course, I will miss his brandy." He lifted the glass and sipped.

"Don't worry, Wyn. After you wed Ivy, you'll be

able to afford this any time you want." Thorndike moved to the fire and sat in a chair facing the low-burning flame. "You'd think the bloody rich Earl of Tamberlake could afford a few lamps."

"Actually, I prefer it dark. That way we don't have to see his face." Wynbrooke sat in the chair opposite Thorndike. "He is a freak. He keeps a duck as a pet, lives in the dark, and doesn't like people. Even his butler is a freak."

Thorndike snorted. "The whole house is filled with freaks. Look at his cook. A worse-mannered peasant I have never met."

"But you have to admit the food is good."

"I will concede that point." Thorndike lifted his glass. "Here's to the freaks and their quality of life."

Wynbrooke was silent for a moment. "Tamberlake's face doesn't seem to trouble Lady Ivy."

"She does seem willing to overlook a lot."

"That trait could come in handy after we're married."

They both laughed, then Wynbrooke sobered. "Marriage. I didn't think it would come this far."

"You know it's the right thing to do. The *ton* expects it, and your mother expects an heir." Thorndike stared into the fire. "Well, with luck you'll only have to bed her once."

"If I had luck, she'd be a woman of loose morals and come to me already bedded and with child."

"No chance of that. A year is all it should take."

"A year. Gad, how will I stand it?"

"Try not to think about it." Thorndike finished his brandy. "A year isn't long at all."

"But the thought of bedding her . . ." Wynbrooke gave a theatrical shudder.

Thorndike chuckled and stood. "Just think of the rewards."

"Yes, the money will be handy." Wynbrooke finished off his brandy.

"And the safety." Thorndike took the snifter from Wynbrooke and returned both to the salver, then pulled Wynbrooke to his feet. "Come, let's go back to bed." He leaned forward and kissed Wynbrooke on the lips.

When they broke apart, Wynbrooke sighed. "You're so good to me, Roger. I don't know what I'd do without you." He draped his arm around Thorndike, and the two men left the room.

Tamberlake set down his glass before he dropped it. Leaning back, he closed his eyes. Impossible. This night had been beyond belief. When he came down, he'd walked straight to the salon, poured himself a brandy, and sat in the winged armchair in the darkest corner of the room. The fire burned low in the hearth, but he needed no other light. He had wanted only silence in which to think and a drink to soothe him. Now he didn't think a drink was enough.

With a wry smile, he thanked whatever fate had sent him downstairs tonight. He was willing to sit here all night if he had to, but he would stop her.

If Ivy thought he would leave her be now, she was sorely mistaken.

Chapter 15

Tamberlake's eyes fluttered open. His head swam, and disorientation swamped him. As he tried to make sense of his surroundings, he turned his head and nearly cried out in pain. His neck was stiff. Blinking to dispel the last vestiges of a poor sleep, he saw the fire in the grate, or better said, the gray embers of a spent fire. He remembered where he was and why he was there.

The heavy drapes gave him no sense of the time. He jumped from the armchair and this time did let out a groan from between clenched teeth. His leg throbbed, and his neck felt as if someone had fastened an iron shackle around it. He limped to the window and threw the drapes open. The sun was high overhead, its light shining over the explosion of spring color in the hills and mountains. The yard was empty. The doors to the carriage house stood open. Only his carriage stood in the stalls.

Damn. Ivy was gone.

Tamberlake went to the bellpull and yanked on

the wire. "Fletcher," he yelled in accompaniment of his action. "Fletcher."

The butler shuffled into the room a few moments later. "You rang, sir?"

"Where are my guests?"

"They left, my lord. Several hours ago. They told me not to disturb you as they had taken their departure from you last evening."

"Damn." Tamberlake glanced out the window. He was too late. Unless . . . "Have my horse saddled, then come upstairs and help me dress."

"Yes, sir." Fletcher bowed his head and left the room.

Tamberlake grabbed his cane and, ignoring the pain in his thigh and neck, hurried to his room. He threw off his dressing gown and pulled on his undershirt.

He hadn't ridden much since his accident. His leg no longer had the strength for long periods of posting, but on a horse, he could catch her. A horse with a single rider could cover more ground than a carriage over this terrain. He would stop her and . . .

He paused. How could he explain his behavior? As much as he abhorred Wynbrooke and Thorndike, he had no desire to ruin them by revealing their indiscretions. But neither could he let Ivy marry Wynbrooke.

By the time Fletcher came upstairs, Tamberlake had stopped his frenzied activity and sat on the edge of his bed.

"Sir? Are you ill?"

Tamberlake shook his head. "No, but I think I'm approaching this wrong."

"Sir?"

He gave the butler a sly smile. "I think it's time to visit my mother."

Two weeks later, he climbed into his carriage and sat on the cracked leather. He hadn't sat on these cushions since he arrived five years earlier. Gad, had it really been that long?

The carriage lurched into motion, and his heart did as well. His heart pounded in time with the horses' hooves, and sweat beaded on his forehead. He clutched his cane in a stranglehold. He wasn't sure he could go through with this journey.

How could he not go? A letter wouldn't suffice. Lord Dunleigh would hardly take the word of a stranger over that of the man betrothed to his daughter. But to go to London . . . Tamberlake sat back.

Quack.

From the roof of the carriage, Humphrey made his anxiety known. The sound brought the first smile of the day to his face. In packing up the house for the journey, he had decided he must take the animals. Humphrey was too much a spoiled pet to survive without care. Catching the mallard had been easy. Humphrey had climbed right into the cage. The duck was used to sleeping in it, after all, but when the door closed on the bird, Humphrey had shown his displeasure. He had quacked and flapped his wings until he'd exhausted himself.

But the duck had been easy to subdue compared with the polecat. Shylock wouldn't appear, not even for his favorite treat—a newt that Tamberlake had spent several days turning over log after log in pursuit of. Luckily he and Beaker had started to chase the elusive animal two days before departure. They finally caught the animal by tossing a tarp over him and stuffing him into a cage. And in a note of irony that didn't escape Tamberlake, Shylock calmed at once and had gazed at his two captors from behind the wires with almost friendly eyes.

Shylock traveled beside Humphrey in a covered cage. Tamberlake wasn't sure the animals would adapt to life away from Wales, but he couldn't leave them behind.

Tamberlake lifted his leg to stretch across the seat. He was taking almost the entire household with him to Marsgrove, his ancestral seat. Fletcher, Beaker, and Mrs. Beaker rode in the other carriage. Fletcher had arranged for the maids and gardeners to stay on, as well as hiring a couple as caretakers. Fletcher had proven to be an efficient butler, but he doubted his mother would appreciate the man's talents.

Ivy must be at home by now. Tamberlake wondered what she was doing and how the preparations for her wedding were coming. He smiled again at that thought and closed his eyes. He had much to do before he saw her again.

"I did not expect such irresponsible, childish behavior from you," said Lord Dunleigh. "Especially after I gave you my permission."

"Yes, Father." Ivy sat on the edge of the settee.

Her gaze flew to the window more often than was polite, but her father wouldn't notice her lack of attention.

"Traipsing about the country like a gypsy. What were you thinking? Were you trying to bring scandal upon the family?"

"Yes, Father." At his scowl, Ivy blurted out a different answer. "I mean, no, Father."

"You're just lucky Wynbrooke is such a patient man."

And that Wynbrooke had enjoyed the brandy and food in Wales enough. "Yes, Father."

"The next time you run such an errand you will take the train. Efficiency. That's the key."

"That isn't bloody likely," said Christopher, pushing himself upright from his insolent slouch at the hearth. "Ivy isn't going to have another errand like this one."

Her father's face grew red. "Dash it all, Christopher, that isn't what I meant, and you know it."

"I'm just saying it's highly unlikely that Ivy would find herself in such a situation again." Christopher crossed and took a seat beside her.

"And it seems to me you could have taken the situation in hand and hurried your departure along." Lord Dunleigh paced in front of the settee and pointed at his son as he passed.

"What would you have had me do, Father? Forge the carriage pieces myself?" Christopher raised a single eyebrow.

"You might have had a thought for me. Your simple trip lasted far longer than warranted. People were beginning to wonder about you. But I don't suppose I could have expected the correct behavior from you." Lord Dunleigh frowned at his son.

"We're back now, Father. At least I didn't lose you any more money." Christopher gave his father a lazy grin.

"And don't think I'm not aware of that. I may have to send you away longer next time."

Christopher's grin disappeared.

Lord Dunleigh stopped and glared at Ivy. "Can you imagine how embarrassed I was to explain your errand?"

"We're sorry to have worried you, Father." Ivy smoothed her gown.

"So what is he like?" Her father clasped his hands behind his back and rocked back and forth on his heels.

The sudden change of topic amused her. How mercurial of her father to seek information about the man. Ivy didn't want to play along. "Who?"

"Tamberlake, of course. He's a rich man. Does he show any interest in returning to London?"

"No." Ivy gazed out the window again. She wasn't sure how she'd react if he came to London. She wasn't sure she was strong enough to see him again.

"A pity. I would have liked to feel him out for support. A man with such money as he must have influence, and I could have shown him how to use his."

"Isn't Wynbrooke enough?" Christopher eyed his father with ill-disguised impatience.

"Old family, good name, to be sure, but it never hurts to make new contacts. Tamberlake would have been a victory." Father gave her a knowing look. "Is he as bad as they say?"

Ivy wrinkled her brow in confusion. "He isn't bad at all."

"His looks, girl. His looks. Are they as terrible as they say?"

An angry retort rose to her lips, but she bit it back and gave her father an innocent look. "Oh, no, Father. They're much worse."

Christopher covered his mouth with his hand as a fit of coughing overtook him.

Her father took on a look of concentration. "I can understand why he stays where he is then. Perhaps I should write him a letter of thanks. Yes, an excellent plan. I can begin a correspondence with him." Lord Dunleigh gave Ivy a nod of thanks. "Good move, Ivy. You've opened up a channel for communication with the man. I believe I can take advantage of your little adventure."

"I'm glad I could help, Father," said Ivy, without the slightest hint of sincerity.

"Your mother wants you in her boudoir, Ivy. Some nonsense about a dress." Lord Dunleigh left the room, muttering his plans to himself.

"You are wicked, Ivy." Christopher turned to her with a grin. "I almost couldn't disguise my laughter."

"He wouldn't have noticed in any case."

"Probably not. He couldn't decide if he was annoyed with us or grateful we made a valuable contact."

She didn't respond.

Christopher took her hand. "You haven't been yourself since we left Wales. You're pale and you're not eating. Are you ill?"

"No, I'm fine. I'm just not terribly happy."

"It's Tamberlake, isn't it?"

Heat shot into her cheeks. "What do you mean?"

"I saw the looks you gave him toward the end of our stay. You like the fellow."

With a sigh, Ivy rose, and started to pace. "He was different. He talked to me and listened to me. Unlike anyone here."

"I like that." Christopher crossed his arms over his chest.

She smiled despite herself. "Not you, silly."

Her brother stood and joined her. "I know, Ivy. He was a remarkable man. I enjoyed his company as well."

"You speak as if he were dead."

"No, but you may as well consider him so. You are betrothed now."

"I know." She couldn't prevent the tears that sprang to her eyes.

Christopher hugged her. "It's not so bad. You'll have your own house soon. And I'll come visit. Often."

She laughed. "I do love you, Christopher."

"I know." He released her and smiled. "You'd better go to Mother. When it comes to clothes, she doesn't have much more patience than Father."

Ivy nodded. "She will just have to wait a few more minutes. I have something I must do first."

Christopher left the room. Ivy stepped to the secretary and removed a sheet of paper. Sitting at the writing shelf, she dipped the end of a pen into the ink and paused. After a moment, she started writing.

Lord Tamberlake,
  I thought I should inform you that you needn't worry about that matter we discussed on my last night at Gryphon's Lair. The issue has resolved it-

*self as I hoped, and you needn't fear any unex-
pected arrivals.*

*Yours,
Lady Ivy St. Clair*

She read the note over once, blotted it, folded
it, and sealed it shut. With a neat hand, she ad-
dressed the letter. Her mother waited. Wiping a
tear from her eye, she glanced at the paper in her
hand. She wondered how she would feel if the re-
sult had been different.

"Lady Ivy?" Mrs. Pennyfeather came into the
salon. "Your mother is wondering what's keeping
you."

"I'm coming." Hiding the letter in the folds of
her dress, Ivy forced a smile to her lips and crossed
to Mrs. Pennyfeather. As they walked through the
front hall, Ivy dropped the letter on the butler's
table. He would see it mailed. She shot a quick
glance to the woman beside her, but Mrs. Pennyfeather seemed not to notice.

The two women climbed the stairs. Ivy could
hear her mother from the top step.

"I just don't know what to do with that girl."

Mrs. Pennyfeather smiled at Ivy, then led her into
the sitting room. "I've found her, Lady Dunleigh."

"Thank goodness. I don't know what I'd do
without you, Agatha."

"Agatha?" asked Ivy.

"Mrs. Pennyfeather, of course. She's been such
a boon to me since you've returned. Your father is
letting me hire her to help with the preparations
for your ball." Ivy's mother reclined on a chaise
longue. She stuffed a bonbon in her mouth and
chewed with some force. The chubby woman had

a pout on her face as she looked up at her daughter. "Really, Ivy, I've been waiting for just forever," she said in chocolate tones.

"Mother won't let me pick the material for my gown until you pick yours," said Georgina. The younger girl's blond curls bounced around her face as she tossed her head. "I don't think it's fair I have to wait. Ivy doesn't care anyway."

"But it's for her betrothal ball, my darling." Lady Dunleigh spoke to her youngest daughter as though she were soothing a pet. "Your gown will be just as pretty. You'll see."

A fifth woman stood in the room. *She must be the couturière,* thought Ivy. The woman clicked her tongue as she fussed over the materials.

"Now, Ivy dear, we must decide which of these colors suits you." Lady Dunleigh waved her hand to the seamstress. "Madam Renault can help us."

Ivy looked over the heaps of colorful fabrics that lay strewn about the room and sighed. "Couldn't you select one for me?"

Her mother gave her a look of exasperation. "I suppose that would be best. Your taste is questionable at most. Just look at the thing you're wearing now."

Ivy looked down. The dark green dress was a little drab perhaps, but it kept her warm. She shrugged.

"Hopeless." Lady Dunleigh looked over the material. "I'm thinking a yellow, or perhaps a peach color."

"An excellent choice," agreed the seamstress. She lifted a bright bolt of fabric. "This one, perhaps?"

Ivy nearly flinched. "I'll look like a canary in that."

"Hush, Ivy. You don't understand these things." Lady Dunleigh shook her head. "No, a little duller perhaps. We can't have the color outshine the wearer."

Ivy watched as her mother rejected one color after another. After several minutes, Ivy noticed Mrs. Pennyfeather inch to the side. The woman pointed to a bolt of a pale rose fabric. Ivy glanced down and felt a wave of relief wash over her. "What about this one?"

Her mother examined it. "Hold it up to her."

The seamstress held the fabric up to Ivy's face.

Lady Dunleigh nodded. "Perfect. It might put some color in those pale cheeks of yours."

"Is it my turn now, Mother?" asked Georgina.

"Go ahead, dear."

Georgina lifted one fabric after another. Ivy shook her head at her sister's excitement. "May I go now, Mother? I've picked out my fabric."

"No, you may not. We have to discuss style and accessories still. Really, Ivy, you could show some enthusiasm. It's your ball, after all."

"Yes, Mother." Ivy sighed. She moved some fabrics from a pouffe and sat.

"You might learn something from your sister, as well. Pay attention."

"Yes, Mother." Ivy propped her elbows on her knees and cupped her chin in her hands.

"Sit up, Ivy."

"Yes, Mother."

It was going to be a long day.

Chapter 16

Marsgrove. The carriage wheels crunched as they turned onto the gravel driveway and drove beneath the ornate arch of the gate. The house wasn't visible yet, but Tamberlake leaned forward to look out the window. To the left he caught a glimpse of the statue of Ares that stood in a copse. Some of the trees must have died, since it had never been visible from the road before. He would see that new ones were planted.

A small herd of red deer raised their heads at the carriage's approach, then scattered farther into the fields. Their number was good, he was pleased to see.

The trees thinned, and as the carriage followed the curve in the drive, he saw the house. Marsgrove lay on a rise with an immaculate expanse of circular lawn in front of it. A gardener looked at them, then went back to pruning the shrubs. The carriage pulled around to the front and stopped. Tamberlake didn't wait for a footman to open his door. He found himself eager to be home.

Strange. He had lived in Gryphon's Lair for five years, and as comfortable as he found it, he had never considered it home. Marsgrove was home, even if his mother thought herself firmly ensconced at its head.

He climbed from the carriage and reached back in to grab his cane. The days of inactivity had left his leg stiff, and as he stretched it to walk, he let out a soft moan.

"Shall I call for help, my lord?" asked the coachman from the roof of the carriage.

"No." He tossed a coin to the driver. "See that the animals are unloaded in the rear, put the coach away, then find yourself a pub and have a drink on me. We made good time, Rufus."

"Aye, sir. Thank you, sir." Rufus clicked his tongue, and the horses set the carriage in motion again.

Leaning on the cane, Tamberlake glanced up at the imposing facade. His family had built the house more than three hundred years earlier, and although each generation had added their own touches to it, the house retained its Elizabethan grandeur. Three stories of windows looked down upon the front lawn, and a multitude of chimneys extended skyward from the roof. Tamberlake noticed that one of the false minarets had toppled. He would add that to his list of items that needed attention.

The door opened, and the butler appeared at the top step. For a moment, the man looked at the unexpected visitor with disdain; then his face converted into an expression of shock.

"Good afternoon, Whitson." Tamberlake climbed the steps with the aid of his cane.

The butler's face transformed once again. An

impenetrable mask dropped over his expression. "My lord. Welcome home. Your mother didn't tell me to expect you."

"She didn't know." Tamberlake walked past Whitson to the door. "Have my things brought to the master suite."

Whitson looked uncomfortable. "Excuse me, my lord, but the countess is in the master's chambers."

"I see. Very well, have my things put in another room for today, but don't unpack. I'll move into my chambers tomorrow. See that someone starts to move my mother's things. She can choose any room she wants except mine."

"Yes, sir."

"Where is the countess?"

"I believe she's in the parlor, my lord. Shall I announce you?"

"No, thank you, Whitson. I want to surprise her." His smile wasn't one of eager anticipation.

Tamberlake stepped trough the portal. To his astonishment, a wave of satisfaction washed over him. Marsgrove seemed to welcome him. This was his house, and it felt right that he was here.

As he walked down the hall, a comfortable familiarity stole over him. He had raced across this floor as a child, escaping the monotony of a tutor's lesson or the repercussions of rearranging his mother's bric-a-brac. The warmth of the memories granted his smile a touch of sincerity, instead of the full irony he intended, as he entered the salon.

"Good afternoon, Mother."

Lady Tamberlake gasped and spun to gaze upon the intruder. Her eyes grew wide as recognition set in. For several moments, she said nothing, then she straightened her skirt and gave a delicate sniff. "Auburn. Great heavens, what are you doing here?"

"This is my house."

"Yes, but I'm not prepared for guests."

"I wasn't aware I needed an invitation to come here."

"No, don't be daft. But you might have written me."

"Why? Did you need a warning?"

"I don't appreciate your flippancy." Lady Tamberlake perched on the edge of a chair. "You must admit your arrival is disruptive."

"I'm happy to see you as well, Mother."

"Don't pretend with me, Auburn. Have you come to torment me for some reason?"

Tamberlake took a seat opposite his mother. "What makes you think I came home for you? I have my own reasons for being here."

"And they are . . . ?"

"No, Mother. I'm not sharing my secrets. My arrival doesn't concern you. Not yet, at any rate."

He enjoyed the look of confusion on her face until she composed herself. "Well, how long can we enjoy your company?"

"We?"

She let out a groan of exasperation. "I. How long can *I* expect to enjoy your company?"

"I didn't realize you enjoyed my company."

She drew in a deep breath and glared at her son. "Your impertinence tires me. How long are you staying?"

He smiled. "I can't answer. I may never leave."

"What?"

"I'll be here at least one month, and I hope longer."

His mother couldn't speak for a moment. "This is unexpected."

"More than you know. I understand you've taken over the master suite."

His mother had the grace to redden. "You weren't here. This is my home, and you haven't left Wales in five years. Of course, I took the rooms."

"You might want to tell Whitson which room you want to have your things moved to. I'm sure he'd pick a nice one, but it might not be your choice."

"You can't expect me to move on a whim."

"It's no whim, Mother. I've come home. I've neglected my duties far too long."

"You can run the estate from Wales."

"Yes, but I can't find a bride from there."

Lady Tamberlake's mouth dropped open. "But how can you . . . What will people say?"

Tamberlake stood. "I don't care what people say."

Lady Tamberlake sighed. "Very well, Auburn. I can't stop you. I'm expecting a few friends for tea soon. If you join us—"

"Don't worry, Mother. I have no desire to see your friends. You don't even have to tell them I'm here. In fact, I would prefer you wouldn't."

Relief eased her pinched expression.

"But you'd better reconcile yourself that I've returned, and I no longer have a mask."

Tamberlake left the salon feeling stronger than he had in a long time.

* * *

Tamberlake enjoyed the view from the parlor windows. He had never acknowledged how much he missed Marsgrove. Although he had spent the night in a small room, he had slept well. Now, overlooking the elaborate gardens ready to bloom with the spring, he was happy to be here.

"Auburn, there is a duck in the fountain." Lady Tamberlake entered the room. The frown on her face warned him of her mood.

"Good morning, Mother. Did you sleep well?"

"Did you hear me? There is a duck in the fountain. My guests noticed it yesterday, and when I went out to shoo it away, it came out of the water and quacked at me. I asked the gardener to get rid of it, and he told me you won't allow anyone to touch him."

"The duck's name is Humphrey."

"That creature has a name?"

"Yes."

"And it's going to live in the fountain?"

"If he chooses."

"I won't have it terrorizing my guests."

"Humphrey is a duck, Mother. I doubt he could terrorize a puppy."

His mother glared at him. "Very well. Far be it from me to go against the earl's word." She flounced from the room.

The upheaval had begun.

Later that afternoon, he and Fletcher were in the newly emptied master's chambers organizing his belongings. He was placing books on a shelf when three sharp raps on the door shot through the room. Before he could bid the visitor enter, his mother shoved the door open and strode inside without any sort of preamble.

"Antoine has threatened to quit. He claims that there's a man ordering everyone around in his kitchen. That . . . that Beaker man from Wales."

He would have to remember to lock his door if he wished for privacy. "Who is Antoine?"

"My chef."

"Oh, him. Give him a month's pay. Two months, and tell him we no longer need his services." He returned to shelving his books.

"Auburn, are you prepared to let that oaf, that Beaker man, take over the kitchen?"

"Yes."

"But Antoine's French."

"And Beaker's the better cook."

"You can't mean it."

Tamberlake put his books on a table and faced his mother. "I ate your Frenchman's food yesterday. It was a tasteless mess hidden in sauce. Beaker is Marsgrove's new cook. If Antoine is really French as he claims he is, he will find new employment with little difficulty, especially with the glowing references I will write him."

"But—"

Fletcher lumbered into the room carrying two small Meissen figurines. "Excuse me, sir, what shall I do with these?"

"Who is this?" Lady Tamberlake pointed at Fletcher.

"This is my butler, Fletcher."

Fletcher bowed. "Forgive me, madam. I did not realize I was interrupting."

"You've brought a new butler as well?"

"I did."

"But Whitson has been with us for twenty years."

"I know."

"Are you going to dismiss him for no reason also?"

"No, Mother. I know you prefer Whitson."

"We can't have two butlers."

"Why not?"

She sputtered for a moment. "But it isn't done."

"I have no intention of letting Whitson go, but Fletcher can do things for me."

"Whitson will not be pleased."

"You can tell Whitson that I think his service impeccable, but Fletcher is staying. If Whitson doesn't like the arrangement, he may leave." He took the porcelain statuettes from Fletcher. "I believe these are yours. You forgot to take them with you."

Lady Tamberlake opened her mouth as if to speak, then clamped it shut. She grabbed the Meissen and pivoted on her heels. She left the room without looking back.

He would have laughed, but he realized this was a serious battle of wills between himself and his mother. If he didn't establish himself as the lord of the manor at once, he never would.

The final event of the day occurred in the late afternoon. He was in the garden, stretching his legs, when a series of screams rent the air.

He started toward the stables. Just as he rounded the house, his mother came out of the building, and with a look of fury on her face, she raced toward him. Two groomsmen followed her. Her dress was covered in mud and straw, and her hair looked rather windswept. The problem was no wind stirred the air that day.

"There is a polecat in the stables," she said, grinding out each word between her clenched teeth.

Good. Shylock had decided to stay for a while.

"I was bringing an apple for my horse, when it leapt on me and sniffed my pockets. When I screamed, it jumped into my hair and squealed as it became tangled." Lady Tamberlake swept at the debris on her skirt without much success. "It only came free when I fell into the muck. And it took the apple."

"The polecat is harmless, Mother. He is used to animals and will do an excellent job of ridding the stables of mice. He only has three legs, enjoys treats on occasion, and his name is Shylock."

For an instant, his mother's face showed surprise, but she hid it well in the next instant. "The stable master told me it was a pet of yours, but I didn't believe him. If you will excuse me, I will clean up now." She turned from him, started for the house, then stopped. Facing him again, she asked, "Do you have any other pets you haven't told me about?"

"No, Mother. And I am sorry for any fright they might have caused you."

She didn't give him a response.

Whitson found him in the study a few minutes later. "My lord, your mother regrets to inform you she has a headache and will not be dining with you this evening."

"Thank you, Whitson. Do convey my sympathy to her."

"Yes, my lord." Whitson bowed his head and turned to leave.

"Oh, and send Fletcher to me."

"Yes, sir."

In a few minutes, Fletcher came into the room. "You wished to see me?"

"Can I count on your discretion?"

Fletcher looked taken aback. "I hope I have done nothing to bring my integrity into question."

"No, not at all. I have a few matters of some delicacy I'd like your help with."

"How may I be of service?"

"I need someone capable of making inquiries."

"I know of just the person, my lord."

"Excellent. Please arrange for him to come here."

"As you wish, sir."

Tamberlake sat at his desk, and folded his hands on the writing surface. "Since I have returned, I think it proper I attend social functions. But I shall need the guest lists before I decide whether to attend. Can you arrange that?"

"As your butler, I believe I can gather the information from the staff of any house you wish."

"I really only wish to know if one lady shall be present at certain events."

"May I ask the name of the lady?"

He raised an eyebrow.

Fletcher nodded and gave a little smile. "I understand, sir. Is there anything else?"

Tamberlake nodded. "There is one other item. I need to arrange for some dancing lessons."

Chapter 17

Tamberlake waited behind his desk as Fletcher brought the man into his study. He estimated Savernake was his age. The man had dark hair and dark eyes, and his features betrayed nothing. Not even when Savernake saw his face. Probably handy for the business he conducted. "Please sit down, Mr. Savernake," said Tamberlake from behind his desk.

"Thank you, my lord." Savernake took his place in a wooden-backed chair.

"I understand you knew Lord Stanhope."

"More that I knew *of* him. He was a friend of my father's." Although Savernake's voice gave evidence of good schooling, it held little emotion.

"And your father is . . ."

"The Earl of Warksbooth." Savernake didn't look away.

"I see." Tamberlake examined the man. He didn't show any shame for his illegitimate birth. Tamberlake liked that. "Your reputation precedes you. I've heard you're a man of great discretion."

"Yes."

"The task I have for you requires more information than action." He handed the man a folder with some information on Wynbrooke. "Inside you will find the name and address of Earl Wynbrooke. I need to know the state of the earl's finances."

Savernake nodded. "Easily done."

"There's more." Tamberlake leaned back in his chair and pressed his fingertips together. "I need proof of some of his activities."

"Do you mean gambling debts? Mistresses?"

"Wynbrooke doesn't gamble and he doesn't keep a mistress, but I imagine he does entertain himself at some exclusive men's clubs."

"Brothels?"

"Perhaps. But not filled with women."

Savernake raised an eyebrow, the first reaction Tamberlake could discern. "I believe I understand."

"I don't want to ruin the man. I just need some evidence."

"Very good, my lord. The financial records should be easy to find, but if the man has been discreet, the other information may be more difficult to trace."

"Which is why I require your help. I don't have the time to chase the information at present. Will you do this?"

Savernake paused for a moment. "Forgive my impertinence, but I only take cases I find worthy of my time. May I ask what you intend to do with this information?"

"Wynbrooke is to marry. I intend to save the woman from that fate."

Savernake smiled. "Then I would be honored to help you."

Tamberlake stood and extended his hand. Savernake rose and took it in his. "Thank you, Mr. Savernake."

Savernake bowed and followed Fletcher from the room.

Tamberlake sat again. Excitement stirred within him. His plan had commenced.

Ivy stared at her dress. It was beautiful. Tiny silk flowers and silver embroidery embellished the pale rose skirt and bodice. Her mother had sent up a necklace of aquamarine stones with matching ear bobs for her to wear that night. Real rosebuds lay ready to adorn her hair. Tonight she would be as lovely as she could be.

She gazed into the mirror and frowned.

"Ivy, don't scowl so or your face will freeze that way." Lady Dunleigh directed the chambermaid to empty the bucket into the tub. "First, you bathe, then we'll get you dressed. We have several hours yet. Plenty of time."

Not if you're hoping to make me a Cinderella. Ivy smiled to assure her mother she understood the task in front of them.

"Don't dawdle in the bath. We still have much to do. Ring for a maid when you finish. And don't dawdle."

"You're repeating yourself, Mother."

"Then obviously it's important." Lady Dunleigh swept from the room, shooing the maid in front of her.

Ivy slipped out of her wrapper and slid into the tub. The warm water embraced her, caressed her.

She gave in to the temptation and closed her eyes for a moment. The heat brought back the memories of a night she tried not to recall too often for fear she'd lose her will to carry through with her wedding. But at moments like these, Tamberlake claimed her every thought. And she wondered if he ever spared a thought for her.

With an angry splash, she grabbed a sponge and started scrubbing herself. Perhaps if she scrubbed herself hard enough, she could remember tonight was her betrothal ball and not the time for lost dreams.

She finished her bath in little time and stepped from the tub. With some reluctance, she rang for a maid, knowing once others arrived, she had no hope of peace for the rest of the day.

As she expected, the poking, prodding, and primping began with the arrival of the first maid. Her hair was yanked and pulled into obedience, and, while her corset ensured an unnatural thinness to her waist, the crinoline gave a fullness to her hips not humanly possible.

When the preparations ended, Ivy would have let out a sigh of relief, except her corset prevented a decent breath. Her hair coiled around her head in a perfect halo, the tiny buds decorating the roll in a celebration of spring. Her dress echoed the season.

Her mother circled her, then let out a soft grunt. "Well, it will have to do."

The clock strikes midnight for Cinderella. "Thank you for your confidence, Mother."

"You'll do fine, Ivy. You already have a betrothed. Now we just have to worry about Georgina."

"Right. I forgot. You're throwing me a betrothal ball to find Georgina a husband."

"Oh, my dear." Lady Dunleigh patted Ivy's arm. "I understand your nerves. Of course this is your big night."

Lady Dunleigh hurried to the door. "Now don't be late. Our guests shall arrive soon. I have to see how Georgina is faring. And pinch your cheeks, Ivy. You're ghastly pale."

Ivy was grateful to be alone for a few moments. She gazed in the mirror. Despite her mother's less-than-ebullient words, Ivy felt beautiful.

She only wished Tamberlake could see her tonight.

"Lords and Ladies and Gentlemen, may I present the betrothed couple, Earl Wynbrooke and my daughter, Lady Ivy St. Clair."

Her father's voice resounded into the hall. Wynbrooke nodded at her and started forward. Ivy made sure her smile was firm as she walked into the ballroom on Wynbrooke's arm. Applause greeted them as they entered, and the crowd parted for them as they made their way to the center of the room.

The music started, a waltz, and Wynbrooke twirled Ivy on the floor. She had to admit he was a superb dancer. Soon other couples joined them. Ivy was relieved not to be the center of attention any longer. She watched the guests as she circled by them. Her father had not wasted this opportunity to entertain the elite of society.

When the waltz ended, Wynbrooke bowed to

her. "Well done, my dear. Now that the formal presentation is over, we may relax and enjoy the rest of the evening."

Ivy looked at him in surprise.

He nodded. "I don't like to attract too much attention to myself."

"Neither do I."

"We'll get along just fine, you and I." Wynbrooke escorted her from the dance floor. "Can I bring you something? A drink perhaps?"

"No, thank you."

Ivy's parents crossed to them. Lord Dunleigh smiled. "You made an excellent impression. Wynbrooke, come with me. I think we need to celebrate this with more than the weak lemonade they're serving down here."

"An excellent idea, sir." Wynbrooke bowed to the ladies. "Will you excuse us?"

Lady Dunleigh giggled. "Of course, you dear boy."

Ivy felt a wave of relief as the two men left. Her role was over for the evening. In the next hour, she accepted congratulations from individuals, danced twice, and listened to the teasing from her mother's friends about married life. The buzz of activity never slowed. Ivy wondered how many people her parents had invited because the crush was too great for the ballroom and spilled into the other rooms on the floor and even into the garden. Her mother would be thrilled with the success.

Suddenly the buzz grew; then, like a wave, silence washed across the room until even the music stopped. Ivy glanced around to see what had disturbed the mood of the guests. Her mother gasped beside her.

"Dear heaven. The monster earl." Lady Dunleigh dug into her reticule for a small vial of smelling salts and handed it to Ivy. "Open this for me, Ivy, before I faint."

But Ivy ignored her mother's request. She couldn't keep her gaze from Tamberlake. He walked across the floor with the aid of his cane, never veering from a direct line toward her, looking neither right, nor left, only at her. Heat flooded her cheeks, and she didn't know whether to laugh or to cry.

"Ivy," said her mother with a hiss. "What is he doing here? He'll ruin my party."

Ivy brushed her mother away and walked toward him. Her heart pounded in her chest. She was so happy to see him again, yet the sight of him brought a constriction to her throat. His garb was as elegant as any here, and he wore only the eye patch on his face, she was happy to see. His long hair was tucked behind his ear on the unscarred side of his face, while he allowed his hair to fall over the other side. An innate dignity filled his demeanor, reminding her of a knight paying homage to his lady.

Tamberlake stopped in front of her and bowed. As if she were an automaton, she offered him her hand. He lifted it to his lips and pressed a brief kiss to the back.

"Lady Ivy, I'm happy to see you again."

She didn't trust her voice. "What . . . what are you doing here?" she whispered in a croak.

Before he could answer, Christopher strode to the middle of the floor, oblivious to the stares of the guests. He held out his hand and shook Tamberlake's. "Tamberlake, good to see you. I must say I'm surprised, but it's a pleasant surprise. What brings you to London?"

"I would be no sort of gentleman if I didn't congratulate Lady Ivy on her upcoming nuptials."

Christopher raised his brows. "You've come a long way for a party."

"Perhaps. But as you know, I had the time." Tamberlake turned to Ivy. "May I have the honor of a dance?"

She nodded, still unsure of her voice.

Tamberlake handed his cane to Christopher. "Would you hold this for me while I dance with your sister?"

"Anything to be of service." Christopher grinned and walked to the edge of the dance floor with the cane.

Tamberlake held out his arms. "Lady Ivy?"

She stepped into his embrace. It was as strong and welcoming as she remembered. A shiver ran through her at his touch, awakening memories in her body she had hoped to suppress.

They stood in the middle of the parquet for a moment, then Tamberlake glanced at the musicians. "Play, good fellows."

The musicians scrambled to raise their instruments, and after a few false notes, they fell into the rhythm of a waltz. Tamberlake looked into her eyes. "You must forgive the awkwardness of my steps. I've had to learn to accommodate my leg."

She nodded, and he led her into the dance. He wasn't as graceful as Wynbrooke. He couldn't turn her as quickly, and the steps weren't in an even three-count, but they did dance.

Frenzied whispers replaced the silence of the crowd until the room roared with excited conversations. No one joined them on the floor, but more people crowded into the ballroom to see the monster earl.

She glanced around. "They're all staring at us."

"I never realized how easily one could entertain the *ton*," said Tamberlake in her ear.

Ivy couldn't relax. A disquiet ran through her. "You didn't come all this way just to attend the ball."

"Very well."

His answer didn't reassure her. She gave him a wary look. "Why are you here?"

"I have some unfinished business."

She didn't know whether to feel relief or disappointment that she wasn't the reason he came. "I didn't expect to see you again."

"I imagine you didn't."

She pulled her lip between her teeth.

"Don't look so nervous. Our audience will think I'm the cause of your distress."

"But you are."

He laughed. "I've missed your forthrightness. Trust me, Ivy. I will never do anything to cause you harm." The music ended and Tamberlake led her to her brother at the edge of the dance floor. He bowed to her. "Thank you for the dance."

"But I—"

"Your betrothed approaches." As Wynbrooke stepped up next to her, Tamberlake took her hand and placed it in Wynbrooke's. "Thank you for allowing me to dance with your fiancée."

Wynbrooke cleared his throat, then said,

"Tamberlake, I wasn't aware you were invited to the ball."

"I wasn't. In fact I must go make my apologies to Lady Ivy's mother for crashing her soiree. I was hoping I could take advantage of my friendship with her children and expect forgiveness after the fact."

The musicians started the next melody. Dancers stepped onto the floor, casting curious glances at the group.

"I think we should leave the parquet to the dancers." Tamberlake took back his cane.

"Wait, Lord Tamberlake." Ivy's father hurried up to them. His gaze landed on the scarred half of the earl's face and a wince flitted across his features, but he hid his distaste behind a wide smile. "What a pleasure to meet you."

"Father, may I introduce the Earl of Tamberlake?" Ivy couldn't bear the predatory look in her father's eyes.

"Ivy told me you wouldn't leave Wales." Lord Dunleigh shot her a disapproving glance.

"Plans change. Ivy was correct, but I found I couldn't ignore some pressing business," said Tamberlake.

"Then I should be grateful for the change in your plans," said her father. "I've been meaning to make your acquaintance."

"Why?"

Lord Dunleigh blinked several times. "I—I I . . . your family . . ." He cleared his throat. "You'll need guidance as you resume your place in society. You don't want to bring shame to the Tamberlake name."

"No, indeed. I shall consider your offer with all

the seriousness it deserves." Tamberlake glanced at Christopher, and to Ivy's astonishment, he winked at her brother out of her father's view.

"Excellent. I'll be in touch," said Lord Dunleigh.

"I look forward to it." Tamberlake leaned on his cane and bowed to Ivy. "If you would excuse me, Lady Ivy, gentlemen."

As he left, Lord Dunleigh turned to his son. "Call on him next week. I want you to cultivate his friendship."

Christopher dragged his finger along his chin. "I may be busy in the next weeks, Father."

"You will visit him, or you'll find yourself without funds next month."

"It was a joke, Father."

"Save your levity for an appropriate moment," said Lord Dunleigh. "I've other guests to see to now. Wynbrooke, come with me. You may learn something."

The two men left. Ivy sighed. "If you wouldn't provoke him as much—"

"I wouldn't have as much fun." Christopher patted her arm. "Don't worry, Ivy. I had every intention of visiting Tamberlake. But I might as well let Father think I'm doing him a favor. Can't hurt if he thinks I'm capable of more than taking up space at his dinner table."

"Maybe you could ask him for more responsibilities . . ."

"I have. I asked if I could run Styles. It is my title, after all, but he said the income was too important for him to trust me." Christopher smiled at her. "I'm fine. I just have to find some way to assert my independence. Perhaps I should go to America."

"Oh, no, Christopher. I'd miss you too much."

"It was just an idea."

Neither spoke for a moment. Then Ivy said, "Did you know he was coming tonight?"

Ivy's abrupt change of topic didn't confuse her brother. "No. It surprised me almost as much as you."

Ivy nodded. Her gaze wandered over the ballroom seeking Tamberlake, but she didn't see him.

"It must have been hard for you. Do you need a moment to compose yourself?" asked Christopher.

She shook her head. "I'm fine, although I wouldn't mind taking some air."

"Finally, something I can take care of." Christopher offered her his arm. "May I escort you to the garden, my dear Lady Ivy?"

Ivy let a smile curve her lips. "You are an idiot, my dear Lord Styles."

"Yes, but you love me despite my faults. Come along. The garden awaits."

Chapter 18

Ivy stared up at the front of Tamberlake's house. Whatever she had expected, it wasn't the opulence of Marsgrove. The impressive facade dwarfed her carriage, and the immaculate grounds seemed to stretch before her forever. She felt much like an ant about to enter a palace. Before she could recover her composure, a footman opened the door for her and let her into the front hall. "May I help you, my lady?"

"I'd like to see Lord Tamberlake. Is he in?"

"Whom shall I say is calling?"

"Ivy . . . Lady Ivy St. Clair."

The footman showed her into the drawing room. Ivy's stomach churned. She had hoped to see Fletcher, a familiar face in an unfamiliar place, but she supposed he must be busy elsewhere in the house. She gazed about the room. Chinese porcelain stood upon the tables and elaborate paintings hung on the walls. An enormous mantel clock chimed the quarter hour, and golden cherubs hung in the corners. The black marble fireplace gleamed, and her feet crushed the thick Persian rug. It was even more intimidating inside than out. Coming here was a mistake.

She was about to leave when Tamberlake entered the room.

"Ivy?"

"I shouldn't have come." She gathered her skirts and tried to walk past him.

He reached out and grasped her arm. "Is something wrong?"

"No, no, I just . . ." She paused and turned to him. "Thank you for coming to the ball."

Tamberlake released her. "You came to thank me?"

"No, I . . ." She shook her head. "I'd better go."

"Are you alone?" He looked disapproving.

"Yes. No one knows I'm here. Well, the driver, but he won't say anything. I must go."

"What happened to your forthrightness?"

"I don't know. You are . . . I . . ." She sank onto the settee and dropped her hands into her lap. "I'm frightened of you."

Astonishment marked his features. Then he smiled. "Since when are you afraid of the monster earl?" he asked in a cajoling tone.

"That isn't what I meant. I hadn't expected to see you again."

His expression became unreadable. "I understand. You're regretting your actions."

"Not in the least. I cherish every moment we spent together, and I regret only that I can't have more." She winced, then covered her face with her hands. "I shouldn't have said that."

"Why ever not? I enjoyed hearing it." He sat beside her and took her hand. He peeled her glove from her hand and kissed her palm.

She let out a soft purr, then snatched her hand away. "You mustn't do that."

"But I want to kiss you." He raised her hand again. "Here." He kissed her palm again. "And here." He kissed her wrist. "And here." He unfastened the tiny buttons at her wrist and pushed her sleeve up her arm and kissed the softness of her forearm.

"You can't." But she didn't pull her arm away.

"I am the master of Marsgrove. I can do as I wish." He cupped her face in his palms and kissed her lips.

Even as her conscience protested, she reveled in the taste of him. She had missed him, and now, beside him, she knew a part of her would always be empty without him. She allowed herself one final moment of contact before she pushed away from him with great reluctance. Tears welled up in her eyes as she faced him. "I cannot. Please." The final word was a whisper of desperation.

He released her and gazed into her face. "Don't cry, Ivy. I will never hurt you."

"You will never mean to." She drew in a ragged breath and dashed away a tear from her cheek. "I came to ask you not to see me again."

He didn't answer for a moment. "Now that I've returned, we will run into each other."

"I know."

"Do you trust me, Ivy?"

"With my life."

"Then trust me now. Now and tomorrow and tomorrow." He kissed her again without the earlier gentleness.

His hunger thrilled her. When his tongue entered her mouth, all sense of impropriety fled. How could anything this wonderful be wrong? Her heart soared with freedom. She wanted him, and she didn't care about the consequences.

Tamberlake broke off the kiss this time. She blinked at the abrupt end of the headiness that had engulfed her. With a smile, he brushed a loose tendril from her face and tucked it behind her ear. "I suppose if I ask you to trust me, I have to prove myself trustworthy."

A belated rush of guilt seized her. "You must think me a wanton."

"I think you a beautiful woman whom I desire very much." He pulled her sleeve down to her wrist and buttoned the cuff. Then he slipped her hand into her glove, but not before pressing a last kiss on her palm. "You must go home before they miss you."

"Yes." Ivy stood.

"But you will see me again, Ivy. I swear it."

A shiver of anticipation skittered down her spine. She squelched the heady joy she felt. "But Wynbrooke—"

He placed his finger on her lips. "Trust me."

He took her arm and saw her to the carriage. As he handed her into the coach, he whispered, "Soon," and stepped back and waved.

She left without saying another word out of fear that she would blurt out that she loved him. As the carriage drove off, guilt assailed her. She was a betrothed woman. She knew Tamberlake would never betray her, but she didn't trust herself.

The late afternoon sun shone down as Ivy returned home. Her little journey had taken all day. She rushed into the drawing room just as her family settled into their seats for tea. Hoping no one would notice her hurried entrance after her dash from the carriage, she took her place in an empty chair.

Lady Dunleigh poured the tea. "And I had another note today from Lady Smythe-Jones. She said everyone is speaking of our ball." She passed out the cups to her family.

"Excellent," said her husband as he reached for a small sandwich.

Ivy eyed her mother with disbelief. "Your fears about Lord Tamberlake were unfounded then."

"Goodness, yes. His appearance at our ball is the talk of the town. I could almost kiss the man. Except for his face, of course." Lady Dunleigh giggled.

"Oooh, don't remind me," said Georgina. "I thought I would faint when I saw him."

"His face is fine," said Ivy with some heat.

"Really, Ivy, even you have to admit he looks monstrous," said her father. "But what a coup to have him make his first appearance at our house."

Christopher shot her a sympathetic glance. "Actually, one doesn't notice his face after a while."

"I don't think I could ever look at that face long enough to become accustomed to it," said Georgina, popping a small teacake into her mouth.

"Stop speaking of him as some sort of oddity. He's a man," said Ivy.

"But a man no one has seen for five years," said her father.

"I wouldn't be surprised if they wrote it up in the papers," said Lady Dunleigh.

"A triumph, really. I couldn't have planned it better myself." Lord Dunleigh helped himself to another sandwich.

Ivy placed her tea back on the table untouched. She had no appetite for either the food or the conversation. "He's a charming, intelligent man, that's all."

"I don't see why you're so upset, Ivy," said Georgina. "If I were you, I'd be happy he caused such a stir at your ball. Everyone will remember your name now, and you'll be invited to ever so many parties even after you're an old married lady. And if you are, I think Father should make you take me along. After all, I still need to find a husband."

Christopher barked out a chuckle. "Don't worry, Georgie. Father will find you the perfect husband, just as he did for Ivy."

"Don't call me Georgie. It makes me sound like a boy."

"There, there, Georgina. Don't let Christopher distress you," said her mother.

"No one would mistake you for a boy," said Lord Dunleigh, eating a third sandwich. "They had better not, after all the money I spend on your clothes."

The inane conversation was giving her a headache. Ivy stood. "May I be excused? I find I'm not feeling well."

"Go and lie down then," said Lady Dunleigh. "I'll send something up to settle your nerves in a bit."

Ivy darted from the room, grateful for the peace of the hallway. The day still had a bit of sunlight left, and the garden beckoned.

The air outside was cooler than in the parlor, but the smells of London tainted its sweetness. How she wished she could spend the few months before her wedding at their country house. As she wandered the well-manicured garden paths, she found herself smiling at the memory of climbing the rough, rock-strewn paths of Snowdonia.

Stop it, Ivy. You'll have enough time for nostalgia after you're wed.

But just thinking the words wasn't enough to banish the memories from her mind.

Tamberlake read the papers in front of him. Savernake had provided solid information in a short amount of time, but the information didn't offer him an easy solution to his dilemma. In fact, he knew it would complicate matters, and after Ivy's visit yesterday, he was eager to proceed.

Fletcher approached him. "Excuse me, my lord. You have a visitor." The butler handed him a card.

"Lady Coville." Tamberlake raised an eyebrow. "Show her in."

As Fletcher left, Tamberlake stood and walked to the window. *Lady Coville. How interesting.* He looked out onto an expanse of lawn which had been the site of a garden party five years ago, when Lady Coville had been his fiancée.

He heard the rustle of her skirts and turned from the view. She looked the same, perhaps a little older, but still had her youthful figure and perfect skin. Her eyes were the violet of amethysts, and her lips curved into two soft arcs of plum. Her blond hair curled out from underneath her cap in an artfully elegant coiffure. And he found himself thinking of brown hair and brown eyes, and finding them far more attractive.

"Auburn. It's been a long time." Lady Coville walked toward him. She reached forward with both hands and grasped his.

"Lady Coville."

She let out a gay little laugh. "Surely we know each other well enough to do away with formality."

"Very well, Daphne."

"Much better." She released his hands. Her gaze lifted to his face for an instant, then darted away. A delicate shudder shook her.

"I was sorry to hear of your loss."

"You heard?"

He chuckled. "I may have been in Wales, but I did receive the papers from London."

"Then you know I'm out of mourning for old Coville." She never looked into his eye, and her gaze flitted across his scars, never resting long on his face.

"Old? That's hardly an affectionate term for one's husband."

"Please, Auburn. There's no need for pretense between us. We both know why I married Coville."

"Because you didn't marry me." He said it without rancor. To his surprise, none of the old resentment surfaced.

"Don't be bitter."

He shook his head. "I'm not bitter."

"I was young and foolish."

"You were unable to look at me."

"As I said, foolish."

"Look at me now."

Daphne hesitated a moment, then lifted her gaze. Her violet eyes widened, and her struggle to suppress revulsion played across her face. She flinched and then steeled her features. "I'm sorry. Give me time."

He looked at her with some curiosity. He felt none of the anger he had expected, nor did he care about her inability to face him. "Why are you here, Daphne?"

"I was wrong to marry Coville."

"It's a little late for that now."

"But it's not too late to correct my mistake."

"Your mistake?"

"Not marrying you."

"As I recall, you didn't even wait a month before you became engaged to Coville."

"He was old. I couldn't wait long." Daphne took his arm. "A woman has to look after herself, and I had a scandal attached to my name."

"A scandal of your own making."

"Perhaps. But now I am a widow. That allows me certain freedoms."

"Indeed."

"Think of it, Auburn. We could finally have the dream we shared so many years ago."

"Are you asking me to marry you?"

"Would that be so surprising?"

Tamberlake stared at her. After a moment he smiled. "An interesting proposition. I'll need time to consider it."

Daphne's expression relaxed. "I knew you'd understand. We'd be perfect together."

Before he could answer, his mother came into the room. "Daphne. When Whitson told me you were here, I didn't believe him." Lady Tamberlake embraced the woman. "What brings you to Marsgrove?"

"I heard Auburn had returned."

His mother's joy at seeing Daphne didn't surprise him. She had blamed him for Daphne crying off. "Ladies, I hope you will excuse me. I have something I must take care of." He retrieved the papers from the table and left the room.

Why had Daphne decided to visit him? He didn't believe her story of contrition or her desire to be Countess Tamberlake. No, that was incorrect. He could believe her desire to be countess, but not to marry him. Yet another mystery. He hated mysteries. At least he'd be able to answer his questions about Daphne. It seemed he had another job for Fletcher's man.

Chapter 19

Lady Smythe-Jones hooked her arm in Ivy's. "I can't tell you how much I enjoy hosting my annual sporting day. All these young people make me feel young again, too."

"I'm sure they do." Ivy smiled at the chubby matron. The sun shone down on them and newly blossomed flowers colored the edges of the grass. "It's a beautiful day."

"Of course it is. It wouldn't dare rain on my sporting day. It's far too important. Do you know how many marriages have started right here?"

"I can't imagine."

"And I so enjoy plotting with their mamas and pairing them off." Lady Smythe-Jones patted her arm. "Not you, my dear. You already have your match. And such a good one, although that Wynbrooke seems a little reclusive. You'll change that, won't you dear?"

Not likely, thought Ivy. She glanced at the groups scattered across the wide stretch of lawn. "Is everyone here single then?"

"No, that would be too obvious, don't you think?" Lady Smythe-Jones giggled in what Ivy assumed was a girlish way. "Perhaps your mama will let me have a try with sweet Georgina. She already attracts so many of the young scoundrels."

Ivy glanced over to her sister. True enough. A bevy of young men surrounded Georgina. "That she does."

"So what sport will you participate in? Bowling on the green? Pall Mall? Archery?"

"I'm afraid I'm not much good at any sport." Ivy gazed over to where Wynbrooke played cricket.

"You see yourself as a supporter, do you? I can't blame you. When my Geoffrey was alive I always rooted for him during the hunt."

Her mother waved to them, and Lady Smythe-Jones directed them toward her. Lady Dunleigh sat with a group of women in wickerwork chairs. Lady Smythe-Jones plopped herself into an empty seat. Ivy took a stance behind her. From this position, her hostess couldn't continue to share her matchmaking secrets with her.

"Good heavens, I didn't think *he* would come." Lady Dunleigh sat up suddenly.

Ivy's gaze traveled to the door. Tamberlake. He stood on the top step, surveying the grounds. When he spotted her, he smiled and walked directly toward her. Ivy's eyes widened. What was he doing here?

The whispers in the group grew louder as he neared and stopped all at once when he bowed to them. "A good day to you, ladies." He reached for Lady Smythe-Jones's hand. "Thank you for inviting me." He kissed the back of her hand and released it.

Lady Smythe-Jones snapped her mouth shut. "I didn't think you'd attend."

"And miss this pleasant company?" He turned from the older woman to Ivy and smiled. "Lady Ivy, you look captivating today."

She couldn't prevent the welcoming smile on her face. "Thank you, Lord Tamberlake."

"I do believe you are even more beautiful in the English sun. Wales simply wasn't bright enough to show you off."

Heat flowed into her cheeks. Ivy didn't know what to think. While she enjoyed his attention, she knew his actions would cause more gossip. After the ball, she had heard speculation about their familiarity. His greeting would only produce more. She glanced around the group of women and noticed that none of them, save Lady Smythe-Jones, looked at him.

"So tell me, young man, why did you decide to accept my invitation?" asked Lady Smythe-Jones.

"How could I refuse to come to one of your famous sporting days?"

Lady Smythe-Jones looked pleased.

Ivy watched as he charmed the hostess with his witty comments and, one by one, pulled the ladies into the conversation. Soon they no longer feared to look at him, although their gazes would turn from the scarred side of his face.

"Time for the archery competition."

Ivy didn't know who made the announcement, but Wynbrooke appeared at her side. Thorndike joined him a moment later. Thorndike gave Tamberlake a superior smile and said, "Tamberlake. Didn't expect to see you here. Are you going to compete?"

One of the ladies gasped at the suggestion.

Tamberlake glanced down at his cane. "I hadn't intended to compete."

"Oh, but I insist. Archery doesn't require you to run."

"Young man, you will watch your tongue or you will leave my party," said Lady Smythe-Jones.

"Don't fret, dear lady." Tamberlake turned to Thorndike. "Since you insist, I'd be happy to participate."

Tamberlake planted his cane beside him and started toward the field. Ivy bit her lip to keep from crying out as his cane sank into the ground and he stumbled for a step. But he righted himself and reached the field with the other competitors without trouble. Thorndike and Wynbrooke followed him.

Lady Smythe-Jones latched onto Ivy's arm again. "I do admire his pluck, you know. Carrying on as if nothing were wrong with him."

"Nothing is wrong with him." Ivy couldn't stop her words.

"I'm speaking of his injuries, dear child. I can't tell you how thrilled I am he came. After your ball, I knew I must invite him to my sporting day, but I had no hope he would actually attend. Think of the repute my parties shall have after this." Lady Smythe-Jones giggled like a schoolgirl.

Ten targets stood a good eighty yards away. The gentlemen lined up to take their turns. When Tamberlake stood in line, the whispers once again flew. The gentlemen strung their bows. After looping the string on a bow tip, several of the men dropped the string or couldn't pull it taut enough to reach the other end. To Ivy's bemusement, Tamberlake bent his without so much as a falter.

The gentlemen took their stances. Tamberlake looked a little off center, but he didn't sway on his feet. A servant passed out the arrows. He nocked the arrow and eyed the target. Ivy held her breath.

"Gentlemen, you may release your arrows."

The twangs of the bows sounded like an orchestra in need of tuning. Several servants ran down to the end of the field to measure the results. They noted those closest, then cleared the targets for the next group of archers. When all the gentlemen had released their arrows, the judges announced the numbers of those who would continue to the next round.

"Gentlemen numbers two, three, eight, twelve, fifteen, sixteen—"

But Ivy stopped listening. Tamberlake was number eight.

He took his place among the ten remaining archers. She didn't dare blink as once again the arrows flew.

"Numbers three, eight, fifteen . . ."

Ivy clapped her hands. He was in the final five. Wynbrooke failed to make it to the second round, and Thorndike missed his chance in this round.

The five archers took their stances. Ivy watched him turn his head slightly to give himself a better view with his eye. She pulled her lower lip between her teeth. The arrows flew again.

Tamberlake's arrow glided through the air in a graceful arc. From Ivy's view, it appeared to be a good shot, but she laced her fingers together and held her hands up to her mouth.

"Gentleman number eight is the winner."

Ivy clapped her hands together until her palms ached. She laughed and smiled until her cheeks hurt. He had won.

Tamberlake handed his bow to a servant, retrieved his cane, and made his way to Ivy. Wynbrooke and Thorndike stood beside her. He acknowledged her excitement with a grin, then turned to Thorndike. "You're right. Archery doesn't require me to run."

Wynbrooke clapped him on the back. "Hidden talents, Tamberlake. What other secrets are you hiding from us?"

"If I told you, they wouldn't be secrets, would they?"

Ivy couldn't stop smiling. Tamberlake leaned closer to her ear and whispered, "If I'd had my own bow, I would have done better."

She glanced at him in surprise. "Better than first place?"

He shrugged. "I would have won second and third as well."

The ladies took their turns, then the guests gathered around Lady Smythe-Jones, who stood by a table covered with prizes. She waved at everyone. "I haven't had such fun since . . . well, since my party last year, although I daresay this one will be more talked about."

The guests awarded her polite laughter. She nodded her acknowledgment. "First, the prize for Pall Mall."

Lady Smythe-Jones handed out several awards to the winners of the various competitions. Ivy waited with impatience until the hostess announced the archery awards.

"I know it wasn't a proper York round, but for

the best shooting of the day, I award this golden arrow to Lord Tamberlake. You surprised us all, young man."

Tamberlake took the small replica with a bow. "Thank you, Lady Smythe-Jones. I enjoyed myself."

"I expect to see you here next year to defend your title."

"It would be my honor." Tamberlake turned from the table. He sought out Ivy. Returning to her side, he handed her the arrow. "For you."

Wynbrooke's eyes widened. "That thing is made of gold."

"I can't accept it," said Ivy, but his gesture thrilled her.

"It's a pretty bauble for a pretty lady." Tamberlake closed her fingers over the shaft.

Ivy shivered.

Tamberlake gave her a knowing smile and released her hand. "I noticed you didn't participate in the contest."

"I've never shot an arrow in my life."

"May I show you how? You don't mind if I borrow Lady Ivy for a moment, Wynbrooke?" He didn't wait for the answer. He placed the golden arrow into Wynbrooke's hand and took Ivy by her arm.

"N-no," came the response from behind them.

He led her to the field and laid his cane on the ground. Taking up one of the bows, he strung it, then handed it to her. "Stance is the most important thing. I have to accommodate my leg, but you should brace yourself evenly on both feet. Stand with your shoulder to the target."

Ivy did as he instructed. Tamberlake moved behind her. "Good. Now lift up the bow."

She did, and he reached around her and

nocked the arrow onto the string. "Try to draw the bow."

She pulled on the string, but it barely moved.

"Like this." He placed his arms around her and laid his hands on hers. He drew back the string.

She glanced around. "People are watching."

"Look at the target, not the people," he said in a gentle rebuke. "Can you see the center?"

"Yes."

"Good. Now line up the tip of the arrow two rings above the center circle. Ready?"

"Yes."

"When I say release, let the string roll from your fingers." He adjusted his stance so that he pressed against her. "Release."

She let go the string. The arrow flew, but she didn't see it. His warmth flooded her, blocking everything else from her mind.

"You hit the target." Tamberlake stepped back.

The cool air on her back helped her regain her composure, even as she missed his touch. She squinted toward the target. "I didn't hit the center."

He laughed. "On your first try? I should think not, but I would enjoy giving you another lesson."

Ivy faced him, then noticed the small crowd watching them. "Oh dear. I think we attracted some attention."

"Excellent."

She didn't understand his cryptic remark.

Her mother, with Georgina trailing behind her, hurried up to them. "Ivy, what are you doing?"

"Lord Tamberlake was showing me how to shoot an arrow."

"It didn't look that way," said Georgina.

Wynbrooke came up then. He gave the golden arrow back to Ivy, then frowned. "They're serving refreshments in the house. I find I'm rather hungry."

"Won't you join us, Lord Tamberlake?" asked Ivy.

"No, thank you. I'll find my way back without you."

A look of relief passed over Lady Dunleigh's face. Wynbrooke took Ivy's arm and led her away from Tamberlake. Her mother and sister followed. Ivy glanced over her shoulder. Tamberlake grinned at her.

She couldn't discern the source of his merriment.

Chapter 20

In Marsgrove's front hall, Lady Tamberlake drew on her gloves and looked for her wrap.

"Ready at last?"

She whirled around at the sound of her son's voice. "Auburn. Why are you skulking about in the darkness?"

"I've grown rather fond of the shadows these past five years." He stepped toward her. "Are we ready to leave?"

"I'm going to a ball. What are your plans?"

"The ball as well. It seemed superfluous to use two carriages."

His mother raised her eyebrows. "You're coming to the ball?"

He smoothed the lapel of his black coat. "I'm dressed for it." The stiff collar of the brilliant white shirt bit into his neck, but he refused to tug at it.

She examined him. "Indeed you are, but I hardly expected you to accompany me."

"Consider it a surprise."

"One of many these days."

He took her mantle from the footman and draped it over her shoulders. "Just think of the attention you'll receive if I accompany you."

"I? *I* shan't receive the attention. The *ton* is buzzing with the rumors of *your* return."

"They aren't rumors, Mother. I have returned."

She let out a puff of air in exasperation. "You cause a stir wherever you've appeared."

"You make me sound like a ghost."

"Nonsense. You've just stirred the curiosity of the *ton.* They haven't had anything this exciting to talk about in years."

"Then I should hate to disappoint them. Shall we?" He held out his arm.

His mother looked at him. "At least you've remembered your manners." She took his arm, and they walked to the awaiting carriage.

It was dark when they arrived at the house of Lord and Lady Hillsforth where the ball was being held. A throng of carriages lined the street where they stopped. Tamberlake gave his driver instructions, then helped his mother from the carriage. Music reached his ears from inside the house, and light spilled into the front yard. A good number of servants milled about outside the house. He led his mother to the door, where a footman relieved them of their wrappings.

Farther inside, the murmur of myriad conversations added a sort of harmony to the music. Tamberlake maneuvered his mother and himself to a better position. He observed the glances cast in his direction and the hurried whispers that followed. Good. They had noticed his arrival.

A regally-clad woman swept down upon them. She took Lady Tamberlake's hands in hers and kissed her cheeks. "Honoria, my dear friend, I was afraid you weren't coming."

"I wouldn't miss your ball, Alice," said Lady Tamberlake. With a flip of her hand, she gestured toward Tamberlake. "You remember my son?"

The woman fell silent for a moment, then smiled again. "Of course I do. Lord Tamberlake, I am honored you chose to come to my little gathering."

"Thank you, Lady Hillsforth. Although I would hardly call this a little gathering. It certainly looks as though you're setting the standard for the rest of the season. I daresay you've caused some consternation among the ladies of the *ton* who now must scramble to achieve the same level of festivity when they entertain."

His mother shot him a look of surprise, and Lady Hillsforth blushed with pleasure. "You're too kind, my lord."

"Not at all. I merely speak the truth." He bowed to her.

"Well, do come and enjoy yourself, my lord. There are several lovely girls here who are waiting for dance partners . . ." She glanced at his cane. "Oh, dear."

"No need to fret, my lady. You'll find I'm capable of many things."

Lady Hillsforth giggled. "Go on, then. I see another guest I must greet. Honoria, I'll find you as soon as I'm finished here." Lady Hillsforth moved past them to greet the newest arrivals.

Her mouth open in astonishment, Lady Tamberlake stared at him.

"If you continue to look at me in such a manner,

Mother, someone might think something was wrong."

"You charmed her. I think the time in Wales did you some good."

"It wasn't Wales, Mother." He gave her a half smile and led her deeper into the house. Peering over the heads, he looked for the reason he came. He didn't see her yet.

"Well, are you going to tell me what has wrought such change over you?"

"Not tonight."

Lady Tamberlake fell silent. She gazed up at her son, as if seeing him for the first time, then nodded. "Very well. I shan't ask any more questions. However, I still expect an answer sometime."

"Lord Tamberlake." Daphne waved to them and pushed past several people to reach them. She dipped into a curtsey. "Lord Tamberlake, Lady Tamberlake, what a great surprise to see you. Just as I was beginning to think I'd find no one interesting at this fete."

"Surely that can't be true," said Tamberlake.

Daphne shot him a glance. "No one as interesting as you," she whispered for his ears alone.

"I see an old friend. I'll leave you two here," said Lady Tamberlake. "You don't want an old lady hanging around you." She gave Daphne a pat on the arm and left them.

"I am pleased to see you here, Auburn," said Daphne, latching onto his arm.

He really should have paid more attention to that guest list Fletcher procured. Daphne might complicate matters, especially if she persisted in her imitation of a leech.

"Have you given our little talk some thought?"

"Not enough."

She put on a pretty pout at his answer. "You're making me think you don't care for me."

Her practiced expression left him unmoved. He didn't want to play her game this evening. "Daphne, I didn't come to the ball to discuss—"

"Dance with me." She tugged him toward the dance floor.

"I don't think I should. My leg." He leaned upon his cane.

She stopped short. Looking down at his leg, she gave a delicate shiver. "I had forgotten."

He nearly laughed. Why was she pursuing him with such determination when she clearly wasn't at ease with him? Savernake had not yet brought the answers he sought. He gazed at her pretty face and wondered how long before her inner beauty conquered the flawless facade.

Then he saw Ivy on the dance floor. She was dancing with Wynbrooke. The man was far more graceful than himself, but Tamberlake didn't mind in the least. He turned from Daphne without another thought and headed for the edge of the parquet.

"Auburn? Where are we going?" asked Daphne, trailing behind him. Her curls bounced up and down as she pranced to keep up with him.

She hadn't released his arm. He pried her fingers from his arm. "I've spotted a friend. Will you excuse me?"

"But Auburn—"

He didn't wait. Hearing the music end, he crossed to where Wynbrooke brought Ivy. "Good evening, Lady Ivy, Wynbrooke."

Ivy's face held all the welcome he needed. "Lord Tamberlake. It's good to see you again." She curtseyed.

"We seem to run into you often." Wynbrooke couldn't hide the hint of annoyance in his voice.

"Not as often as I'd like to see Lady Ivy." His voice was loud enough to garner the attention of several guests who stood nearby. He bowed to her. "May I have the next dance?"

"Of course." Ivy glanced at Wynbrooke.

"Go ahead then." Wynbrooke waved them onto the floor with a frown of impatience.

The music started again, and he handed Wynbrooke his cane, enjoying the perplexed look on the man's face. As the first strains of the waltz started, he gathered her into his arms. With his halting steps, he led her in the three-count dance.

"I've missed you," he said. He pulled her tighter. "I've missed holding you."

Ivy lifted her gaze to his. Once again her unflinching scrutiny of his face amazed him. Her smile was genuine. For an instant, she relaxed into his embrace, then stiffened. "You shouldn't hold me so."

"Is that all you can say to me?"

"You know I can say no more. Wynbrooke will see us. People will talk."

He bent lower to whisper in her ear. "Let them. I don't care as long as I can hold you in my arms and dream of doing more." With satisfaction, he watched color climb into her cheeks.

"Auburn, you must stop."

"Stop dancing? Think how the people would stare then."

"You're misunderstanding me on purpose." She frowned at him.

"Yes, I am. And don't frown so. Someone will think I've upset you." From the corner of his eye, he spied Daphne staring at them. He twirled her away from the edge of the floor toward the middle. "There. Now no one can see us."

She laughed. "You're incorrigible."

"That's better. I've missed your laugh as well." He danced in silence for a few steps. "I could grow accustomed to holding you like this."

"You mustn't."

"Ah, Ivy, you still haven't taken me at my word." The music ended.

He leaned forward again and whispered in her ear, "Trust me."

With some hesitation, he released her, but kept his hand on her elbow to escort her off the floor. Wynbrooke waited for them. He thrust out the cane and held it at arm's length as soon as they neared. Tamberlake handed Ivy to him with a bow and took back his cane. "May I bring you some refreshments?"

Wynbrooke frowned. "We are capable of fetching our own drinks—"

"Then allow me to accompany you." Tamberlake stood on the other side of Ivy. Before Wynbrooke could protest, he took Ivy's arm and led her toward the drink-laden table in the next room. Wynbrooke followed behind, never quite able to catch up to them as he dodged his way through the crowd.

Tamberlake handed Ivy a flute of champagne, then took one for himself. Wynbrooke reached them as they took their first sips.

"There you are, man. We thought perhaps you had lost your way." Tamberlake handed him a glass.

"No . . . I . . . the crush . . ." Wynbrooke took a swallow.

"Isn't Thorndike with you tonight? I didn't think you ever went anywhere without him." Tamberlake eyed the man over his glass.

"Roger doesn't much care for such events. He's at home tonight."

"So you're here for Lady Ivy," said Tamberlake.

"Yes. We must make our appearances, you know."

"As the betrothed couple. I suppose those desperate mamas want to prove to the unwilling bachelors how painless marriage is. Not that they have to convince me. I'm looking for a bride myself."

Wynbrooke choked on his champagne. "You are looking for a wife?"

"I may have already found one."

Ivy glanced at his face. The look of anguish almost undid him.

"You've certainly kept it clandestine, if that's the case. I haven't heard a single name attached to yours," said Wynbrooke.

"There is one lady I'm fond of, but now isn't the proper time to mention her name." He glanced at Ivy, then clapped Wynbrooke on the back. "When the time is right, you'll be the first to know. Trust me."

He hoped she understood that those last words were for her.

"This is unexpected, I must say." Wynbrooke grinned at him. "Roger will be so interested to learn of your plans."

Over Wynbrooke's shoulder, he caught a glimpse of Daphne heading toward him. He replaced his glass on the table. "Give my regards to him, won't you? Lady Ivy, thank you for the dance. I don't think you know how much it meant to me." He lifted her hand and kissed the back of it.

"Will we see you later, Lord Tamberlake?" she asked.

"You may depend on it. If not tonight, then elsewhere." He turned from them and intercepted Daphne on her way to the table. "Daphne, may I get you a drink?"

"No, I am not thirsty. Who is that girl you were dancing with?"

"Lady Ivy St. Clair? She is a friend."

Daphne raised an eyebrow as she glanced toward Ivy. "Indeed? A friend?"

"Indeed."

"You told me you couldn't dance."

"I believe I said I shouldn't dance." He leaned upon his cane. "Bad for my leg."

Daphne gaped at him.

"I'll pay for my exertion tomorrow." He offered her his arm. "Shall we find my mother?"

A look of thorough bewilderment crossed her face as she took his arm, and he led her away from Ivy.

Chapter 21

Wherever Ivy went in the following weeks, Tamberlake inevitably showed up. If Ivy was at a ball, Tamberlake danced with her. If she was at a *soirée musicale*, Tamberlake sat beside her. Society no longer stopped when he appeared. Although few could look him in the face, his presence no longer caused the stir it once had. Instead, talk of him concerned a new theme—his relationship to Ivy.

When they were together, he whispered amusing anecdotes or wry observations in her ear, so that she laughed and drew the attention of others standing nearby. He brought her plates of delicacies, or he delivered flutes of champagne to her at the edge of the dance floor while ignoring Wynbrooke at her side.

Ivy didn't know what to think. While she enjoyed his attention, she knew his actions were causing gossip. More than once she heard her name linked with his as she circled a room, and more than once she stopped a conversation by walking into a room. Wynbrooke said nothing to her. She wondered if he even noticed.

However, her father did. Two weeks after this activity started, Lord Dunleigh summoned her to his study.

"Ivy, I want you to explain yourself."

"Explain myself? How, Father?"

"You and Tamberlake. I've heard more than one rumor about the two of you."

Heat infused her cheeks. "He is a friend."

Her father waved a finger at her bright cheeks. "Don't lie to me, girl. I will not have my daughter's name bandied about like some common trollop's."

"I have conducted myself with the utmost decorum since we've returned, Father." Her words weren't a lie. Her father couldn't know of what she'd done in Wales. "I cannot prevent people from speaking about me, nor can I stop Lord Tamberlake from speaking to me."

"People are beginning to wonder if there's more to your relationship. Thankfully, nothing untoward has happened in this house. I've been watching you."

Watching her? "Of course nothing has happened in this house. He hasn't even been here since the ball." Irritation sharpened her voice.

Lord Dunleigh stood. "Mind your tone. You're not married yet. Until you leave here, you are my responsibility, and I won't have you risk my reputation on some foolish whim."

"I thought you wanted to establish a contact with Tamberlake."

"Don't twist my words. I don't need your help to bolster my career. You are a woman and should remember your place." Ivy's father sat in his chair and mopped his face with his handkerchief. "I've sent your brother to speak with Tamberlake. He'll tell me if anything indecent has occurred."

Ivy drew in a deep breath and counted to three. "I have done nothing wrong, Father."

"Good. Then I have nothing to worry about. You may go." He waved her from the room.

As Ivy walked toward her room, thoughts whirled in her head. Her father might have nothing to worry about, but she did. She didn't enjoy being the object of gossip, but she admitted she didn't want Tamberlake's attention to cease either. His request puzzled her. She did trust him, but what was he doing?

"There you are, Lady Ivy. You have a visitor," said Mrs. Pennyfeather. "Your mother is entertaining her in the drawing room."

"Who is it?"

"Lady Coville."

"But I don't know Lady Coville." Ivy didn't like all this unwanted attention.

"Perhaps you'd better speak with her and find out what she wants," said Mrs. Pennyfeather in a gentle tone.

Ivy laughed at herself. "Yes, of course."

When she entered the drawing room, she saw a beautiful woman with a fixed smile on her face. Lady Dunleigh was chattering on about something. Ivy couldn't hear her mother's words, but Lady Dunleigh's gestures and expression were animated enough that she was sure her mother was bragging about something. She hurried forward. "Good morning, Mother. And you must be Lady Coville. I understand you wanted to see me?"

Lady Coville stood. At once Ivy realized the woman's beauty was extraordinary. Against her will, Ivy glanced down at her dress. Brown again.

Not that it mattered. Ivy couldn't compete with this woman even in her finest gown.

"How good to meet you at last, Lady Ivy." Lady Coville's gaze traveled down to Ivy's toes then back again. For a moment, Ivy thought the woman would disapprove of her, but Lady Coville's smile was now genuine.

"I don't believe we've met . . ."

"No, we haven't, but I just had to see the girl everyone is talking about," Lady Coville said.

Lady Dunleigh cast her daughter a chastising look. "Yes, those unfortunate rumors about Lord Tamberlake. I can assure you they are not true. That Lord Tamberlake has made a nuisance of himself, and Ivy is suffering for it."

Ivy frowned. "Mother—"

"No need to trouble yourself, Lady Dunleigh," said Lady Coville. "I don't believe a word of anything those horrible biddies of the *ton* say."

"Thank you, Lady Coville. I could see you are as wise as you are beautiful. Perhaps you would like to meet my younger daughter, Georgina. She is quite the beauty herself."

"Thank you, but now I wish to speak with Lady Ivy. Would you excuse us, Lady Dunleigh?"

"Whatever you have to say to Ivy, you can say in front of me. We harbor no secrets from each other. Isn't that right, Ivy?" Lady Dunleigh beamed at her daughter.

Ivy knew better than to believe her mother's display. Her mother's curiosity would not let her leave. Ivy glanced at Mrs. Pennyfeather in a silent plea for help.

Mrs. Pennyfeather crossed to Lady Dunleigh. "This would be the perfect opportunity to see to those fabric samples. Why don't we gather up the ones we like best and ask Lady Coville's opinion on them?"

"An excellent idea." Lady Dunleigh's face lit up. "Lady Coville, you wouldn't mind helping me choose the best fabric for my new dresses, would you? I need something spectacular for the wedding, and it's obvious your taste is exquisite."

Lady Coville smiled. "It would be my pleasure."

Ivy's mother hurried from the room, followed by Mrs. Pennyfeather. Ivy turned to her guest. "You wished to speak to me?"

"Yes. I have a matter of some delicacy that concerns you."

Puzzled, Ivy looked at her guest. "Would you care to walk outside? I'm afraid my mother can be overzealous about her clothes, and will return in a short while."

"By all means."

The two women stepped into the garden. They walked side by side in silence for a few steps, then Ivy spoke. "I still can't imagine why you've come to see me."

Lady Coville let out a small laugh. "I have to admit it is rather unusual. The gossip I've heard has intrigued me. I had to see if it was true."

"If what was true?"

"That you and Lord Tamberlake are lovers."

Ivy gasped.

"Forgive my bluntness. I could have found more delicate words, but I didn't think you'd mind."

She must have revealed her distress on her face, for Lady Coville reached over and patted her arm. "Please don't worry. As soon as I saw you I knew it couldn't be true. You see, I have a special friendship with Lord Tamberlake myself. I was engaged to him at one time."

So this was the woman who cried off when Auburn was injured. Part of her resented the way the woman had treated Tamberlake, but part of her wanted to thank the woman that she had.

Lady Coville said, "Due to unfortunate circumstances, I couldn't marry Auburn then. But now I am a widow, and I hope to rectify that."

"What?" The words shocked Ivy.

"When he returned, I realized it isn't too late to find happiness with Auburn after all. I went to see him and told him of my intentions." Lady Coville laughed. "But you can imagine my consternation when I heard these rumors about you. I had to come see you for myself, and now that I have, I can set my mind at ease."

"But—"

"And I shall help you in any way I can to bury the gossip. I suppose the best way would be to announce Tamberlake's and my engagement as soon as possible, but until I can, I'll tell anyone who will listen just how mistaken they are about you."

Ivy couldn't think for a moment. Auburn and this woman were to marry? She didn't believe it. She didn't want to believe it.

But who was she to object? She was betrothed to another man. She couldn't marry Auburn. And hadn't he said he had found a bride already?

"I can see my frank words have shocked you. I'll leave you now, but I hope we can consider each other as friends. I'm not much older than you, after all, and soon you'll be married." Lady Coville smiled, but Ivy found it a smug smile indeed.

"Oh, Lady Coville," said Ivy's mother. "What are

you doing out here? I've brought the fabric samples. Do come inside."

"My pleasure, Lady Dunleigh. Your daughter and I have had such an interesting conversation." Lady Coville left Ivy's side and returned inside.

Ivy stared after the woman. She knew she didn't have a right, but she felt betrayed.

Trust me.

But she wasn't sure if she could.

Fletcher found Tamberlake in his study. "My lord, you have a visitor."

"I never realized how popular I would become when I returned. Who is it?"

"Lord Styles, sir."

A genuine rush of pleasure ran through him. "Show him in."

Styles let out a low whistle as he came into the room. "I never knew you lived such a posh life. I shall have to visit more often."

"I have the excesses of generations of ancestors to thank for that." Tamberlake crossed the room to his friend.

"And I thought Mother was the only one prone to excesses." Styles chuckled as he sat in an armchair. "I've heard you're availing yourself of the opportunities you missed while in Wales."

"What do you mean?"

"Balls, parties, and such. You created quite a stir that night at Ivy's ball."

"I imagine I did." Tamberlake smiled and took a seat in the chair opposite Styles. "I have to admit I enjoyed myself. Shocking the *ton* is becoming one of my favorite pastimes."

Styles stretched his legs in front of him. "I know. I've heard the rumors."

"So quickly? Gossip is an efficient machine."

"You're aware of it?"

"Of course."

"Then I should tell you I'm here on my father's errand."

"So this isn't a social visit."

"Of course it is. If it weren't, I wouldn't have told you I'm here to do my father's nefarious business." Styles laughed. "He is a torn man, my father. He wants me to cultivate your friendship, but he needs to know just how true these rumors are about you and Ivy."

"Ahh, the machinations of the *ton*. Let's hope I haven't forgotten how to play."

"Somehow I don't think you've forgotten anything."

"How is Ivy?" Tamberlake didn't miss the raised eyebrow of his guest at the familiar use of her name.

"Ivy's well. I don't think she likes being the object of attention much."

"I'm not sure I do either, but it's necessary."

"Necessary?"

Tamberlake shook his head. "I can't explain now. The gossips have chosen us as their topic. I suppose we'll just have to wait until they find some new fodder."

Styles narrowed his gaze. "It doesn't bother you that Ivy is suffering for this?"

"Of course it does."

"Then perhaps you should stay away from her for a while. Even I've noticed how you always seem to be near her when we are out."

Tamberlake hated deceiving Styles. He drew in a deep breath. "Can I rely on your discretion?"

"Certainly."

He held up his hand. "Don't answer so lightly. If I confide in you, you will be going against the wishes of your family, your father."

"When have I ever followed the wishes of my father?" Styles paused, then scrutinized him. "Does this have anything to do with Ivy?"

"Yes."

Styles nodded. "Ivy hasn't been happy since we left Wales. She thinks she's in love with you."

Tamberlake grinned. "That's convenient, since I intend to marry her."

His guest's mouth dropped open, then he snapped it shut and swallowed. "Pardon?"

"I intend to marry Ivy."

"But—but . . . what about Wynbrooke?"

"You needn't worry about him."

Styles glanced around and said in a low voice, "Are you going to kill him?"

"Nothing so dramatic."

For a moment, Styles was silent, then he snapped his fingers. "The rumors. You're trying to make Wynbrooke cry off."

"I knew you were an intelligent man."

"How can I help?"

"With all the talk, your father will undoubtedly try to keep Ivy away from me. I need to be seen with her."

"Simple enough. Should I talk to Wynbrooke? Plant the seeds of doubt?"

"No, I can handle Wynbrooke."

"So I'll be around to make sure you and Ivy can

be seen together. Let me know if there is anything more you need me to do."

"I will."

Styles stood. "I suppose I should be off. Father will be waiting for a report."

"What shall you tell him?"

"That you are as distressed as he about the unfounded gossip and that we seem to be hitting it off quite well." Styles winked in a most outrageous manner. "He might just be able to form that contact with you after all."

Tamberlake chuckled. "I can see why Ivy likes you."

Before he left, Styles paused. "I don't suppose I can tell Ivy about your plans."

"I would prefer to ask her myself."

"I quite understand. Right. I'm off then. No need to see me out." Styles left the room.

Tamberlake felt as though a burden had been removed from him. Having Styles's approval of his plans relieved his conscience about putting Ivy through the gossip mill. A little. But it was time for the next step in his plans.

It was time to see Wynbrooke.

Chapter 22

Rosmartin Park wasn't half the size of Marsgrove, but its lines boasted a history that could be traced back to the time of the first King George. Still, here and there the house exhibited signs of neglect. A shutter hung off its hinges on the second story, and a crack had started between the bricks at the corner of the house. In a few years, Rosmartin Park would need extensive repairs if Wynbrooke didn't see to the structure now. The gardens were overgrown, and roses ran wild over the few benches. Tamberlake looked over the land. Most of it was unused. Wasted.

As the butler showed him into the drawing room, Tamberlake noticed more signs of distress. Doilies covered threadbare spots on an ancient sofa and a layer of dust covered the shelves. The art on the walls was of high quality, but a clean rectangle of wallpaper betrayed where a painting had hung. The empty spot revealed the dinginess of the rest of the paper. He wondered if the painting had been sold for expenses.

Tamberlake couldn't picture Ivy in this setting. No, better said, he didn't *want* to picture her here. He looked at his host. "Good of you to see me on such short notice."

"Nonsense. We're old friends now. At least I can claim an older friendship than most people in the *ton*." Wynbrooke chuckled. "I have to admit I was curious why you sought me out."

Thorndike crossed his legs and leaned back in his chair. "You're full of surprises these days, my lord. We never thought you'd make so many public appearances. It's hard to miss the buzz you've caused."

He should have guessed Thorndike would question his actions. Thorndike probably also guessed this wasn't a social call. Tamberlake sat. "Circumstances change."

"Indeed they do," said Wynbrooke. "So why have you come to see us?"

Tamberlake almost cringed at the casual use of the plural pronoun. "It is a matter of some delicacy."

Wynbrooke and Thorndike exchanged glances. "How can I help?" asked Wynbrooke.

"I want you to break off your betrothal to Ivy."

The silence was palpable. Then Wynbrooke laughed. "An excellent jest, Tamberlake."

"I'm not jesting."

Wynbrooke stared at him in disbelief, and Thorndike had a stunned expression, as if he had just been struck by something large and painful.

After a prolonged stretch, Wynbrooke said, "Pardon me?"

Tamberlake smiled. "I've shocked you."

"I don't think 'shock' is a strong enough word," said Thorndike.

"And I don't think I quite understand," said Wynbrooke. "Why should I break off my betrothal?"

"Because I want to marry Ivy, and she has a strong sense of duty. She would never do anything to go against her word. So that leaves you."

"I?"

"Yes. *You* have to break it off with her."

"But I don't want to break it off." Wynbrooke's voice sounded more like the bleat of a lost lamb.

Trying to maintain his patience, Tamberlake gazed at the man. "My actions of the past weeks haven't been for my own amusement or the amusement of the *ton*. I wanted to give you ample cause to cry off. No one can blame you for breaking the betrothal when I have done all I can to ensure Ivy's name and mine are linked. You've heard the rumors?"

"Yes, but they don't trouble me." Wynbrooke winked at Thorndike.

Tamberlake was sure he wasn't intended to see that gesture. "I *want* the gossip to trouble you. Surely you have had doubts about the marriage."

"Not really. In fact, I don't see what the fuss is about. I find nothing objectionable in Ivy's behavior."

"Because she has done nothing untoward." Tamberlake heard the hint of impatience in his voice. He drew in a deep breath. "What I meant is that society can lay more than enough blame on Ivy and me to justify your actions."

"No, Lord Tamberlake. I've no desire to end the betrothal," said Wynbrooke.

Tamberlake sighed. "I didn't think you would make this easy."

"You're not making any sense, my lord," said Thorndike. "Wyn doesn't wish to end his relationship with Lady Ivy, yet you don't seem to find that a deterrent."

"It's not." He leaned forward in his chair. "I have no desire to be ruthless, but I am never unprepared when I want to achieve something. I've made inquiries and know of your financial straits."

The two men stared at him again. Tamberlake shook his head. "With some work, you can overcome your difficulties. Rosmartin Park is a fine estate. If it had better management, you could live well off its income."

"You want me to work?" A look of revulsion flitted across Wynbrooke's features. He shuddered. "I hire someone to do that for me."

"It seems to me you can ill afford the salary of another employee, especially if you could do it yourself."

"And it seems to me that you have been too long out of society to know what is considered the proper way to occupy one's time for an aristocrat," said Thorndike. "Wyn shouldn't have to work. He is an earl."

"One can afford to be stubborn about such things if one has the money." Tamberlake pulled out a sheet of paper from his breast pocket, unfolded it, and handed it to Wynbrooke. "This is a list of books I believe would help you. My source of information tells me Rosmartin Park has shown a deficit for the past seven years. If you look into the techniques outlined in these books and periodicals, you can turn a profit in a year."

Wynbrooke sputtered, opening and closing his mouth like a fish out of water. "I have no intention of working like a common laborer."

"That is your choice, of course," said Tamberlake. "On the day I marry Ivy, I shall settle five thousand pounds on you. I think that's ample compensation for the trouble I'm causing you. That money should see you through until the estate is profitable again."

Wynbrooke barked out a guffaw. "Five thousand? I shall have three times that when I marry her and access to more. Her father won't let her live in squalor, and I'm sure he'll be more than happy to help us on occasion. And when he dies, her brother inherits. You know how close they are."

"Wyn's right, my lord. He stands to gain more if he marries her," said Thorndike.

"As do you, I suppose." His patience was at an end.

"What do you mean by that?" asked Thorndike. "I won't benefit when Wyn marries. If anything, he will have less time for his friends when he has a wife to see to."

"I doubt that." Tamberlake leaned forward and looked Wynbrooke in the eyes. "Not his *special* friends."

Wynbrooke's expression took on a look of panic. His gaze shot to Thorndike, then back again. His complexion grew red. "I don't know what you mean."

"Don't you?"

"What are you saying?" asked Thorndike. All traces of politeness vanished from his features, and a definite hint of alarm rang in his voice.

"I saw you. Both of you. At Gryphon's Lair. On your last night, in the salon. You each had a brandy, engaged in some idle chatter, which was rather revealing, and then—"

"Enough." Wynbrooke popped out of his chair. He started to pace the room. "What do you intend to do with your information?"

"Nothing. If you don't break it off with Ivy, I'll have no choice but to go to her father. What he does with the information I have no control over."

"He won't believe you," said Thorndike. "Your word isn't enough."

"Perhaps not, but I have proof."

"I don't believe you. We've been careful."

"Indeed you have, but my man is more thorough than you are careful. I have evidence Lord Dunleigh won't ignore."

Wynbrooke looked pale. "Dear God."

"How do we know you won't expose us anyway?"

"I shall send you the evidence after I marry. I have no desire to ruin you."

"You already have." Wynbrooke whirled on him. "How do you expect me to exist on five thousand pounds?"

"As I explained, Rosmartin Park can provide you with an adequate income," said Tamberlake.

"And if you change your mind . . . ?" asked Thorndike.

"You will just have to trust me."

"Easier to say than to do, especially after you've threatened us." Thorndike glared at him.

Tamberlake couldn't blame the man for his lack of faith. "My only interest is the welfare of Ivy."

After a moment's silence, Wynbrooke spoke from the corner, where he had paced. "I have a proposition."

Tamberlake raised an eyebrow.

"I don't see why anything has to change at all," said Wynbrooke. "If I married Ivy, I wouldn't be averse to letting you have her."

"What?" Tamberlake scowled.

"It would solve all our problems. I would still get the money I need, you could be with Ivy, and it would save me from bedding her. You could even have a child. Then I could have my heir. No one would be the wiser, and we would all get what we want."

Disgust roiled in Tamberlake's gut. Anger shot through him like a flash of lightning. "Do you actually believe Ivy would go along with such an agreement? Do you believe I would?"

"Why not?"

"Because I want to marry her, to make her my wife. And any children we have will be raised by me and her, not you."

"You leave us with little choice then," said Thorndike.

"I leave you *no* choice." Tamberlake stood. "I expect to hear news of the betrothal's end within a week. No need to see me out, gentlemen. I wish you good day."

At Marsgrove he retreated to his study. Pouring himself a sherry, he walked to the window. Another gray English day, but it brought him comfort to be back in his home.

"How did it go, sir?" asked Fletcher.

"As I expected." He shook his head. "I wonder about the shortsightedness of people."

"Indeed, sir. Can we anticipate an announcement soon?"

"We can."

"May I add my congratulations then?"

Tamberlake raised an eyebrow. "Thank you, Fletcher."

"Mr. Savernake has sent more information for you." Fletcher handed him a thick sheaf of papers.

"So quickly? This Savernake is efficient."

"Yes, my lord. He makes a good living providing information."

Tamberlake tossed the papers on his desk. "I'll read them later. I've faced enough distasteful business today."

"I'm sorry to hear that, sir. Your mother wishes to speak with you."

"Before dinner? She'll ruin my appetite." He ran his hand through his hair. "Tell her she can come see me now if she wishes."

"Very good, sir."

Fletcher left the room. Tamberlake didn't have to wait long for his mother.

"Where have you been? I've been waiting to see you all day." Lady Tamberlake faced her son.

"I had something to take care of, Mother. I'm sorry if I caused you any inconvenience."

"You didn't, so don't bother to apologize." She took a seat in a leather armchair. "I saw Daphne yesterday."

"Did you?"

"You needn't pretend interest in my activities, either. As I said, I saw Daphne yesterday, and she told me you two spoke of marriage."

"We did."

His mother looked annoyed. "And you didn't have the decency to tell me about it?"

"It doesn't concern you, Mother."

"Of course, it does. I'm your mother."

"Only by birth," said Tamberlake. He sighed, then lifted his hand in a gesture of defeat. "I'm too tired to engage in verbal warfare with you."

His mother gave a delicate sniff. "I merely wanted to give you my approval. You know I've always liked Daphne."

"What if I don't marry Daphne?"

Lady Tamberlake's eyes widened. "I do hope you don't intend to make her your mistress. I can't approve of that."

He almost laughed. "No, Mother. Rest assured I wouldn't trouble you about my mistresses, if I had any."

She clasped a hand to her chest. "Thank heaven for that."

"What I meant to ask was what if the woman I choose to marry isn't Daphne."

His mother stared at him. "Not Daphne?"

"Would you accept a different woman at Marsgrove?"

"Frankly, Auburn, I never considered it a possibility."

"Consider it now."

She sat in silence for a moment. "It's that girl, isn't it? The one from the ball?"

"Lady Ivy St. Clair."

"But she's already betrothed."

"I know."

"Then this conversation seems pointless."

"Humor me."

Lady Tamberlake shrugged her shoulders. "I don't know the girl. Why is my opinion so important?"

Tamberlake paused. "I intend to make Marsgrove

my home. You are welcome here for as long as you wish, but if you can't accept my wife, I will ask you to leave."

"As is right." Lady Tamberlake folded her hands in her lap.

He stared at his mother.

"Don't look so surprised. Marsgrove is yours, and your wife will be its mistress. You can be assured I know my role as dowager." She stood and crossed to him. She placed her hand on his unscarred cheek. "We have our differences, Auburn, but you are still my son."

He didn't know how to respond.

His mother laughed. "I don't believe I've ever won one of our verbal battles. I shall have to remember this strategy." She left the room.

For a moment he didn't move. Then he laughed at himself. He had had quite the day.

Chapter 23

Ivy closed her book as Mrs. Pennyfeather came into the sitting room.

"Lord Wynbrooke has arrived," said the woman.

"Wynbrooke is here?" asked Ivy in surprise. "We weren't expecting him."

Mrs. Pennyfeather nodded. "I thought you might want to know."

"Has he asked for me?"

"No. He's asked to speak to your father first."

This information wasn't reassuring. An alarm sounded in her mind. "Did he mention why he came?"

"No, Lady Ivy," said Mrs. Pennyfeather. "But he didn't look happy."

"Perhaps I should go down." Ivy glanced at her dress. Drab, but clean. She headed downstairs. She didn't think Wynbrooke's visit boded well for her.

She reached the drawing room before her father. Wynbrooke faced the window. "Lord Wynbrooke? What brings you here today? May I get you some tea?"

"No, thank you, Lady Ivy." Wynbrooke crossed to the sofa, sat down, then popped up again. "I was hoping to speak with your father, but you may stay if you wish. It concerns you, after all."

Her disquiet grew. She sat in a straight-backed chair. "Have you had some unfortunate news?"

"No, I . . . Perhaps it would be best to wait for your father."

"I am here." Lord Dunleigh entered the room. "Wynbrooke, good to see you. I understand you have something to tell me. Nothing unpleasant I hope."

Wynbrooke pulled out a handkerchief and balled it in his fist. A sheen of perspiration glazed his forehead, and he shifted his weight from foot to foot. Ivy watched him pull the handkerchief from one hand to the other, then he wiped his brow. His mouth opened and closed several times, but he didn't speak.

Ivy's father frowned. "What is it, man? Are you ill?"

Wynbrooke cleared his throat, then moistened his lips. "I regret to inform you that I can no longer marry Lady Ivy."

"What?" bellowed her father.

Ivy stared at Wynbrooke. The initial shock of his words stunned her, but a swift flood of relief now filled her. She wouldn't have to marry him. She wanted to cheer.

She peered at her father, and her elation evaporated.

Lord Dunleigh's face was mottled, and his eyes looked ready to bulge from their sockets. "You want to break off the betrothal?"

"Yes," said Wynbrooke, looking more uncomfortable. He wiped his brow again.

Lord Dunleigh shot a glance at her. She shrank back into her seat. He shook his finger at her as though he might say something to her, but then he faced Wynbrooke again. "Why?"

"I cannot ignore certain distressing stories that have come to my attention. As you know, the Wynbrooke name is an honorable one, and I cannot risk any blemish upon it. When we made the alliance, I believed Lady Ivy would make an exemplary countess."

"I quite understand," said Lord Dunleigh between clenched teeth.

"I dislike having the name of my betrothed linked to someone other than myself."

"Tamberlake," muttered Lord Dunleigh.

Ivy stirred in her chair. "Father, I—"

His father whipped his head around to glare at her. "Silence. I don't want to hear from you." He drew in a deep breath and faced Wynbrooke again. "Are you sure? I could help win you influence. If you could overlook her behavior of these past weeks—"

"No, I'm quite sure. I was never much interested in wielding authority in any case." Wynbrooke stuffed his handkerchief into his pocket. "As fond as I am of Lady Ivy, I'm afraid I couldn't marry her now."

"But the scandal. Think of what the scandal shall do to your name." Lord Dunleigh's voice took on a pleading tone.

"Better a short scandal now, than that of a cuckolded husband later."

Ivy cringed. Her father sputtered in indignation, looked at her, then pursed his lips and blinked furiously.

"As you knew when we first talked, I prefer the quiet life. I shall stay out of society until the stories die down." Wynbrooke took two steps toward the door and straightened his coat. "I shall not forget your graciousness, Lord Dunleigh. You may count on my support in the future. I do not blame you for the outcome of this affair."

"You are too kind," said her father.

Wynbrooke bowed to Ivy. "Forgive me, Lady Ivy."

She nodded.

Wynbrooke left the room.

Ivy didn't dare look at her father. She kept her gaze lowered, less in shame than in fear that her joy would shine in her eyes and her father would notice.

Lord Dunleigh popped out of his seat and paced the room. "What do you have to say for yourself?"

"What can I say, Father?"

"Nothing. I wouldn't believe you in any case. You told me before I had nothing to fear, but you were wrong, weren't you? Oh, the shame." He clamped his hands around his head.

"But, Father—"

"No, no more. I don't want to hear your lies." He pulled the bell cord. Mrs. Pennyfeather appeared a moment later. "Get my wife and children."

Lady Dunleigh was the first to appear. She hurried to her husband, her eyes wide with worry. "What is it, Dunleigh? Mrs. Pennyfeather seemed to think you were having an apoplectic fit. Are you ill? Look at your color. Your face is red."

"I'm not that lucky," he said and glared at Ivy.

"Ivy? What have you done now?" asked her mother. "Can't you see your father is ill?"

She was spared from answering as Christopher and Georgina entered the room. "Is this important? I was just looking over a book of the newest fashions," said Georgina with a pout.

"Sit down and behave yourself," said her father with a snarl.

Georgina's eyes widened, and she took a seat.

"Your father's ill," said Lady Dunleigh.

"I am not ill," he barked.

Christopher shot Ivy a questioning look, then took the chair next to her.

Lord Dunleigh paced in front of them for a few steps in silence, then pivoted on his heels to face them. "I never thought I would live to see the day my children would bring ruin upon this family."

"I haven't lost any money, if that's what you're asking, Father," said Christopher.

"This isn't about you." Lord Dunleigh pointed at Ivy. "Wynbrooke has cried off."

"He did?" Georgina couldn't keep the excited horror at her sister's scandal from her voice.

"He did?" Christopher turned to Ivy. "Well done," he whispered so only she could hear.

Lady Dunleigh began to wail. She waved her hand as if it were a fan. "My smelling salts. Someone bring me my smelling salts."

"Pull yourself together, Phoebe. We don't have time for your theatricals now." Lord Dunleigh frowned. "I don't see how we can avoid the scandal Ivy has brought upon us."

Ivy's mother pulled out a lacy handkerchief and sniffed into it. "I suppose we should turn down any invitations we receive and send our regrets to those we've already accepted."

Georgina lost all look of merriment at her sister's predicament. "What?"

"Well, we can't go out now." Lady Dunleigh blew her nose. "How long do you think we need to remain hidden?"

"Until the gossip dies down. Until the *ton* finds someone new to talk about. A month should suffice."

"A month?" cried Georgina. "What am I supposed to do for a month without anything to do?"

"You might try reading a book," whispered Ivy.

Christopher stood. "I don't see why we have to seclude ourselves. I for one think we should face the gossips and show them we don't care."

Lord Dunleigh snorted. "You don't know anything, boy."

Christopher narrowed his gaze. "I am not a boy."

"Then stop acting like one." Lord Dunleigh dismissed him with a wave. "Then we are in agreement?"

"No. I don't see why I should stay home because Ivy's done something stupid." Georgina pouted. "It's not fair."

"Don't fret, Georgie. I'm sure the scandal will make you all the more intriguing to the boys," said Christopher.

Georgina turned her wide eyes on her brother. "Do you really think so?"

"Quiet, you two," said Lord Dunleigh. "Good. Then we shan't speak of this again." He marched from the room.

Lady Dunleigh shook her head. "Oh, Ivy. Now what are we going to do with you?"

Ivy's thoughts raced, and she bit back a smile. "Perhaps . . . but no, I wouldn't want to cause more trouble."

Her mother dabbed at her eyes. "I don't see how you could cause any more than you already have."

"But if I went away for a while? Stayed away from the *ton*?" Ivy bit her lower lip.

"We have no place to send you. Everyone is in London for the season. Your father wouldn't let you go to the country house alone," said Lady Dunleigh.

"I could go to *my* house."

"Your house?"

"The one Lord Stanhope left me. I could go to Devon and seclude myself." She hoped her eagerness didn't alter her tone.

Lady Dunleigh grew pensive. "You can't go alone."

"I could take Mrs. Pennyfeather. She's had nothing to do really since my ball." Ivy held her breath.

"Mrs. Pennyfeather would be an acceptable chaperone." Lady Dunleigh paused for a moment.

"So I may go?"

"Let me speak to your father." She took Georgina's arm. "Come, Georgina. Let's pick out what you shall wear when we can show our faces again."

Ivy turned to Christopher when they were alone. "Are you angry with me, too?"

"Not in the least. I am envious perhaps."

"Of what?"

"You're going away."

"That's not for certain."

"Yes, it is. You've provided them with the perfect solution." He hugged her. "You're not upset by their reactions?"

"Not really, although I could have done without Father's display."

"He enjoys himself when he can throw his power around."

Ivy laughed. "You're terrible, Christopher."

"I know. Father's told me enough." Christopher stood. "I really am glad you won't be marrying Wynbrooke."

"I am, too."

And inside her, the hope flared that perhaps now . . . perhaps she . . . maybe . . .

Tamberlake.

Styles shook Tamberlake's hand. "I received your message. Wise of you to invite me to Marsgrove. You aren't the favorite topic at our house at the moment."

"I didn't think I'd be welcomed just yet. Shall we walk?" Tamberlake led his guest outside and down a gravel path. "How is Ivy holding up?"

"She's stronger than you think. Despite Father's anger, she's happy about the broken engagement." Styles laughed. "Yesterday Ivy was reading. Father launched into a tirade about her behavior. Ivy set her book aside, listened without making a comment, then picked up her book and continued to read. Father hasn't tried to talk to her since."

He didn't know whether he wanted to laugh at her pluck or wring her father's neck. Of course, killing the father of the woman one intended to marry wouldn't do. "I don't like to be the cause of unpleasantness for her."

"You aren't. Ivy left today."

"What?"

"She convinced Father the scandal would die sooner if she left London. She and Mrs. Pennyfeather are taking up residence in the house she inherited from Lord Stanhope."

He felt a rush of frustration. This was unexpected news. It didn't change his plans, merely slowed them for a bit. "Where is the house?"

"Devon."

"I suppose I must travel then."

"You're going to see her?"

"I have to ask her to marry me. Although I suppose I should take care of your father's dislike of me first. I think I should wait another day."

"Knowing how my father likes to peddle his importance, I don't think you should have any problem setting up an appointment to see him."

As they passed the fountain, Humphrey quacked, jumped out of the water, and followed behind the two men.

"You brought the duck with you. I still hold he's better trained than most dogs," said Styles.

"He is." Tamberlake threw the bird a chunk of bread and continued along the path. "Your father may not be willing to see me after he learns what I have to say to you."

Styles glanced at him. "I thought you brought me here to ask about Ivy."

He shook his head. "No, I have another matter I need your help with."

"Now you have piqued my curiosity."

"In a bit. We've almost reached our destination."

They walked along a serpentine lake. Humphrey

decided the water looked better than their company, so he plunged through the reeds into the water. He swam toward other ducks.

"Every time we pass the lake, he acts as though he's forgotten I have a lake. And when I return along the path, he climbs out and follows me back to the house. It's as if he thinks I've brought him to play with friends." Tamberlake threw the remaining bread onto the water.

The path turned and led them into a small wood. A little way into the trees, they reached a clearing. A statue of Ares stood in the center of a circle of gravel. An artful ruin arched over the statue's head and marble benches stood scattered around the statue.

"What do you think of it?" asked Tamberlake.

"It's a peaceful spot."

"No, really look around you. What would you change?"

Styles shot him a look of bewilderment, but examined the area again. He shrugged his shoulders. "I wouldn't change the folly. I would add more trees there"—he pointed to his left—"so you couldn't see the road, and I would want a little more color in here. Perhaps some flowers, or maybe even a reflecting pool. And I'd plant ivy or wisteria to climb the arch."

He stroked his chin. "I hadn't even thought of that. Excellent ideas."

"Now may I ask what this is about?"

"You're how old now?"

"Twenty-three." Styles looked even more bewildered.

"So I'm seven years your elder and soon to be your brother-in-law."

"If Father will let you."

"I'll marry Ivy with or without your father's approval. But he'll grant it. No, I'm speaking of you now."

"Me? Tamberlake, you're not making any sense."

Tamberlake nodded. "I have a holding outside of Huntingdon. For the past two years it has steadily been losing money. It still turns a profit, but I can no longer trust my steward. I'd go myself, but I have more important matters I need to see to here."

Styles laughed. "Such as marrying Ivy."

"Precisely. So I want you to go and find out what is happening to my land."

"Me?" Styles gave him a look of astonishment.

"Yes. You have my permission to make whatever changes you deem necessary to restore prosperity to the land and people."

"You would trust me with this?"

"Without hesitation."

"Are you sure?"

"I can't go myself, and I can think of no one I could depend on more."

"I'll go."

"But it may require a year, even longer, for you to set things right."

"Doesn't matter. I have nothing to do here, and it will save me from listening to Father lecture me about my idle ways."

"Thank you, Styles."

"When shall I go?"

"As soon as you wish."

"Tomorrow then." Styles let out a whoop. "You don't know what this means to me."

Ahh, but I think I do. "The day after will suffice. You will come back for the wedding."

"Wouldn't miss it." Styles clapped him on the back. "And if Ivy doesn't marry you, I may just have to."

Tamberlake laughed. "God, no."

"You're right. You're a little too hairy for my tastes."

He felt a camaraderie with Styles he had almost forgotten existed. Friendship. "I have the information for you in my study. Let's return so you can examine it. We'll collect Humphrey on the way."

Chapter 24

Tamberlake stood in the entry hall. He listened with some amusement as Ivy's father thundered through the house.

"The boy was here yesterday. How could he have left so quickly? It's that Tamberlake. He's behind all this. He's trying to destroy me."

"Calm yourself, dear," came the voice of Ivy's mother. "It probably isn't true."

"Of course it is. It's all part of some insidious plan to ruin me. First, he seduces my daughter and makes her the central figure in a scandal. Then, he lures my son from my side. Probably to some seedy den of iniquity. How will this look in Lords?"

"Lower your voice, Dunleigh. What will the servants think?"

"Madam, this is my house, and if I wish to shout, I will. The servants be damned."

"Dunleigh," said Ivy's mother with a gasp. "You'll give yourself an apoplectic fit."

"If I choose to give myself a fit, I shall. Stop coddling me," said Lord Dunleigh. "Your son is gone, and your daughter fancies she's in love with that Tamberlake scoundrel."

Tamberlake handed the butler his gloves and hat. "Please tell Lord Dunleigh I am here to see him."

"Whom shall I say is calling?"

"Lord Tamberlake."

A brief expression of surprise flitted across the butler's features, but he nodded and left the hall. "Excuse me, my lord."

"What do you want?" barked Lord Dunleigh.

"Lord Tamberlake to see you."

"He's *here*? What the blazes is he doing *here*?"

"Shall I tell him you're not in, my lord?"

"No. Send him in. Send the bounder in."

Tamberlake stood outside the room. The butler reappeared and nodded. Tamberlake ambled into the room as if he hadn't a care in the world. "Good day, Lord Dunleigh, Lady Dunleigh."

"How dare you show your face here?" said Dunleigh. Red splotches glowed on the man's face.

Tamberlake turned to the man. "I? I have done nothing of which I am ashamed."

"You've dragged my daughter's name through the mud, and now you've lured away my son as well. You call that nothing?" Dunleigh wagged his finger at him. "What do you want now? To seduce my wife as well?"

Ivy's mother gasped. "Dunleigh." She fanned herself with her hand.

"In the first place, I would never do anything to harm Ivy." Tamberlake crossed to Dunleigh and faced him. "In the second place, Styles made his own decision to leave this house. Perhaps you should look closer to find whom to blame."

Lord Dunleigh opened and closed his mouth like a fish. His eyes bulged from their sockets.

Tamberlake ignored Dunleigh's agitation. "I've come to ask for your daughter's hand in marriage."

Lady Dunleigh hiccuped once, then stared at Tamberlake.

Dunleigh raised his arm in triumph. "Hah. She isn't here. You chased her away, you know. She can't show her face in London, so she's off in seclusion."

"I doubt I could chase her away. Ivy is a strong woman. I rather think if she left, she wanted to go."

Her father glared at Tamberlake. "You can't expect my approval after everything you've done?"

"Yes, I can," said Tamberlake in an even tone. "Ivy will make me the perfect wife."

"Not without my consent," said Dunleigh. "And I won't give it."

Tamberlake pulled a few sheets of paper from his coat pocket. "You'll change your mind once you've read these." He placed the papers on the table. "I will admit to causing Wynbrooke to cry off, but I won't apologize for it."

"What of the harm you've done to my name? The *ton* speaks of nothing else."

"But when I marry Ivy, the *ton* will think it a love match. The gossip will change into admiration. You can use that to your advantage."

Lord Dunleigh stopped his pacing. His face returned to a more normal color. He seemed to be pondering this possibility. "What are these papers?"

"They show the state of Wynbrooke's finances. I assure you they are accurate."

Lord Dunleigh snatched the papers from the table. "This won't change my mind."

"Read them."

Ivy's father glared at him one last time, then cast his gaze to the papers. His eyes widened, and his mouth dropped open. He flipped to the second sheet. "I can't believe this," he muttered, but he didn't lift his gaze from the page. At the third page, his face grew red once again, and his breathing was audible throughout the room. "The scoundrel. The villain. I won't stand for it. And to think I was going to marry Ivy off to that worthless rogue."

Lady Dunleigh looked on in amazement. "What has happened?"

Dunleigh waved the papers in the air. "Wynbrooke's penniless, barely scraping by. The man played me for a fool. I had no inkling he was marrying Ivy for her settlement. I shudder to think how much money I might have wasted on him." Dunleigh tossed the papers on the table and turned back to Tamberlake. His angry expression melted at the sight of him. "I don't know what to say. You've done us a great favor."

"So is Lord Tamberlake evil or good now?" Lady Dunleigh looked from one man to the other.

"My dear woman, don't you understand? He has saved us from Wynbrooke. Tamberlake is a hero." Lord Dunleigh nodded.

"And Ivy . . . ?" asked Lady Dunleigh.

Lord Dunleigh turned to Tamberlake. "Do you still wish to marry Ivy?"

"Yes."

"Then you have my blessings."

"Thank you, sir."

"I think a fall wedding would be lovely," said Lady Dunleigh. "Or perhaps a winter wedding. The bride can arrive in a sleigh—"

"No, Lady Dunleigh," said Tamberlake. "I don't wish to wait that long. I will marry Ivy next week."

"Next week? But that's impossible," said Ivy's mother.

"I have a special license."

"But I can't possibly have a dress ready by next week. And Ivy needs a trousseau," said Lady Dunleigh.

"She can wear whatever she wants. Her dress doesn't matter to me, and I will take care of all Ivy's needs after we are wed." Tamberlake paused. "But perhaps we should ask Ivy."

"She's in Devon," said Dunleigh.

"I know. I travel there tomorrow."

"This is so sudden. I'm not sure I can follow everything that has happened," said Lady Dunleigh.

"It doesn't matter if you understand. Ivy's marrying Tamberlake." Lord Dunleigh clasped his hands behind his back and rocked on his heels. "Hah, what an accomplishment."

"If you say so, dear." Lady Dunleigh looked confused. "What of Christopher?"

Lord Dunleigh frowned. "Yes, there is the matter of my son."

"Styles agreed to help me with my estate in Huntingdon. I have pressing business here that precludes me from seeing to it. He is a good friend."

"Yes, of course." Dunleigh laughed as if he were

privy to a joke. He extended his hand toward Tamberlake. "My dear fellow, how can I ever thank you?"

Tamberlake took the man's hand and shook it. "I considered it my duty."

"You are a good man, Tamberlake," said Dunleigh. "Soon I shall call you 'son.' "

"Then it's settled. I shall send word when and where the ceremony shall take place." Tamberlake nodded to Ivy's father. "Lord Dunleigh, thank you for seeing me."

"It is I who thank *you*, Tamberlake." Ivy's father beamed at him. "You've proven yourself a boon to this family."

"Now if you will excuse me, I need to ready myself to travel. No need to see me out." Tamberlake stepped into the hall, where the butler handed him his gloves and hat. Behind him he heard Lady Dunleigh.

"But it will be such a small affair."

"Don't fret, Phoebe. You can have your grand wedding for Georgina." Dunleigh's voice boomed with pleasure now. "And I shall have Tamberlake at my side."

Tamberlake shook his head. He must really care for Ivy if he was willing to endure her parents.

The stone-and-thatch cottage had thrilled Ivy the moment she saw it. A stream ran past the two-storied building, and an abundance of flowers grew in riotous abandon. The small house had more than enough space for her. She had unpacked her belongings in the largest bedroom, then unpacked a new case of books to fill the shelves next to an enormous fireplace in the salon. There was no dining room, but a large wooden table stood in the kitchen where she and Mrs. Pennyfeather took their meals. She was glad of the company, for Mrs. Pennyfeather not only entertained her with stories of her past employers, but the woman knew how to cook. Ivy acknowledged she'd be rather hungry if she had to fend for herself.

Hampton-in-the-Moor was a small village, and as yet the villagers hadn't been friendly, but they hadn't been unpleasant, either. Ivy enjoyed long walks on the moors and quiet afternoons with a book. With no one to cast judgment on her attire or dismiss her opinion—and especially without the specter of an unwanted marriage—Ivy savored a freedom she found heady. She missed Christopher, but not the constant noise of living with her family—the squabbles, the inane chatter, her father's bellows. Here birds filled the hedgerows with song, and the gurgling of the stream was her constant melody.

The week since their arrival had sped quickly past. Mrs. Pennyfeather had taught her to bake bread, and they tasted the region's famous clotted cream. Ivy picked up her often-neglected needlework and finished a good portion of the embroidery, much to her satisfaction. She made plans for a henhouse for chickens to provide them with fresh eggs, and hired someone to fence in some of her land for a cow. With Mrs. Pennyfeather's help, she cleaned and aired out the entire house until it smelled as fresh as the country air. The bucolic life agreed with her. She could only thank Lord Stanhope for thinking of her in his will.

But in her quiet moments, her thoughts turned to Tamberlake. What was he doing? Where was he now? Was he thinking of her? When she walked, she remembered their walks in Wales. When she read, she pictured his library. And when she lay in bed at night, she relived his every touch.

Her fear was that as she settled in she'd have more and more quiet moments, so she sought out activities to keep her occupied. This morning she pulled on her oldest garb, a simple brown skirt with a white blouse. The sky was patchy with clouds, but she wanted to plant flowers before the rain fell, and if she had time, start on cutting back the roses that had grown rampant in years without attention. By the kitchen door, she gathered a trowel and shears and a large tarp on which to collect the cuttings.

"Don't forget your bonnet," said Mrs. Penny-feather.

"But there's no sun."

"A beam breaks through every now and again. And tie it well. There's a mischievous breeze blowing."

"Yes, ma'am," said Ivy with a smile. She grabbed a sunbonnet and pulled it on her head.

A gust tugged at her hat the moment she stepped outside. She put her implements on the ground and tied the ribbon under her chin. The flower bed ran along the low stone wall. A number of seedlings waited for her. Mrs. Pennyfeather had procured a clematis, some garden pinks, and chrysanthemums. The clematis she would plant by the wall and hope the climber would soon cover the stones in a profusion of color.

Spearing the trowel into the dirt, she dug a small hole. She had never planted anything before, and the smell of the overturned earth was a new and wondrous aroma. Following Mrs. Pennyfeather's instructions, she dropped a seedling into the hole and packed the dirt around it. If the plant grew, she could thank luck more than her skill.

The sound of hoofbeats down the lane reached her ears, but she didn't look up. She concentrated on placing the next little plant into its new home.

"I don't believe I've ever seen a more charming sight," a male voice said from the other side of the stone wall.

Ivy's heart raced even before she looked up. Tamberlake.

Chapter 25

For a moment neither spoke, then Tamberlake laughed. "I hurried here with all due haste, and now I find myself at a loss for words." He lifted his right leg over his horse and slid off the left side of the mount. He looped the reins over the gate post.

"You came." Ivy stood, brushing dirt from her skirt. "I didn't know if I should let myself hope."

He unstrapped his cane from the saddle and entered the yard. "I've seen your father."

"And he let you leave unscathed?" Ivy laughed. "What spell did you cast over him? I might have need of it in the future."

"No spell, just facts." Tamberlake took her hand. "He's forgiven me everything."

"Now I know you must be some sort of sorcerer. When I left, my father was condemning you to the far corners of purgatory."

"Furthermore, he's given me his permission to marry you."

Ivy fell silent. She stared at him with wide eyes. He could almost see the questions whirling around in those brown depths. Finally, she burst out, "Do you really want to marry me?"

Tamberlake laughed. "It's customary for the man to ask the woman. And I must apologize. I should have asked you first without embroiling your father in our union." He faced her and placed his hands on her shoulders. "Ivy, will you marry me?"

Her mouth broadened into a grin. "Yes. Oh, yes." She threw her arms around his neck and kissed him.

The unexpected onslaught filled him with delight. He pulled her to him and returned her kiss. His body reacted as it always had to her, this time with the added force of the unsated hunger of the past weeks.

When they broke free, she looked up at him. "But how? How did you make my father change his mind?"

"I suppose I do owe you the truth."

"The truth?" She stepped back and looked at him with a wary curiosity.

"The rumors, Wynbrooke breaking the betrothal, Christopher in Huntingdon, I planned it all."

She appeared stunned. "How? No . . . why?"

"Because I couldn't let you marry Wynbrooke. You would have been miserable."

"I see." A furrow appeared between her brows.

"You never would have cried off, so I had to give a reason for Wynbrooke to call off the wedding. I knew I would cause a stir when I returned. I just had to make sure your name was linked to mine. The *ton* would do the rest."

"But Wynbrooke didn't seem to care about the rumors."

"I know." Tamberlake paused. "Wynbrooke has other secrets that made him easy to manipulate."

"Secrets?"

"His financial straits, and another."

"Which is?"

He hesitated. "Wynbrooke and Thorndike are lovers."

Ivy's eyes widened, and then she frowned. "That explains much."

"The rumors allowed him to retain his dignity, but I would have exposed him if he didn't break it off."

"And my father?"

"Once I explained to him Wynbrooke's financial troubles, he proclaimed me a hero. I didn't tell him the other."

Ivy turned away from him. "But why? Why do you wish to marry me?"

He thought for a moment. He couldn't very well tell her that she would make an ideal wife, that her background in society would be an asset, that his body ached for her as no woman before. "We suit each other. So what say you, Ivy? Shall we wed?"

"I'm not sure we suit each other at all. I shall always be grateful for the experiences we shared, but you mustn't think you have to marry me." As she faced him, her eyes welled up with tears. "I thought you were different from other men."

He stilled. "What are you saying? I came here to ask for your hand."

"Do you recall asking me to trust you?"

"Of course."

"I did. I trusted you. But you didn't trust me."

"But I—"

"Do you know what I have been through these last weeks? The object of gossip, ridicule, and speculation. I have been yelled at, laughed at, pointed at, and stared at. I reacted to it all with as much grace as I could muster, but I hated it. Didn't you perhaps consider how much easier I could have borne it all if you had simply told me?"

He stepped toward her, but Ivy lifted her hand. "My whole life I have been used by others. First, my father used me to make connections, then Wynbrooke used me to give himself a proper shield in society and to shore up his finances. Now I find you've used me in your manipulations. You didn't trust me enough to ask for my help."

"I saved you from marriage to Wynbrooke."

"For that I shall be ever grateful. You're right. I would have been miserable married to him." Ivy drew away from him. "Thank you, Lord Tamberlake. You have done me a great service."

His ire stirred then. "I am not the only one who skillfully maneuvered a situation to get what he or she wanted."

"What do you mean?"

"That night in Wales. I seem to recall you casting aside the rules of society to get what you wanted— a night to call your own, a night to hide away in your memories without a care for anyone but yourself, without a thought to the one you left behind, without a thought for me."

Her cheeks flamed. "That's not how I intended—"

"You started this game of using people."

"I didn't use you."

"Didn't you? You took pity on a crippled monster—"

"You're not a—"

"Save me your empty words. At least Lady Coville admits she sees me as a monster." He exited through the gate and tossed the reins over the horse's head.

The sky had turned gray now. With some difficulty, he placed his left foot into the stirrup and swung his weaker right leg over the animal. From atop the horse, he looked down at her. "And to think I believed Styles when he told me you loved me. What a fool I've been."

"Christopher told you?" Ivy started after him, but in the next moment a clap of thunder roared through the yard. Behind her a window of the house shattered. But there had been no lightning.

"Ivy, get down!" Tamberlake glanced around, but could see nothing among the trees.

A second shot rang out. Ivy screamed. He whirled around to see if she had been hit and saw her fall to the ground. "Ivy!"

His horse reared, and he felt himself slip from the saddle. His weak leg couldn't grip the horse's side. As he fell, he heard her shout, "Auburn," but he hit the hard dirt. His head jerked back. A sharp pain exploded in his skull, then darkness consumed him.

He must be in heaven.

He lay on a soft cloud, warm and safe. Through half-closed lids he saw nothing but white. An angelic hand wiped his brow. He sighed in contentment.

"Thank the stars, he's waking."

Tamberlake blinked and looked into the face of Mrs. Pennyfeather. As the room came more into focus, he saw he lay in a bed with an enormous white duvet on top of him. He turned his head and saw Ivy strangling a cloth in her hands and holding back tears. On the other side of the bed stood Fletcher. Somehow he was the one thing that made no sense. "Fletcher? What the devil are you doing here?"

"Making sure you didn't die, my lord."

"Die?" He tried to sit up, but dropped back onto the pillows with a moan. His head pounded. He reached up and felt an enormous bump on the back of his skull. Squinting, he looked at Ivy and remembered the scene in the garden, the storm, and the gunshots. He sat up and grabbed her hands, ignoring the nausea that threatened to conquer him. "Are you hurt?"

"I'm fine." She pulled one hand free and stroked his face. "Please lie back down."

He did as she said, but didn't release her other hand. "Where am I?"

"In my cottage." Ivy wiped his brow with the damp cloth.

"How long have I been . . . ?" He looked around the room again. Fletcher still seemed out of place. "How did you get here, Fletcher?"

"Mrs. Pennyfeather fetched me from the inn, sir."

He stretched out gingerly. Pain tweaked his movements, but no more than a few minor aches. The bedclothes soothed his skin. He frowned. "Where are my clothes?"

"Your clothes are in there." Fletcher pointed toward a cupboard.

"Who . . . ?"

"I undressed you, sir."

Tamberlake looked at Ivy. Her cheeks bloomed with color. She shrugged. "There's no need to deny it. I did as much as I could before he arrived. I couldn't have undressed you by myself any more without jostling you terribly."

"Thank you." He pushed himself up onto his elbows. "I should get up now."

"No. You are to stay in bed until the doctor can see you," said Ivy.

"A doctor? No, I'll be fine in a few moments." He gazed at Fletcher again. "Our rooms?"

"I've given them up, sir. Lady Ivy has offered us housing here. Your things will be along shortly."

"I don't think I . . ." He stopped. His stomach roiled. Fletcher stepped to the side of the bed and held out the chamber pot to catch the contents of his stomach.

Mrs. Pennyfeather said, "Come, Lady Ivy. His lordship needs a moment. We shall fix him a tray. I imagine by the time we return, he shall be lying still." The woman led Ivy from the room.

In the kitchen, Ivy sliced some bread while Mrs. Pennyfeather put eggs into boiling water on the stove. "He'll recover, won't he?"

"I wouldn't worry about his lordship. Once he eats, he'll regain his strength in little time."

After laying a napkin over the rough wooden surface, Ivy laid out butter and jam on the tray. She placed the bread plate beside them, and Mrs. Pennyfeather added two soft-boiled eggs. Ivy carried the tray to Tamberlake.

"Invalid fare," he said and grimaced.

"Eat. You need to regain your strength." She buttered a slice for him.

Looking much like a young boy forced into doing something good for him, he bit into the bread. "The last thing I remember is seeing you fall, and then I slipped from my horse. I thought you'd been shot."

"I didn't fall. I merely got down as you suggested. Then your horse reared. I thought *you'd* been shot."

"No, I fell. I don't often ride because my leg isn't strong enough, but I was in a hurry to reach you. When the animal reared, I couldn't keep my seat. My head . . ."

"Your head hit a rock."

"That explains the bump I feel." He looked at the eggs and winced. "I won't touch those."

"As you wish, my lord," said Fletcher.

"How did I get here?"

"When you fell from the horse, I shouted for Mrs. Pennyfeather. When she came outside, you opened your eyes. We helped you stand, but you didn't seem quite yourself. We thought it best to get you to a bed. Mrs. Pennyfeather thought it likely you hadn't traveled alone, so she ran to the inn, where she found Fletcher."

"Why don't I remember any of this?"

"Because of that bump on your head." Ivy tried to feed him another bite of bread, but he turned away.

"The gunman. Did anyone find him?"

"No, my lord," said Fletcher. "I reported the attack at once, but the local magistrate seems to think some hunter must have made an error."

"It was no error. He fired twice. The first shot destroyed the window. If the shot was in error, there would have been no second shot." He pushed the tray away. "How about a rasher of bacon?"

"Not until you've recovered," said Ivy.

"I am recovered." He paused. "How long was I unconscious?"

"Just a few moments," said Ivy. "But you fell asleep several times, and this is the first conversation you've had where you've made sense."

"This makes sense to you?"

"Lady Ivy has been by your side since we put you into bed," said Mrs. Pennyfeather, dabbing at her eyes with a handkerchief.

With that answer his memory came back fully. He glanced at Ivy. She looked haggard and spent. And never more beautiful. He turned to the older woman and handed her the tray. "Mrs. Pennyfeather, may I plead to your sense of pity and ask you to remove this food. Fletcher will help you."

Fletcher nodded at Mrs. Pennyfeather. "At once, my lord." The two servants left the room.

Ivy pulled her lower lip between her teeth.

"I thought you hated me," said Tamberlake.

The tears that had threatened earlier spilled over her lids. "I was angry, and I said some hateful things."

"As did I. Anger can make a fool out of the most noble man."

"Or woman." Ivy smiled through her tears. "I *was* angry."

"And my pride demanded I retaliate." He took her hand. "I should have trusted you."

"Yes, you should have." She paused. "Of course, I was so committed to doing my duty, I may not have played along."

His thumb stroked the back of her hand. "I'd like to say that was my reason for not telling you, but I can't. I was too caught up in rescuing you, too caught up in playing the hero, to think how you might have felt."

"And you did rescue me." She gave a shudder. "Can you imagine if I had married Wynbrooke?"

"I try to think of it as little as possible." Tamberlake lay back. "I won't force you to marry me either if you don't wish."

"So you can be free to marry Lady Coville?"

"Dear God, no." He sat back up and grimaced with pain. She darted forward to wipe his brow, but he waved away her attention. "Whatever gave you that idea?"

"She told me you planned to marry."

"Yes, she told me the same thing. As if I would marry the woman who jilted me when I needed her the most."

"But Lady Coville—"

"Forget Lady Coville." He pulled the cloth from her hand and wiped the tears from her cheeks. "You are the first woman who could look at me without seeing a monster."

"You're not a—"

With a smile he placed his finger on her lips. "I know." He took her in his arms. Over her shoulder, he saw his eye patch hanging from the bedpost. He pushed her away and touched his face. Nothing covered his scars. Pressing his palm to his eye socket, he said, "Why did no one tell me I am uncovered?"

Ivy gasped—a loud, horrified, theatrical gasp. "Good heavens, you've exposed yourself to me. I've been compromised. Now I suppose you have to marry me." She stared at him in mock horror.

Tamberlake laughed. "I was right. You do suit

me." He stroked the inside of her wrist. "Shall I show you just how much?"

"Not until you are recovered."

"And if I tell you I'm feeling better with every moment?"

"Then I'll know you are delusional, and I'll call for help."

He grinned. "Very well, my lady. I shall acquiesce to your wishes this time."

"Why does that leave me less than reassured?"

"Because we are so well suited, you can read my very thoughts. Marry me, Ivy. Marry me and banish darkness from the monster's life."

Her eyes filled with tears again. "You're not a monster. I suppose I shall have to marry you just to keep telling you that."

He kissed her cheek. "Go rest, Ivy. You need it as much as I."

She nodded and left the room. Only after she departed did she touch the spot where he'd kissed her. They were indeed well suited. If he suited her any better, she might burst into flames.

Chapter 26

Ivy stared at her plate. A week ago she had been in a house in Devon. Today she was sitting at her father's table, eating food she couldn't taste, wearing a new name and an old dress. Countess Tamberlake was the name, and the dress she wore was the same she had donned for her betrothal ball a lifetime ago, only now it served as a wedding gown. Not that it mattered. The newspapers wouldn't write about this wedding. Only her family and his mother had been present. And Fletcher and Pennyfeather. No, the papers would write about them after the announcement hit.

The ceremony had been short and Ivy remembered only snatches of it. The chapel was small, but beautiful. For some reason, she could still recall the splashes of light across the floor from the stained glass window, but not the words of the vicar. She remembered hearing Tamberlake say his vows and making her own, but little else, such as how she walked down the aisle. Nerves, she supposed.

But she didn't understand why she was so nervous.

"Are you going on a honeymoon?" Ivy heard her mother ask. "Extended trips to the Continent are all the rage now."

"No. I . . . that is, we have something to take care of first," said Tamberlake.

"When I marry, I will make sure my husband takes me on a honeymoon," said Georgina.

"These are extraordinary circumstances, Georgina," said her mother.

"Yes, but I don't see why I couldn't have a new dress for Ivy's wedding," said Georgina.

"There wasn't time," said her father. He turned to Tamberlake. "Take my advice, son, and leave the women to their clothes. I'd wager even Wellington himself would have been afraid to stand between a woman and her dresses." Lord Dunleigh laughed at his own joke.

Ivy wished that she had something stronger to drink than the wine in front of her, or at least that she could crawl under the table.

"Of course Ivy isn't interested in clothes," said Georgina. "If she were, she would have waited until she could get a new dress made."

"I suspect Ivy has more important things to think about than clothes, Georgie," said Christopher.

"Such as?" asked Georgina, looking surprised at the notion.

Such as who shot at Tamberlake and me. Ivy sipped her wine.

"Don't trouble your pretty little head about it, Georgina," said Lord Dunleigh. "I'll find you a husband who will spoil you in the manner you desire."

Ivy glanced down the table at her husband and wondered if he now regretted marrying her. She probably should have warned him about her family. At least he liked Christopher, and he had dealt with her father before today. Her gaze landed on Lady Tamberlake. The woman hadn't said a word since the ceremony. Ivy decided that the dowager countess should have had the warning instead.

The interminable meal ended, and the carriage waited for the wedded couple. Ivy's mother made a show of crying as she kissed her daughter. Her father was too busy imparting final bits of wisdom to Tamberlake to say good-bye. Ivy climbed into the carriage with a sigh of relief. She smiled at her mother-in-law, then faced out the window. Christopher stood just outside and waved. In the few moments they'd had together before the ceremony, Christopher had spoken of nothing but his new responsibilities. His face lit up as he told her of the estate in Huntingdon and the ideas he had already executed. She would miss her brother, but she had never seen him happier. Waving back, she wished him nothing but the best.

The carriage rocked as Tamberlake climbed in. He sat beside her, then knocked on the roof with his cane to signal the driver.

No one breached the silence for half an hour. Tamberlake leaned back and dozed. With London behind them, Ivy kept her gaze focused on the passing countryside, but couldn't avoid noticing Lady Tamberlake focused *her* attention on the new countess. Finally Ivy turned to her mother-in-law. "Do I have something on my face?"

Lady Tamberlake laughed. "No, but I will have

the grace to admit I was staring. I don't believe I've seen much of you in society."

"I don't expect you have."

Tamberlake stirred. "Be nice, Mother."

His mother gave him a look of exasperation. "Am I not allowed to ask my daughter-in-law questions?"

"Just remember—*she's* the countess now."

Ivy glanced between them.

Lady Tamberlake made a brushing gesture with her hand. "Ignore him. He tends to be moody."

Ivy gazed at her mother-in-law with interest. "I know."

"You are a surprise to me, Ivy. May I call you Ivy?"

"Of course. There would be far too many Lady Tamberlakes if you don't."

"As I was saying, you're a surprise to me, Ivy. How did you meet my son?"

"Lord Stanhope sent me on an errand to Wales."

"Stanhope? But he died several months ago."

"Yes, it was a sort of legacy. I had to deliver a portrait in order to inherit."

"And once in Wales you charmed my son."

"I wouldn't say 'charmed' is the correct word."

"What word would you use?"

She thought for a moment. " 'Pestered,' maybe. Or 'befuddled.'"

"Try 'tamed,'" said Tamberlake.

"Hardly that, my lord," said Ivy. " 'Wore down,' perhaps?"

Lady Tamberlake raised an eyebrow, an expression Ivy had seen on her son more than once. "You're clever."

Ivy shrugged. "I try to be."

The carriage turned onto the drive to Marsgrove. She fell silent. Although she had seen the estate before, now she was its mistress. Once again the facade impressed her with its elegance.

The carriage stopped, and a footman opened the door. Tamberlake climbed out first, then helped his mother from the coach. Ivy drew in a deep breath and descended. The staff lined the stairs leading to the house. At her appearance they applauded.

"Welcome home, Lady Tamberlake," whispered her husband.

She made her way down the middle of the two rows of servants. She shook hands with each one and thanked them for their congratulations. When she saw Beaker and his wife, she beamed at them. "It's nice to see two familiar faces in this crowd."

"Aye, miss . . . I mean, my lady," said Beaker. The happiness on their faces mirrored hers.

Fletcher stood on the top step. He had driven home directly after the ceremony. When she reached him, he bowed. "May I offer my felicitations as well, my lady?"

"Thank you, Fletcher."

He opened the door for her and let her into the entry hall. Tamberlake followed her.

She let out a puff of air. "How did I do?"

"You charmed every one of them."

"I don't know. I think I may have befuddled them."

"Or tamed."

They shared a laugh.

Lady Tamberlake came in behind them. "Well, no newly wedded couple should have to worry about their mother hovering over them, so I'm going to my room. You won't see me again until tomorrow. Good night, dears." She kissed Ivy on the cheek. "I do believe you'll be good for my son." She swept up the stairs and disappeared down a hall.

Ivy let her gaze roam over the entry hall. The vastness of the foyer overwhelmed her.

"Would you like the tour today or tomorrow?" asked Tamberlake.

"Tomorrow, please. I don't think I'm ready for it today."

"Come. Let me show you your rooms." Tamberlake took her hand and led her up the stairs. Before they ascended, he turned to Fletcher. "We'll have dinner in my room tonight."

"Very good, sir."

Her rooms were so much more than she expected. They entered the sitting room first. Roses bloomed on the wall, and a great marble fireplace stood along one side. From there, a door led to the bedroom. Roses dominated this room as well. A bed occupied its space beneath a green velvet canopy. Her clothes hung in a separate dressing room, but they only occupied a quarter of the space, much to her chagrin. As the new countess she would probably have to expand her wardrobe. A door led to a bathing chamber and a smaller door led to a toilet. She had never seen one of these newer models. She pulled on the chain, listened to the water rush from the overhead cistern through the bowl, and watched it disappear down the plumbing. Her father would be desperate to update his house once he saw this.

But the final door intrigued her most. When she opened it, she saw it connected her room to the master's chambers. With some disappointment, she realized that they wouldn't be sharing their bedroom.

They shared dinner in his sitting room, and then she returned to her chambers to prepare herself for the night. As she pulled on a gossamer nightgown, she realized she was trembling.

You'd think you were a virgin with no inkling of what to expect this night, Ivy. She finished dressing in a huff. She was no coward, and tonight she would be with the man she loved. Perhaps that was the reason for her nerves. He had never said he loved her. She suspected he did—hadn't he proven it to her with his actions? But she didn't believe he was quite ready to give up his pretense of needing no one. In any case, she knew he cared for her, and he was now her husband. Without further hesitation, she opened the connecting door.

He stood by the fireplace, holding a glass of wine. When he heard her, he turned. His long dressing gown opened to his chest. Soft whorls of chest hair curled on his skin. The gown closed in a V at his taut abdomen. As he propped himself against the mantel, the folds of the gown revealed his muscled calf, and Ivy had the distinct impression he wore nothing beneath the robe. His long hair hung loose around his neck, and his eye patch gave him a look of excitement and danger.

Ivy sucked in her breath. "My lord pirate," she whispered in awe.

His deep chuckle rumbled through her. "If I am your pirate, then you must be my treasure, for in-

deed you have entranced me like no other woman."
He left his glass on the mantel and turned to her
with his arms held wide.

She rushed into his embrace. His arms closed
around her, and once again she savored his strength.
A sense of rightness filled her as he tipped her
chin up and kissed her. Her hand slipped into the
opening of his robe, and she splayed her fingers
against the warmth of his chest.

Her heartbeat quickened as he traced a trail
with a fingertip from her back to the edge of her
breast. Through the filmy material of her gown, he
cupped the soft roundness. Her nipple puckered
into his palm. He slid his other hand lower down
her back until it rested on her buttocks. He pressed
her to him. The silk of his robe did little to hide
the proof of his desire.

His erection rubbed against the apex of her
thighs, teasing her until she heard herself let out a
soft moan. He stepped back from her and held out
his hand. "Come."

She placed her hand in his, and he led her to
the bed. At the side of the bed, he untied his belt
and let the dressing gown slip to the floor. He
stood in front of her, naked and beautiful.

His hands grasped the material of her nightgown and lifted it over her head. He let the gown
pool onto the floor between them. Bracing his
right leg against the mattress, he lifted her from
the floor and laid her in the bed. Then, kneeling
beside her, he rolled on top of her.

His weight covered her like a velvet blanket. He
lowered his mouth to her breast where he suckled
and pulled her nipple into a taut peak. With one
hand, he reached between her legs and cupped

the curly mound. The heel of his hand kneaded small circles as his fingers explored her deeper regions. She let out a ragged breath and lifted her hips to press herself tighter against him. When his finger slipped inside her, she cried out and felt herself close around him.

"Not yet, sweeting," he whispered and withdrew his hand.

Her body ached for more of his touch. She tried to raise herself to him, but he just chuckled and shifted his mouth to her other breast. He maneuvered his hips over hers and let his erection glide in and out between her legs, stroking her bud with each pass.

She didn't know how much longer she could stand the sweet torment. Her hands slid over his hips, trying to guide him closer to her nest, but he was too strong for her. Desperate to fill the longing within her, she reached between their bodies and closed her fingers around his shaft.

He drew in a sharp breath. "Guide me in."

She did as he asked. Through her fingers, he slipped inside her. He pulled her hand free and trapped it above her head. He drove into her, stretching her, filling her, until hip met hip. Again and again he withdrew, only to plunge into her depths anew.

She met his movements until the world disappeared and only sensation remained. Emotions spiraled in a wild whirlwind until they so overwhelmed her, nothing remained but to shatter, and with a cry she did. Above her, Tamberlake thrust himself into her a final time and sent his seed deep within her.

For long minutes, neither spoke. They lay with

limbs entwined, breathing deeply. With gentle kisses, Tamberlake sucked the final morsels of sensation from her mouth. "Ah, Lady Tamberlake, you do suit me."

It wasn't the declaration she had hoped for, but it would do. For now.

Chapter 27

The tour of Marsgrove took the entire morning. Tamberlake didn't show her the servants' quarters, but he took her through the rest of the house, even to the cellar where the foundation rested on the catacombs of a medieval abbey.

"The size of Marsgrove is astonishing," said Ivy as they walked toward the outbuildings.

"My ancestors were lucky. When Cromwell came into power, the earl fancied himself a man of the people. By the time of the Restoration, that earl had died and the new earl was the king's staunch supporter."

"Sounds like what my father would do," said Ivy.

"Come along. There's something I want to show you inside the stables."

The smell of clean straw as they entered gave evidence to the care and skill of the grooms. The stable master bowed to them. A row of horses poked their heads over the half-doors. Farther down the row a stable boy mucked out a stall. Tamberlake reached into his coat pocket and pulled out a bit of paper. He unfolded it to reveal a piece of fish.

Ivy opened her mouth in surprised excitement. "Shylock is here?"

He placed the fish on a beam. "I couldn't leave him behind."

They waited for a moment, but saw nothing.

"Excuse me, my lord?" The boy walked up to them.

"Here now. Don't ye go bothering the master," came a sharp reprimand from the groom.

"No, it's fine," said Tamberlake. "What is it . . . What's your name, lad?"

"Jim, my lord."

"Well, Jim, what did you want to tell me?"

The boy snatched his cap from his head and worried it between his hands. "It's just if you were wanting to see Shylock, I could help, sir."

"Why is that, Jim?"

The boy shuffled his feet. "I sort of got him trained, my lord."

Tamberlake raised his brows. "Indeed?"

"Aye. He comes when I whistle."

"That must have taken some time."

"Aye, my lord. He didn't want to trust me at first."

"You weren't neglecting yer duties, were ye, boy?" asked the stable master.

"No, Mr. Bates. It's just . . . "

"Just what?" barked Mr. Bates.

"Well, his lordship don't ride much," said the boy. "And after I finished mucking out the stables—begging your pardon, my lady."

Ivy smiled. "You were saying . . . ?"

"I mean, after I would finish cleaning the stalls,

I would try to make friends with the beastie," said Jim.

"And you succeeded?" asked Ivy in surprise.

"He still won't let me carry him around, but he comes when I whistle. I always gave him a little treat, you see." Jim flushed a bright red. "I mean, your ladyship."

"Could you show us?" asked Ivy.

Jim puckered his lips and let out a soft whistle. In a moment, Shylock's masked face appeared from under a pile of hay.

"Good boy," said Jim. He took the fish and held it out to the sleek creature.

Shylock rose up on his rear leg, sniffed the offering, then grasped it in his front paws. Jim reached out and stroked the animal on the head. Shylock allowed it for a moment, then scurried away with his prize to hide under the hay again.

"Amazing," said Ivy.

"You seem to have a way with animals," said Tamberlake.

"Me mother says I'm always bringing home some creature or another." Jim smiled in sheepish manner.

"Keep up the good work, Jim. If you have this much talent with animals you may find yourself master of the horses someday." Tamberlake mussed up the boy's hair.

"Do you think so? I mean, thank you, my lord." Jim grinned.

As they left the stables, Ivy said, "I didn't know you were good with children."

"Neither did I. He's the first one that hasn't run away from me in years." He said nothing for a moment. "Do you ride?"

"I know how, but I don't often."

"I used to ride daily. It is perhaps the one thing I regret most about my accident." Tamberlake gazed at the stables. "Marsgrove had the finest stables. We still have a good number of horses. If the urge should strike, the groomsmen will find you a suitable mount."

She took his arm. "You don't speak often about your accident."

"There's little point in dwelling on what can't be changed." He shrugged. He wouldn't tell her he still suffered from nightmares on occasion.

As if she sensed his reluctance to speak about the subject, she asked, "So if you brought Shylock, does that mean Humphrey is here also?"

He smiled. "In the fountain outside the orangery."

She laughed. "What did your mother say when she saw the animals?"

"Let's just say she wasn't thrilled."

They walked around the back of the house to the formal garden outside the greenhouse. Humphrey quacked when he saw them and hopped from the fountain. Tamberlake bent down to stroke the feathers on the duck's back.

"Humphrey makes five," said Ivy.

"Five?" He looked up at his wife with curiosity.

"Familiar faces at Marsgrove. Six, if I count you."

He straightened and drew her into his arms. "Count me by all means. In fact, maybe I should count for two."

He kissed her.

* * *

Three days later, Ivy poured tea for her mother-in-law.

"I saw the notice in the paper this morning," said Lady Tamberlake. "You can expect the attention to begin at once."

"Do you really think so?"

"Don't sound so reluctant. The *ton* will be curious. They all knew of your betrothal to the Earl Wynbrooke and the consequent severing of ties. Even I knew of it, but I was forewarned by my son."

"I had rather hoped for more time before I had to appear in public."

"Nonsense. They will love you. You can be forgiven any scandal now that you are wed. Besides, no one would dare say anything against the Countess of Tamberlake."

Ivy wished she had Lady Tamberlake's confidence.

Whitson entered the drawing room. "Lady Coville to see you, Lady Tamberlake."

Ivy didn't know to which Lady Tamberlake he spoke.

The dowager countess patted Ivy on her knee. "Send her in, Whitson."

Lady Coville swept into the room as if she owned Marsgrove. Color rode high in her cheeks, and rage danced in her eyes. "Tell me it isn't true."

Lady Tamberlake gazed at the woman. "Daphne, how unexpected. Won't you join us for some tea?"

"I didn't come here for tea. Where is Auburn?" asked Lady Coville.

Ivy folded her hands in her lap. She struggled to maintain a calm demeanor and not let the panic she felt overwhelm her. Even in high fury, Lady Coville was beautiful.

"He'll be along in a moment, I'm sure. Won't you sit down?" asked Lady Tamberlake.

Lady Coville stared at her as if she were a deranged woman. "This is not a social call, Lady Tamberlake."

"I gathered that much from your excited entrance. You've suffered a disappointment." Lady Tamberlake poured tea into a third cup and offered it to the woman.

"Disappointment? You told me Auburn was looking for a wife. You said you'd be happy to see me in that position," said Lady Coville.

"And I didn't lie to you. Auburn was looking for a wife, but I could not control whom he decided on."

Lady Coville glared at Ivy. Ivy refused to shrink under the woman's scrutiny. "What did you do? Why did he marry you?"

"I don't know," said Ivy in all honesty. "I think I understand him well."

"You couldn't. You're a nobody. Why would he choose you when he could have had a woman like me?" Lady Coville paused, then let a wicked smile curve her lips. "You tricked him, didn't you? You're more devious than I thought. He wouldn't have married you unless he had to. What did you do? Did you lure him to your bed and let your father catch you?"

"Really. I should think you'd know Auburn is too clever to let himself get caught," said Ivy in a cool tone.

"He was to marry me. I was supposed to be the countess."

"Control yourself, Daphne. Don't make me regret my friendship with you," said Lady Tamberlake.

"Don't you see? She's fooled everyone with her drab dress and her mousy looks."

"That's enough," said Ivy. She stood. To her surprise, she didn't feel anger toward the woman, only a sort of pity—the same sort she would feel for Georgina when Georgina couldn't understand something. "What were you thinking? That you'd come into my home, insult me, and demand I give my husband an annulment? Or worse, a divorce? Go home, Lady Coville. With your beauty, you should have no trouble snaring another husband. You can't have mine."

Lady Coville's mouth dropped open. "You can't speak to me this way. Do you know who I am?"

"Yes. Do you know who *I* am? I am Ivy Seaton, Countess of Tamberlake."

"Well said." Auburn stood in the doorway. He grinned at Ivy, then proceeded into the room. "Good day, Daphne."

Lady Coville put on a pretty pout. "Auburn, you can't mean what you said."

"That I wish you a good day?" He continued forward until he stood by Ivy. "Daphne, I think you owe my wife an apology."

"What?" Her face transformed into a mask of rage. She didn't look so beautiful now. "We were to marry. She stole you from me."

"You misunderstood. We were never going to marry."

"But you said—"

"No, *you* said. I said I would consider it. I did, and I decided marriage to you wouldn't be beneficial."

"Your mother told me she gave us her approval."

"My mother wasn't the one to decide. I made my own choice of bride." Tamberlake paused. "But your offer made me curious. Why would you want to marry me when you can't bear to look at me? Shall I tell you what I discovered?"

Lady Coville grew pale. "What?"

"That your husband left you very little money when he died and the present Earl Coville doesn't like you much. Perhaps you should have been a little kinder to your stepson."

"That wasn't the reason I wanted to marry you. I never stopped loving you."

Tamberlake shook his head. "You don't love me. You didn't love me when we were betrothed. We were fond of each other, but you never loved me."

"How can you say that?"

"Because it's the truth. You can't even look at me, and you want me to believe you love me?" Tamberlake sat on the sofa. "Go home, Daphne, before you make a bigger fool of yourself than you already have."

Lady Coville turned red. "I'm not the one making a fool of myself. You are. You'll see when she cuckolds you, when she finds a man who is whole. At least *I* never lied to you."

"Get out," said Ivy.

The woman turned to face her. "You will regret this." Lady Coville pivoted on her heel and stormed from the room.

For a moment no one spoke. Then Lady Tamberlake offered the untouched cup of tea to her son. "Well, that was unpleasant, wasn't it?"

"I thought you liked her, Mother," said Tamberlake.

Lady Tamberlake shrugged her shoulders. "I did."

"You wanted me to marry her."

"That was before I knew about Ivy." Lady Tamberlake sat back. She let out a long sigh. "A short while ago, before you returned home, your atrocious cousin, Raymond, came to Marsgrove. When I asked him the reason for his visit, he said he wanted to see what changes he would make when he became earl. Can you imagine that buffoon as earl? He believed, as did most of the *ton*, you would die without an heir and he would inherit."

"And you, Mother? What did you believe?" he asked.

"I won't deny it. I thought the same. I thought you'd never find a woman to marry you. When you returned home and Daphne showed an interest in you, I encouraged her so Raymond couldn't inherit."

"Because he would turn you out."

"That's partly true. I would have nowhere to go. But he would make a terrible earl." Lady Tamberlake rose. She crossed to her son. "And despite my selfishness, I am glad you found Ivy. She suits you much better than Daphne ever could." Lady Tamberlake left the room.

"Well, that was interesting." Tamberlake sipped the tea and grimaced. "Too cold."

Ivy didn't know what to think. She didn't know whether to be outraged at Lady Tamberlake's lack of belief in her son or to be pleased that Lady Tamberlake approved of her. Her conflict must have shown on her face.

"Don't be too upset with her. My mother is nothing if not honest. I think if we didn't have our verbal battles we wouldn't know how to talk with each other." Tamberlake poured the cold tea into a nearby plant and refreshed his cup. "Besides, she's right."

Ivy bristled with indignation. "She most certainly is not. I don't see why anyone would think you couldn't find a wife—"

Tamberlake laughed. "No, not about that. Raymond *would* make a terrible earl."

Chapter 28

The nightmare began in the same way. Before the images became clear in his mind, Tamberlake whimpered in protest.

He was coming home from a party, his head lolling against the cushion of the carriage seat. The soft glow from the carriage lanterns lit the interior. He was drowsy and happy. Why shouldn't he be? Young, handsome, rich, and he was engaged to a beautiful girl.

Tamberlake stirred in his bed. As he watched the unfolding scene in his mind, he tried to warn the young man to be vigilant, but the young man closed his eyes and let a foolish smile spread across his lips at the memory of a few stolen kisses.

Blow out the lamp, you fool, screamed Tamberlake in his mind, but no one listened.

The carriage hit a bump and rocked from side to side. He paid no attention to the motion. But the rocking persisted, then the coach started to tilt. The young man opened his eyes in panic as the carriage toppled to its side and continued to roll over an embankment. His head struck the side as he tumbled within the coach. He heard glass shattering, and then he screamed as pain slashed across his face. Clutching his eye in agony, he felt the wet slickness of blood between his fingers. But only for an instant, for in the next moment, the motion of the carriage flung his hand from his face. Tossed about in the belly of the coach, he heard a snap, and pain erupted in his thigh.

Tamberlake moaned. He knew the worst came next.

When the carriage settled, it lay on its side. The young man sprawled across the interior, not daring to move. He looked down at his leg, and nearly passed out. The white end of a bone stuck out through a tear in his trousers, and his leg twisted beneath him at an unnatural angle. He could only see out of one eye.

Move, urged Tamberlake in his sleep.

Smoke gathered at the top of the inverted carriage. The young man groaned and started to cough. Orange flames licked at the curtains on the broken windows, but he hadn't seen them yet.

Move, shouted Tamberlake again, but he couldn't hear his own voice.

The flame crept closer to the young man's face, singeing his hair. He turned toward the heat and screamed as the side of his face received the full blast of the growing flames.

"Auburn, wake up."

Tamberlake rolled over and blinked. Ivy stood over him, shaking him, yelling at him.

"Auburn, wake up."

He sat up. "I'm awake." His neck was wet with sweat, and his heart raced in fear.

She sat beside him on the bed and brushed his hair from his face. "Are you ill?"

"No. I'm fine." He looked away from her.

"You cried out several times. I heard you through the door. When I came in, you moaned, then screamed. You frightened me."

"It was only a nightmare." He didn't face her. "Go back to bed."

"Are you sure? I could—"

He whipped his head around. "Go back to bed!"

Ivy jumped up and clapped her hand over her mouth. "I'm sorry." She started back toward the door.

"No, wait."

She stopped.

"Please . . ." He drew in a deep breath. "I'm sorry. No one . . . no one has ever seen me like this." He reached for her and she returned to the side of the bed. He pulled her down beside him. "I had a nightmare. It's one I've had many times before."

"This has happened before?"

He nodded.

"What happens in your dream?"

"The accident." He buried his face in his hands. "I relive every moment. The pain, the fear, it's all real again. And each time I think, *This is the night I won't make it out of the burning carriage.*"

"But you do. I mean, you did."

"That doesn't stop the dream." He paused, unsure whether to tell her more. "Just after the accident, I dreamed it every time I slept."

"And now?"

"Seldom. But when I do, it's as real as it was when it happened."

Ivy laid her head on his shoulder.

He put his arms around her. "Stay with me tonight."

She nodded. He pulled back the covers for her, and Ivy climbed in beside him. Her head rested on his arm, and she curled her back against his stomach.

He settled back and folded his arms around his wife. As he closed his eyes, he realized he didn't feel his normal apprehension at falling asleep. This was the perfect cure to any nightmare. He'd have to discuss this with Ivy. No more separate bedrooms for the Countess and Earl of Tamberlake.

The next day, Fletcher found them in the library. He bowed to Tamberlake. "Excuse me, my lord. Mr. Savernake is here. I showed him to your study."

"Thank you, Fletcher." Tamberlake stood and held out his hand to Ivy. "I think you should hear this as well."

When they entered the room, Mr. Savernake rose from his chair.

Tamberlake nodded to the man. "Mr. Savernake, my wife."

"A pleasure to meet you, Lady Tamberlake." The visitor bowed to her.

"Please sit. What have you learned?" asked Tamberlake.

"Very little, my lord." Mr. Savernake pulled out a sheet of paper. "Lord Wynbrooke was indeed absent from his estate on the date you mentioned, but I found no evidence of his presence in Devon. He still might have been there, but I couldn't find proof."

Ivy turned to Tamberlake. She gave him a

slanted glance. "You think Wynbrooke is behind the shooting?"

"I think it a strong possibility."

"I can't imagine Wynbrooke doing such a thing." Ivy shook her head.

Tamberlake faced his visitor. "Did you find out anything else?"

"Nothing to help discover the identity of the gunman," said Savernake. "Do you wish me to continue my investigations?"

"Yes."

"Then may I ask a few questions?" Savernake turned to Ivy. "Do you know of anyone who might wish you harm, my lady?"

Tamberlake straightened. "You can't think someone tried to kill my wife?"

"My lord, at this moment, we can't be sure whether the shots were meant to kill you or your wife. Or possibly even both of you."

Tamberlake opened his mouth to respond, but Ivy's voice interrupted him.

"What about Lady Coville?"

Savernake wrote the name in his notebook. "Is this the same Lady Coville you asked me to find the information on earlier?"

"The same." Tamberlake sighed. "She came by yesterday and expressed her ... disappointment over my marriage. But my wife and I weren't even betrothed when I went to Devon."

"Nevertheless, she may have sensed what was happening. I'll look into it," said Savernake. "Anyone else?"

Ivy remained silent for a while, then shook her head. "No one that I can think of."

"And you, my lord?"

"The only enemy I've made recently is Wynbrooke." He felt Ivy's gaze. "And yes, Lady Coville."

"What of your cousin?" asked Ivy in the next moment.

"Raymond?" Tamberlake was surprised.

"Who is this Raymond?" asked Savernake.

"My cousin, Raymond Seaton. He stands to inherit if I die without heirs."

Ivy turned to Savernake. "Lady Tamberlake told us he came to Marsgrove not long ago to see his inheritance. This was before Lord Tamberlake returned to society, you understand."

"A definite possibility." Savernake closed his notebook and rose. "Very well. I'll see where Lady Coville and your cousin were while you were in Devon and continue my investigation of Lord Wynbrooke. Good day, my lord, my lady."

Fletcher saw the visitor to the door. Ivy crossed to her husband and put her arms around him. "Do you really think someone was trying to kill us?"

"I can think of no other explanation." He kissed the top of her head.

"I'm frightened." A tremor shook her body. "Do you think he will try again?"

He wanted to protect her, but knew he couldn't hide the truth. "Yes, I do. I think that's why I had the nightmare. After my accident, I had it every night, but now I only dream it when there's turmoil in my life. I'd say getting shot at qualifies as turmoil."

"How can you be so glib?"

"What else can I do? I can let the fiend control me with fear, or I can joke about it."

"It's not that easy for me."

"You must take your mind off of it." Tamberlake looked around and handed her a small stack of sealed papers. "Look at these. They arrived today."

Ivy stared at the top sheet. An ornate monogram embellished the parchment. She broke the seal. "It's an invitation from the Duke of Grantham."

"Good old Budgie."

"Budgie?"

"I went to school with him. A more hopeless creature you could never chance to meet. He was heir to a dukedom, and his parents despaired that he would never be ready. I believe he inherited last year."

"Was he a good friend at school?"

"Well, 'friend' isn't the right word. I saved him from the torment of some of the other boys, and he started to follow me around. He never did me any harm, even if he was a pest at times."

"Why was he called Budgie?"

Tamberlake thought for a moment. "He had this hideous coat lined with budge. The thing was old, and most of us were convinced it smelled, but he wore it anyway. He could have easily replaced the thing, but he loved that ratty old coat. And besides, the name suits him."

"He's having a ball, and he's invited us. Do you think we should go?"

"If you want to."

"But if someone is trying to kill us . . . you . . . whomever, do you think it wise?"

Tamberlake took her hands. "We can stay here and let our fear grow, or we can go out and force the man to show his hand. Savernake is a thorough man. If there's something to find, he will. In the meantime, we shall be vigilant."

Ivy thought for a moment. "I think I would like to meet this Budgie."

"It might be fun at that. But don't say you weren't warned."

Ivy looked at the other two papers. "They're invitations as well. Looks like your mother was right."

"What did she say?"

"That the *ton* would forgive us any scandal and be curious about us. I expect more will come tomorrow. Do we have to attend them all?"

"Of course not. No one expects to see much of me yet. I'm still regarded as somewhat of a recluse. I'll leave the decisions to you." He paused. "You look surprised."

"Father never let Mother decide which invitations to accept. Heaven forbid she turn down the wrong one, or worse, attend one with no one of importance." Ivy laughed. "Then we shall see His Grace, Budgie, and I'll decide on the rest later."

Chapter 29

With trembling fingers, Ivy smoothed her dress. Lady Tamberlake had helped her pick out the material and the style. Ivy thought it looked fine, but she would have liked Mrs. Pennyfeather's opinion on it. She glanced up at the enormous chandelier above her. The tiny gas flames illuminated the foyer. She wondered how long it took the servants to light it. Anything to keep her mind from the people about to see her.

"The Earl and Countess of Tamberlake."

Ivy held her breath. This was their first appearance since their wedding. Her grip tightened on Tamberlake's arm.

"Don't worry. You'll do fine."

They entered the ballroom of the duke's immense house.

"Where is he? I haven't seen Tamberlake in years," came a voice from among the crowd.

"The duke," whispered Tamberlake in her ear. A short, pudgy man with a round, friendly face came toward them. "Tamberlake, I—egad, man, what happened to your face?"

Ivy stiffened beside her husband. She was about to lash out at the duke, but the man continued.

"I heard you were injured, but I didn't know what had happened. You're terribly ugly now, aren't you?"

"I was never handsome before, Your Grace," said Tamberlake with a smile.

"Balderdash. You had all the women swooning around you. And what is this 'Your Grace' nonsense? Call me Budgie as you always did." The duke clasped Tamberlake's hand and pumped it vigorously. "I meant to go see you when you were hurt, but by the time I got around to visiting, you had disappeared. Doesn't matter now. Damned good to have you here."

"It's good to see you, too, Budgie."

Budgie turned to Ivy. She didn't know how to react to him. On the one hand, his reaction to her husband's face irritated her. On the other, the rest of his greeting was filled with genuine pleasure and friendship. And Auburn didn't seem to care.

"And this must be your wife." Budgie bowed over her hand. "Lady Tamberlake, such a pleasure to meet you."

Ivy chose politeness as her course of action. "The pleasure is mine, Your Grace."

"Budgie, please. You must call me Budgie. Your husband is a dear friend of mine. I shall never forget how he helped me at school." The duke stepped back and tripped over his own feet. He stumbled into an artificial column upon which sat an elaborate flower arrangement. The column wobbled. Guests standing nearby screamed and scrambled to get out of the way. The flowers crashed to the

floor first. Then, toppling like some ancient arti-
fact on an unsteady base, the column fell. After
the dust settled, two large pieces of plaster deco-
rated the ballroom like the ruins of Pompeii.

Budgie let out a puff of air. "I'll wager that just
set me back a few pounds. Good thing I have a pot
of money."

Ivy stared at the duke. Budgie didn't seem to be
any more upset than if he had just swatted a fly.

"What have you been doing lately, Budgie?"
asked Tamberlake.

"Became the duke last year when my father died.
Been in mourning since then. This is the first ball
I've held. I had to hire someone to do the work, of
course. Couldn't have done it myself."

As she watched Budgie speak, Ivy noticed the
duke had no problem looking her husband in
the face. Budgie's demeanor radiated warmth and
ease with him.

"Mother wants me to find a wife, but those
young things scare me," said Budgie. "I think I
scare them as well, because after I talk with them a
little while, they seem to lose interest in me. What
I'd like to find is a young widow who knows how to
handle a man."

Ivy's mouth nearly dropped open, but Tamberlake whispered in her ear, "He doesn't mean it that
way."

Budgie glanced at Ivy, then waved his finger in
excitement. "You found yourself a wife, even with
your face. She's very pretty, and I'll wager smart,
too. Do you suppose I should get myself one of those
eye patches and see if it helps?" Budgie squinted
his left eye, then covered it with his hand. His face
screwed up in an effort to gaze around the room.

Tamberlake laughed. "No, Budgie, I don't think it would help you. I'd concentrate on telling everyone how rich you are."

"Do you think that will get me a wife?"

"Undoubtedly."

"What do you think, Lady Tamberlake? You fell for the patch, didn't you? Although now that I think of it, Tamberlake has quite a bit of booty at that."

She was saved from answering when the footman announced another name.

"More guests. I suppose I should go greet them," said Budgie. "But I will find you later. I want to hear more about your life, Tamberlake." The duke scurried off.

"And that is Budgie," said Tamberlake. "Thick as a goat."

Ivy looked after the man. "Was he always like that?"

"Only if he liked you."

They circled the room. Tamberlake introduced her to friends, none of whom seemed as wholly accepting of him as Budgie had been, and Ivy saw some of her acquaintances. Overall, curiosity far outweighed the disdain over her actions of the past month. Lady Tamberlake had been right.

"So you decided to come out and show society what a happily wedded couple you are," came a woman's voice from behind them.

Ivy turned toward the familiar voice. Lady Coville sipped from a glass of champagne. Her deep blue gown accentuated the creaminess of her skin and the gold of her hair.

"Good evening, Daphne," said Tamberlake.

"My, aren't we polite this evening?" she asked in

a mocking tone. "You'd be better served if you greeted me with the cut direct."

"I have no desire to hurt you," said Tamberlake.

"It's too late for that," Daphne said.

"There you are." Budgie's jovial voice boomed over Daphne's hushed tones. "I've been looking for you. So what were we talking about?"

"Finding you a wife," said Tamberlake. An intriguing glint flashed in his eye. "Budgie, I don't believe you've met the Lady Coville."

Budgie turned and gaped at Daphne. "Gad, you're beautiful. Did I invite you?"

"Yes, Your Grace." Daphne dipped into a curtsey.

"Good, good. I told my secretary to invite everybody because I'm hopeless at these things. I'll have to tell him he did well."

"Lady Coville is a widow," said Tamberlake.

"You don't say." Budgie stopped as if he suddenly remembered his earlier words. "You don't say. Then this is my lucky night. May I have a dance, Lady Coville?"

He swung out his arm and jostled Daphne's elbow. Her champagne sloshed over the edge of the glass, spilling down her bodice. Daphne shrieked. A spreading stain darkened the blue of her dress.

"I'm such a great, clumsy oaf," said Budgie, and he pulled out a handkerchief from his pocket and began to blot up the drops from Daphne's chest.

"Your Grace!" exclaimed a woman nearby.

"What? Did I get some on you as well?" His hand still worked at Daphne's chest.

Tamberlake leaned to his friend. "Perhaps if you stopped pawing Lady Coville's chest . . ."

"What?" Budgie looked at his hand, and a most

horrified expression appeared on his face. Ivy couldn't tell whose face was redder, Budgie's or Daphne's.

A footman appeared at Budgie's side. "Your Grace, if you will permit me, I shall lead the lady away to freshen up."

"Yes, yes, by all means." Budgie crumpled the handkerchief into the palm of his hand and almost stuffed it into his pocket, then thought better of it, switched hands, and tried a different pocket.

"If you'll permit me again, Your Grace . . ." The footman held out his hand.

Budgie dropped the soggy cloth into it.

"Thank you, Your Grace," said the footman. He turned to Lady Coville and gave a crisp bow. "If you would follow me, my lady."

With a crestfallen expression, Budgie watched the footman lead Daphne away. "I've muffed it again, haven't I?"

"Well, she'll certainly remember you after this, and that's half the battle," said Tamberlake with a smile.

"Do you really think so?" asked Budgie, his voice ringing with hope. "She's so pretty."

"Just keep mentioning that pot of money you have," said Tamberlake.

"And send her a totally impractical gift as an apology," added Ivy. She smiled at the amused glance her husband sent her.

"Excellent idea." Budgie rubbed his hands together. "What sort of impractical gift are you thinking of?"

"I don't know," said Ivy. "Perfume, or a silk shawl, or—"

"Jewelry? Would jewelry make a good gift? Women seem to like that sort of thing."

"A first-rate thought, Budgie. See, you're grasping this courtship thing already," said Tamberlake.

"Right. I'll go tell my secretary right now, shall I? Excuse me." Budgie walked off, practically dancing with every step and oblivious to the people scurrying out of his way.

"What if Daphne does become duchess?" asked Ivy.

"What if she does?"

"It's not really a just retribution for her conduct, is it?"

"You think not?"

"To make Daphne a duchess?"

Tamberlake smiled. "How would you feel if you had to spend a lifetime with Budgie?"

"I'd be screaming after an hour." Ivy laughed, then sobered. "But Budgie is sweet."

"Yes, he is."

"I wouldn't like to see him hurt by anyone. If Daphne weds him—"

"Daphne isn't a bad woman. A bit misguided, perhaps, but not bad. Besides, Budgie may be a little thick-witted, but he's a highly moral man. If, and mind you we are a long way from seeing it happen, Daphne were duchess, she had better mind herself. He won't stand for any duplicity."

"Still, it would be easy to fool him. I would hate to see him unhappy."

"Exactly. Budgie inspires loyalty, and his staff is more than capable of taking care of him. They would never allow him to be made a fool of." Tamberlake took her hand. "You see, Budgie's greatest strength is that he knows he's stupid, and so he surrounds himself with people who aren't."

Ivy absorbed this for a moment, then laughed again. "Can you really imagine Daphne as his duchess?"

"Yes, I can. And if she's half as intelligent as I think she is, she will see it, too." He kissed her hand. "Do you really want to spend the evening talking about Budgie and his possible wife?"

A tremor of excitement skittered through her. "No."

"Then I think we've made enough of an appearance." Tamberlake led her through the maze of guests toward the door.

Chapter 30

With Ivy snuggled against his side, Tamberlake wouldn't mind the hour-long drive back to Marsgrove. He wondered how she'd react if he tried to seduce her in the coach. He'd wait until they were outside London to investigate.

When they left the lights of the city, the road became dark. The carriage lamps shone forward a short distance, but darkness hid most of the road. Usually he liked the darkness, but tonight it seemed menacing. Perhaps it was the lingering effect of his nightmare, or knowing it was on just such a night his accident occurred. Either way, Tamberlake felt restless. His disquiet sent all thoughts of seduction from him.

"Is something wrong?" asked Ivy.

"No," he said softly and stroked her arm.

"It's so quiet. I'm beginning to think we should have stayed at Budgie's party."

He shot a glance at her in the darkness. The night *was* quiet. He could only hear the dull thud of the horses' hooves against the dirt.

"What the devil?" The driver's voice rang out from his perch. The coach slowed.

"Rufus?" Tamberlake leaned toward the window.

"Stand and deliver," came a voice from in front of the coach.

A highwayman? Here? Now? This was absurd. There hadn't been highwaymen on these roads in decades. *Stand and deliver*? Had he learned his trade from Gothic novels?

"Do as I say, and no one will be hurt," the voice said.

"What's happening?" whispered Ivy. She started to move toward the window.

He pulled her back down. "I don't know yet, but stay down."

In the next moment, Rufus cracked his whip, then the carriage lurched forward. Reaching for Ivy, Tamberlake fell back onto the seat. From outside, he heard a curse, then the sound of a rifle shot. Something hit the side of the carriage. This was no highwayman. Someone had ambushed them.

The carriage rolled forward, but from the roof, Rufus let out a shout. The horses neighed, and the squeal of the brakes on the wheels ripped through the air. The carriage shook and rattled, then bumped high into the air.

Crack. Tamberlake might have thought lightning had hit them, but he knew the sky was clear tonight. It wasn't a shot this time. It sounded more like breaking wood.

The carriage jerked to a stop, throwing Ivy to the floor. She screamed.

"Ivy," he cried. Because of the darkness, Tamberlake couldn't make sense of what was happening. Then a vertigo hit him, and he felt as though the world was spinning.

He knew this feeling. He had experienced it once before. The carriage was toppling.

"Hang on," he shouted.

The carriage rolled onto its side. He braced himself and tried to hold onto Ivy. She slipped through his grasp. With a small cry, she fell past him and hit the side of the coach. He could only hold his position for an instant longer, then fell on top of her.

The carriage rocked for a moment, then settled on its side. With care, Tamberlake picked himself up. Ivy lay in a crumpled heap all around him. Through the tangle of her skirts and crinoline, Tamberlake couldn't tell if she was injured.

"Ivy."

She didn't answer.

"Ivy," he shouted. He knelt beside her and lifted her head.

"Yes, I'm here," she whispered.

"Lie still." He couldn't see very well, so he ran his hands over her arms and legs. He found no blood. "Can you move?"

"I think so." Ivy pulled her legs under her and pushed up to her hands and knees. "My head hurts, though, and I feel a little dizzy."

"Don't move." Tamberlake stood until his head touched the other side. The carriage door was above his head. He unhooked the latch and tossed the door open. He could easily lift her out, then push himself up.

Poking his head out, he looked around. The moon was waning and offered little illumination. He couldn't see his driver. "Rufus?"

A light flashed from the trees to his right. Less than a second later, he heard the report. Wood splintered on the carriage. He ducked down.

"Auburn," yelled Ivy.

"I'm fine. I think whoever wants to kill us is out there."

"What are we going to do?"

"I don't know yet." He had to think. If he tried to climb out now, the gunman would try to shoot again, but if he stayed here, the assassin would find him easy prey.

A scent reached him, a smell that left him more terrified than when the carriage rolled. Smoke. The carriage lamps must have ignited the wood.

Memories assailed him. His breath grew uneven, and a phantom pain slashed across his face. He struggled to restrain his panic.

"Auburn," said Ivy. "What's wrong?"

He must have fallen to his knees, for when he turned to her, her face was even with his. "The carriage is on fire."

She cradled one side of her head with her hand. "We have to get out."

His thinking cleared. He needed to save her. "Listen to me, Ivy. I'll climb out first, then pull you up." That way he would shield her with his body. He only hoped the gunman wouldn't shoot him before he saved her.

"But if the gunman is out there . . ."

"We have no choice." Tamberlake held her by her shoulders. "Once you're on top, jump down and run, understand?"

"I won't leave you."

"We don't have time to argue. Do as I say."

Smoke poured into the small enclosure. Ivy coughed and muttered something incomprehensible. He couldn't wait any longer. "Stand up, Ivy."

He hoisted himself onto the top side of the carriage, then lay flat. He reached into the opening. Ivy tried to stand and crumpled to the ground.

"Stand up, Ivy!" He shouted at her as if he reprimanded her. "You must stand up!"

She struggled to pull herself up. Even in the dim light he saw the tears coursing down her face. "I'm so dizzy."

She must have hit her head harder than he believed at first. "Be strong. Stand up for just a moment."

Gritting her teeth, she did as he said. He reached into the doorway, hooked his arms under hers, and pulled Ivy up through the opening. He gathered her into his arms and jumped from the top of the overturned carriage.

His weak leg crumpled as they landed. He rolled so that his body took the brunt of the fall, but Ivy groaned. Flames now spouted from the open doorway at the top.

"Did I hurt you?"

"I don't think so," she whispered. "But my head is spinning."

"We must move from here." Tamberlake picked her up, but the jump must have injured his leg, for he buckled to the ground again. "I can't carry you. Can you run?"

"I can try."

"Then go. Toward the trees. That way." He pointed away from the direction of the gunshot.

She started away from the carriage. Tamberlake pushed himself off the ground and followed with his uneven gait. His cane was now additional fodder for the fire that was consuming the coach. His leg ached, but he ignored the pain.

The light from the blaze threw an uneven glow across the ground. He could see why Rufus had stopped so suddenly. A large tree lay across the road, and the wheel of the carriage had shattered. The horses danced in agitated frenzy. They were still attached to the burning hulk of the carriage. They whinnied and stamped their feet, and their eyes flashed with terror. He couldn't let them burn.

"Ivy, hide yourself. Stay away from the fire," he yelled. As he started toward the animals, he saw his driver lying across the road.

Another loud shot split the night. Dirt and grass flew up at him.

"Auburn," screamed Ivy.

"I'm fine. Stay where you are." He didn't know how much longer the gunman would miss him, but he had to save Rufus.

The man lay sprawled on the ground. Tamberlake hooked his arms under Rufus's shoulders and pulled. As his weight fell on his weak leg, he stumbled back. He groaned at the pain, but continued to pull Rufus away from the flames. When he reached the outer rim of the fire's light, he stopped and put the driver on the ground.

Crack. Wood from the tree rained over him in a shower of splinters. The shot had been louder this time. The gunman must be getting closer. Tamberlake knew his luck couldn't hold much longer.

The horses screamed in fear, a horrible and pathetic sound. He needed to save them. He stepped toward the fire. The crackle and roar of the flames as they ate the carriage deafened him.

The fire heated the side of his face as he reached for the buckles on the first harness. He sucked in his breath as the hot metal burned his fingers. He undid the first buckle, then reached for the second.

One horse reared, nearly trampling him under her flying hooves. He stepped back. "Easy, girl, easy. I'm here to help."

At the sound of his voice, the horses let out a high-pitched whinny. He reached for the leather again and the next buckle.

The fire crept closer to him. The heat was so intense it singed the hair on his arm. Tamberlake worked as fast as he could, but his fingers grew clumsy.

There. He pulled the trace free of the carriage. He slapped his hand on the mare's rump. "Get up, girl."

The horse neighed and pulled on the leather straps. They hung loose. Sensing she was free, she bolted forward, knocking Tamberlake aside. He forced himself to remain on his feet. The other horse whinnied after its companion. He hobbled to the other side and started on the second harness.

"Why can't you just die, Tamberlake?" The barrel of a rifle shone in the brightness of the fire.

Tamberlake whipped his head around. Thorndike?

Thorndike stepped in front of him. "Where's Ivy?"

"Safe." Tamberlake resisted the urge to glance toward her.

"I don't want to kill *her*, you fool." Thorndike lifted the rifle.

Tamberlake never stopped working on the harness. The first buckle was unfastened.

"Why aren't you trying to save yourself?" Thorndike peered at him. "You must know I'm going to kill you."

Tamberlake looked at the man. In the brightness of the firelight, Thorndike's eyes glowed red like those of a demon, but Tamberlake felt no fear. "I can't run away, so why bother?"

"You'd save these dumb animals instead?"

"They don't deserve to die. You want to kill me anyway. What difference does it make if the fire does it for you?" He had to shout over the noise of the fire to be heard. The heat burned his face, but he forced himself to keep working on the harness.

"Look at me," yelled Thorndike.

Tamberlake raised his gaze. He was looking down the barrel of the rifle.

"You see, we did have another choice after all." Thorndike smiled.

Just then sparks flew from the fire and landed on the horse's rump. The animal neighed and stamped its feet. Thorndike glanced toward the movement. In that instant, Tamberlake grabbed the barrel and yanked it from Thorndike's hands. He tossed the weapon into the flames.

The unused cartridges exploded in the fire, sending tongues of flames shooting into the air. The horse reared. Its withers hit Tamberlake, knocking him to the ground. Tamberlake rolled from the fire, and turned back to see the animal striking out with its front hooves, then beating the ground as he landed. It reared again, wrenching itself free of the harness. Neighing, the horse ran from the burning wreckage after its companion.

Out of breath, Tamberlake lay back, and tried to inhale slowly, but coughed instead. His arms stung from the burns, and his leg ached as much as it ever had. He lay on the ground, knowing he should move, knowing any moment Thorndike would arrive to murder him.

Groaning with the effort, Tamberlake pushed himself to his hands and knees. Mustering all his strength, he stood and looked for Thorndike. He couldn't see the man anywhere. Then his gaze fell to where the other horse had stood. Thorndike lay on the ground close to the fire. At that moment, a section of the coach collapsed, throwing burning embers onto Thorndike's arm. The man screamed and tried to roll away.

Tamberlake limped to where Thorndike lay. Blood poured from a wound on the man's scalp and his breathing was labored. His leg stuck out at an unnatural angle, and through a tear in his shirt, Tamberlake could see the imprint of a hoof on his chest. The horse had trampled him.

Thorndike's eyes focused on him. "Damn you, Tamberlake."

Tamberlake ignored the taunt. Grimacing against the pain shooting through him, he pulled Thorndike away from the flames. With every inch, Thorndike let out a moan. When they were far enough away, Tamberlake laid Thorndike onto the ground, then let himself fall beside him.

"You ruined everything," said Thorndike with a rasp. "You've ruined Wyn."

"He ruined himself."

"Ivy's money could have saved him. And as your widow, she would have brought him more." Thorndike coughed, and a thin stream of blood trickled from the corner of his mouth.

"It was you in Devon." It wasn't a question.

"Yes."

"You wasted your time. Ivy knows about you and Wynbrooke. She never would have married him."

Thorndike's eyes filled with tears. "Damn you again. He doesn't deserve such a fate. He can't work."

"No, but you could have."

"I wanted to save him." Thorndike coughed again. "I loved him. I truly loved him."

Tamberlake felt compassion stir within him. Despite knowing this man had tried to kill him, despite the destruction Thorndike had wrought this night, he pitied the man.

"Tell Wyn . . . tell him . . ." Thorndike drew in a breath that was little more than a rattle.

"I will." Tamberlake looked down at him.

"Thank you," whispered Thorndike. He let out a final soft breath, and his eyes focused, unseeing, on the stars.

Tamberlake pushed himself off the ground. Ivy. He needed to see Ivy. Before he could walk a yard, she was there. Stumbling, his every step unsteady, he limped to her. She ran forward and closed the gap between them. She threw her arms around him. They fell to the ground.

"I told you to stay away."

"You didn't say *please.*" Her tears washed a clear path through a streak of soot on her cheek.

Despite the enormity of the night's events, he chuckled.

She looked at the body on the ground. "Thorndike?"

He nodded.

"Is he . . . ?"

"Dead."

"He tried to kill you."

"I know." He stroked her hair.

Ivy blinked at the light of the fire. She struggled to sit up. "Are you hurt?"

Putting his arms around her, he leaned her against his chest. "No, but you are." His fingers probed her scalp until she winced.

"It's nothing."

"Nothing? You should feel the bump I found."

She shook her head gently. "Why? Did he explain why?"

"I'll explain it all later, but now I want you to remember this." He kissed her then, a gentle, caring kiss. "I almost lost you."

"Then you do care for me."

He looked at her in surprise. "How could you think otherwise?"

"You've never said . . ." She dropped her gaze.

He cupped her face in his hands. "You are my light, my joy, my air. You brought me back to the world when I wanted to be dead. You saw behind the mask I wore and found a man. You made me whole again."

Her tears grew in strength. "I love you, Auburn."

"And I love you, Ivy." He kissed her again.

Chapter 31

"You have visitors, my lady," said Whitson.

"Thank you," said Ivy. A few moments later her mother and sister came into the drawing room.

"Married life seems to agree with you, Ivy," said her mother, taking in the elaborate furnishings of the room.

Ivy smiled. Since the events of three nights ago, married life hardly seemed normal. Although Rufus would recover in time, and the hair would grow back on Tamberlake's arms, her husband was at this moment at Rosmartin Park. Wynbrooke had collected Thorndike's body and taken it back with him to his home. Most of the *ton* knew only that they had had a carriage accident that night, for they had both agreed Wynbrooke didn't deserve undue scrutiny. Thorndike had acted alone.

"Have you recovered from the accident?" asked Lady Dunleigh.

"Yes, Mother. I'm fine now."

"And Tamberlake?"

"He's well." Ivy indicated chairs for them to sit on. "What brings you this way?"

"Oh, we were just out doing some shopping and thought we'd stop by," said Georgina.

Ivy raised an eyebrow. "Marsgrove isn't anywhere near London and shopping, Georgina. What do you want?"

"I told you she was too clever to believe that story," said Georgina with a frown.

"It's Mrs. Pennyfeather," said Lady Dunleigh.

"What of her?"

"She's gone."

Ivy shot to her feet. "She's missing?"

"No, no." Lady Dunleigh waved her hands. "She resigned yesterday."

Giving her mother a puzzled glance, Ivy sat. "And?"

"Well, she can't leave. I need her help. She took care of so many details that I found tiresome, so I could concentrate on finding Georgina a husband."

"Hire someone else," said Ivy.

"But I was used to Mrs. Pennyfeather. I told her I wouldn't give her a recommendation, but she just smiled and said she didn't need one. So I thought . . ." Lady Dunleigh paused.

"You thought what?"

"Well, she liked you best, and you seemed to get along so well. Perhaps if you talked to her, you could convince her to come back."

Ivy shook her head. "If Mrs. Pennyfeather wants to leave, you can't stop her, Mother. Besides, I don't even know where she is."

"But you could find her if you wanted to," said Lady Dunleigh.

"You just don't want me to get married," said Georgina with a pout. She sniffed and pulled out a handkerchief.

"You don't need Mrs. Pennyfeather to get married," said Ivy, not in the least moved by her sister's playacting.

"But, Ivy—" began her mother.

Ivy lifted her hand. "If I see Mrs. Pennyfeather I shall talk to her, but I doubt I shall run into her. In the meantime, you'll need new dresses."

Georgina's expression cleared at once. "Why?"

"Tamberlake and I shall be hosting a ball soon. As the sister of the new countess, you'll need to be especially pretty. I'll make sure to invite many eligible bachelors for you."

"Oh, Ivy, you are a good sister." Georgina threw her arms around her.

Lady Dunleigh dabbed at the corner of her eyes. "My girls. You make me so proud."

"You'd better get that shopping done." Ivy rose.

"An excellent idea," said her mother. "We'll return to town and see if anything inspires us. Then we'll help you settle on a theme."

Ivy pasted a smile on her face. "An excellent idea."

"Georgina, what would you think of an underwater ball?" asked Lady Dunleigh as they left the room. "Blues and silvers always looked so nice on you."

"I could dress as a mermaid . . ."

As their voices faded, Ivy shook her head. At least she was successful in diverting their attention and getting rid of them, although she didn't know what Tamberlake would say to an underwater ball.

Tamberlake stretched his leg out in front of him. Since the accident three nights past, it had troubled him more than usual, but then again, he *had* overused it. He winced slightly as the muscle pulled, but it was a good ache—an ache that showed it was strengthening.

He was drained after his morning's meeting with Wynbrooke. He had told the man the truth about the attempt on his life, and also Thorndike's final words. Wynbrooke's eyes had filled with tears, but he thanked Tamberlake for his discretion. Once again, Tamberlake had felt pity move him for the man's genuine grief, and he was glad they had decided to conceal the truth from the *ton*. Without any hesitation, he handed over all proof of the man's activities.

The door to the study opened. "You're back," said Ivy, and she ran to him. She kissed him, pressing her breasts into his chest.

A long moment later, he chuckled. "If you greet me like this every time I come back from an errand, perhaps I should leave more often."

"Don't you dare," she answered with a laugh. "Christopher sent a letter. He's doing well, but he wants to know if you want him to repair the byre for use again."

"I shall have to write and tell him it's his decision." He pulled her down beside him. "Did you know Mrs. Pennyfeather was here?"

She looked taken aback. "No. How odd. My mother came to see me about her this morning."

Before he could respond, Fletcher came into the study. "Excuse me, my lord."

"Yes, Fletcher."

"Two things, sir. First, this letter has arrived for you and Lady Tamberlake." He held out a salver with a folded parchment on it.

Tamberlake took it. "Thank you, Fletcher."

"Second, I've come to tell you the time has come for me to leave your service."

"What? But why, Fletcher? If my mother's been troubling you, I'll—"

Fletcher smiled. "No, sir. You will recall that I used to work for Lord Stanhope. He left me enough money to retire quite nicely. I took on this position because it suited me, but you don't need me any longer. Whitson is a fine butler, and you don't really have need for two."

"But I—"

"I believe the letter will explain it better. It has been a pleasure to serve you, sir. I wish you and your lady much happiness." He bowed and left the room.

Tamberlake stared after him. "I always thought the man a little odd, but I never expected this."

"Mrs. Pennyfeather resigned from my mother's employ as well." Ivy wrinkled her brow.

"Perhaps we should read the letter." Tamberlake broke open the seal and unfolded the sheet.

My dear Tamberlake and my dear Ivy.

"It's to both of us." He put his arm around her and pulled her closer. "Come read with me."

Ivy snuggled in next to him and gazed at the sheet.

If you are reading this letter, it is because you two are now happily wed and my solicitors have sent it on to you as instructed. (Of course, this is a ridiculous sentence, because if you aren't, you wouldn't even know of the existence of the letter. In any case, I will assume you are reading this and proceed on that assumption.)

"Stanhope never could resist levity," said Tamberlake.

I hope you've forgiven me for my meddling by now. A while ago I realized you two suited each other, but I also knew you needed help to find each other. Thus my scheme. I'm only sorry I can't be there to see the results.

"What a sweet man," said Ivy.
"That's not how I felt when you first arrived at Gryphon's Lair," said Tamberlake with a chuckle.
"No, I imagine not." Ivy smiled at him.

Mrs. Pennyfeather and Fletcher remain in my employ. I arranged it through my solicitors and with their collaboration. So you see, they worked for me all this time. Their job was to help bring you two together. Now that the job's done, I have another task for them.

"That explains Fletcher's resignation," said Tamberlake.
"And Mrs. Pennyfeather's," said Ivy.
"I can't believe Stanhope was so devious," said Tamberlake.
"I'm glad he was."

*Enjoy your lives, my young friends, and I hope
you will never forget my small role in bringing
about your happiness. May love be ever yours.*

Yours in eternity,
Lord Stanhope

A small paper dropped from between the sheets and fluttered to the floor.

"What's this?" asked Ivy as she picked it up. She glanced at the writing. "Oh, my goodness. It's a note from Mrs. Pennyfeather."

"What does it say?"

Ivy scanned the note. "She hopes we can forgive her because she stole the carriage parts in Wales as part of her role to keep us together."

"Finally. Now I can sleep better." Tamberlake laughed.

"There's more. Fletcher had followed us to Wales and paid our original driver to leave." Ivy laid the note in her lap. "That explains much."

"Stanhope was quite the devil."

"It's hard to believe, isn't it?" asked Ivy.

"Not if you knew Stanhope." Tamberlake rose from the sofa and moved to the sideboard. He poured two small glasses of sherry. Handing her a glass, he lifted his own. "To Lord Stanhope. Thank you."

She lifted her glass. "Thank you."

They each drank a sip. Ivy said, "I wish I had met the man."

Tamberlake nodded. "I think you would have liked him."

He was about to say more, but a movement outside his window caught his attention. He stepped closer to the pane. Mrs. Pennyfeather was climbing into a carriage with the help of Fletcher. But the man looked different somehow. His hump was missing, and he no longer wore those clumpy shoes. His hair was tamer now as well, and he wasn't wearing his spectacles. Tamberlake stared. If he didn't know better, he'd swear Fletcher looked a lot like . . .

"Stanhope?"

"What about him?" asked Ivy.

Tamberlake shook his head. Impossible. But as he watched the carriage drive away, a smile spread across his lips.

ABOUT THE AUTHOR

Gabriella Anderson makes her home in Albuquerque, New Mexico, with her husband, three daughters, two dogs, two guinea pigs, a rat, a bird, and assorted fish. When she's not writing romance, she volunteers at her daughters' school library, plays volleyball, and tries to avoid cooking and housekeeping. She holds a master's degree in teaching German and German Literature, and she's even appeared on *Jeopardy!* and *The Family Feud.* Fluent in English, Hungarian, and German, as well as knowing Latin, Gabriella loves the way language works, especially when she can use it to put a story on paper.

You can reach her at P.O. Box 20958, Albuquerque, NM 87154-0958 or through her Web site at www.gabianderson.com.